STARSHIP FOR RENT 4

STARSHIP FOR RENT
BOOK 4

M.R. FORBES

D1525525

Published by Quirky Algorithms
Seattle, Washington

Cover illustration by Tom Edwards
Edited by Merrylee Lanehart

CHAPTER 1

The Void pressed down on me, the walls of hopelessness and insanity closing in. No light, no sound, no sensation of movement. Just an endless, yawning void that threatened to swallow me whole. Despair reached out for me, claws scraping the edge of my psyche. Dark, fanged jaws loomed over my soul, tempting me to cower before these hidden monsters. I fought to remember what Ben had told us about traveling through the rifts.

Don't give in. Remember who you are.

It was all an illusion. The darkness of the mind pulled to the surface and weaponized.

As abruptly as it began, the illusion shattered. Head Case burst out of the rift with a jolt, the pinpricks of distant stars once more filling the viewports. At first, I simply stared, hardly daring to believe we had survived. Markan's star fire had come within seconds of literally melting the ship's face off, and ours with it. Remembering the sigilship, my panicked eyes shifted to the rearview, just in time to see the rift fade behind us, Markan nowhere in sight.

Now we were safe.

Beside me, Matt exhaled, hands slowly unclenching

from the controls. Behind us, Tyler let out an exuberant whoop, pumping his fist in the air. "That was incredible! I can't believe we made it!"

"That makes two of us," I managed, sinking bonelessly back into my seat. My heart still raced a mile a minute, the adrenaline of our narrow escape leaving me jittery.

"Can we please never do that again?" Ally asked.

I had no idea when she and Tee reached the flight deck, but looking back, I found them still in their armor, strapped into the theater seating beside Lantz and Karpov.

Ben's voice crackled across the comms, concern evident in his tone. "Is everyone alright? Noah? Matt?"

"We're okay," Matt assured him. "Shaken, but in one piece."

"Yeah, somehow," I added, a slightly hysterical laugh bubbling up my throat. "Though I think I aged about ten years in the last ten seconds."

Ben chuckled with profound relief. "You and me both. Are Tyler and Ally with you?"

"Yes," I replied.

"I need you two to go find Twama," he said. "She's a spy for Markan, and needs to be restrained."

"What?" Tyler cried. "Damn. I guess you'll need to find someone else to paint your toenails, Red."

Ally shoved him playfully with her shoulder. "Maybe you can do it next time."

"Uh-huh," Tee countered with a grinning wink. "We're on our way, Cap." He released his seat harness and stood before pausing. "Hey, quick question. What the actual hell was that back there? I thought you didn't have the juice to make another rift."

"I don't on my own," Ben replied. "Noah, did you notice that glowing blue monolith in Markan's workshop?"

"Yeah," I replied. "It made my skin tingle."

"I think it was some kind of chaos energy siphon or

reactor. It was leaking chaos energy like nobody's business. I pulled in as much of it as I could while we were there. It's the only reason I was able to subdue Markan long enough for Lavona to reach him and get a hand over his mouth. The reactor was still spilling chaos energy into surrounding space while we made our getaway. Thanks to the sigibellum, I had enough to create the rift. I tried to transport us back to Earth, but I don't think it worked. Levi, where are we, anyway?"

"Inconclusive," Levi replied. "I am still collecting sensor data."

"Markan said he tried to use a rift to get back to the Spiral," I recalled from our meeting. "But it always dumped him back in Warexia."

"That's right," Ben agreed.

Matt frowned, a furrow appearing between his brows. "Okay, back up a second. I'm a little lost. Why is Markan trying to get to the Spiral?"

"The short version? Markan is a Gilded who served in the Sigiltech War. He entered a rift and got pulled into Warexia, just like us. Only he's been here for a thousand years."

"Hold up," Tyler said. "What's a Gilded?"

"Like Saruman," I replied.

"Oh. Damn. That's bad."

"Ally, Tee, get going," Matt said. "We don't want Twama roaming around loose to contact Markan again."

"But the story's just getting good," Tyler complained.

"I'll fill you in later," I said. "Unless you want Twama to tell the thousand year-old wizard where we are so he can rift in and finish the job?"

"On my way!" He announced. "If Ally would stop lollygagging…"

She glared at him again, and they hurried from the flight deck.

"Okay, that explains the sigilship," Matt said. "And I suppose he's getting his chaos energy from the siphon?"

"In part," Ben replied. "But the Warden also gave him a boon which let him slip free of our favorite wanna-be god in the first place."

"You mean the Warden gifted him with chaos energy?"

"Sort of. Markan was already Gilded. I think the nanites made him into a walking sigibellum."

"That was a dumb boon to give him."

"The Warden doesn't control the boons. The nanites do. Markan said he thinks the person who receives the boon gets what they subconsciously desire the most. It just doesn't always manifest as expected."

"So Markan gets his mojo back and uses it to build a massive criminal empire, plus he finds a place to hide where the Warden can't find him. Is that about right?"

"Bingo bango boingo. Give yourself a prize."

"Okay, so that makes sense, in the crappiest way possible. But what's the Warden's connection to chaos energy? I'm getting the feeling it's not just hard to access here like you originally thought."

"Right again, my friend. The Warden has siphons of his own. He's using chaos energy to power...well...everything he makes."

"So he's a wizard, too."

"We don't know that," Ben countered. "He might be more of a scientist, making use of an otherwise elusive element. The important point is that he's sucking most of it up, and Markan is obviously pulling in the rest. All that's left for folks like me are the small puddles left behind."

"Hey guys, I think we have an answer to where we are," Lantz said. I hadn't noticed that he'd moved from the cheap seats to the engineering station while we were talking.

"What is it?" Ben asked.

"Remember how I told you that the Warden always

starts pinging our network when we drop out of hyperspace?

I nodded, a sinking feeling in my stomach. "Let me guess. He's knocking on our door again."

"With an entire marching band," Lantz confirmed. "Wherever we are—"

"We're still stuck in this damned galaxy," Matt finished, disappointment thick in his voice. "And still stuck with the Warden."

"Maybe not," I said, reaching into my pocket.

"No, we're definitely in Warexia," Lantz said. "Guaranteed."

"I meant, we may not be stuck with the Warden." I withdrew the device Lavona had managed to grab during our confrontation with Markan.

All eyes turned to me. I held up the small, innocuous-looking machine. "Markan called this a nanite disabler. He said it could sever the Warden's link to the nanites in our bodies and prevent him from being able to control or track us. We can go to the Wardenship, and there's nothing he can do about it."

"That's unbelievable," Matt said. "Are you sure it works?"

"No. But Markan claimed it did, and he had no reason to lie. And he did manage to escape the Warden, so it lines up."

"In that case, we know what to do next, don't we? Use the device to ditch the Warden and set a course for Aster-ock. We can meet up with Goloran there before heading for Levain's secret station."

"Not yet," Ben replied. "We're all relieved we escaped from Markan, but we're hardly out of the woods. In fact, right now we're stuck dead center between an immovable object and an unstoppable force."

"And the immovable object doesn't hate us yet," Matt agreed. "I see your point."

"We don't want to get on the Warden's bad side until we're sure of how to proceed."

"But we need to get to the Wardenship," I said. "It's the key to going home."

"We hope it'll be the key to going home," Ben countered. "We have no proof of that. Lantz, is there any way to open audio comms access for the Warden but keep him cut off from video and all other internal systems?"

"You know the second we let the Warden in, he's going to give us another task," I said.

"I'd say the odds are pretty high."

"So why do you want to let him talk to us?"

"Because then we're in control of the communications, not him. With the disabler, we know we can cut him off at any time. But he doesn't know that."

"So we use the Warden, the way he's been using us."

"Exactamundo. Lantz?"

"I'll need a few minutes," Lantz replied.

"Okay. I'm coming back down to the flight deck." Ben's comm disconnected, leaving the flight deck in a fraught silence.

My thoughts turned to Lavona, badly injured in sick bay. And Larev, who had traded his life for hers. The Hemid had done the right thing, while I'd listened to her screaming at me to run. I'd promised myself I would make my parents proud, but I knew in my heart I had let them down, as much as I had let Lavona and myself down.

Sitting around and feeling sorry for myself wouldn't help anything. Like the song in Tee's car the night we'd left the hospital. I'd been knocked down.

And now, I had to get back up.

CHAPTER 2

The flight deck doors whisked open. Ben entered with Meg, who helped support him as he made his way to the command station. Rena trailed behind them, her face etched with concern.

"Ben, you okay?" I asked.

"It still took it out of me to pull in enough chaos energy to open the rift," he replied. "I'll be fine."

"Rena, you should have mentioned your father was a Gilded," Matt said upon seeing her.

"I...I didn't know," she replied. "He never displayed any kind of special abilities in my presence, and he told me the scars were a sign of social status where he was from."

"He didn't lie about that," Ben said. "Even during the war, there were very few Gilded."

"You keep mentioning some war," I said. "What was it?"

"A conflict between the ruler of the Manticore Spiral and the creator of Sigiltech. He tried to use chaos energy to seize the galaxy by force, but was ultimately stopped."

"I can't imagine how you defeat one of those sigilships."

"With a lot of regular ships," Ben answered softly. "And a lot of casualties."

The response chilled me. "Right."

"Hey, Captain," Tyler said over Ben's comm badge. "We have Twama in custody. She swears she's innocent."

"Of course she does," Meg said, rolling her eyes.

"Restrain her in the hangar," Ben replied. "We'll deal with her later."

"Aye aye, Cap," Tee answered.

"Captain, I have the switch ready to allow the Warden access to the comms," Lantz reported.

"Wait," Rena said before Ben could open the channel. "What about my father?"

"What about him?" Ben asked.

"I understand you're all eager to go home. But my father is a bad man who does bad things for his own self-interest. He's hurt so many and will continue to do harm until someone stops him."

"We tried," Matt said. "We failed."

"We're not strong enough to beat him," Ben agreed.

"But you managed to escape him," Rena urged. "You have the same abilities he does."

"On a much lower scale."

"Only because he has these siphons and you don't. What if you had a siphon?"

"That would help, but I imagine they're all back at your dad's station or on his ship. He has no reason to keep them anywhere he isn't."

"But you said the Warden uses chaos energy as fuel. Which means he has siphons. Maybe if you tell him what happened, he'll give you one."

"Or maybe when we tell him we were face-to-face with Markan and didn't end him, he'll trigger our kill switches," Matt said. "We should use the disabler before we talk to him, just in case."

"I'm not ready to risk using the disabler," Ben said.

"The Warden said he wouldn't be too harsh with us if we failed, as long as we tried," I said. "Maybe Rena is right. We should tell him what happened and ask for a siphon."

"We know the Warden can be unpredictable," Ben said. "And I don't think he's any less selfish than Markan. He just got here first."

"He didn't start the war on Viconia," I pressed, remembering Lavona.

"We can't trust what he said about going easy on us. Especially when we failed against his arch nemesis. Anything we do is a risk, but I think honesty might be the greatest risk of all."

Ben ran a hand through his curly hair, clearly conflicted by the options. As renters, the ultimate decision technically rested with me, Tee, and Ally. But I wasn't about to pull that card on this one. I doubted Ben would honor it, anyway. We were way past that point.

"I have an opinion, if you'd like to hear it," Lantz said.

"Go ahead," Ben replied, relieved to have a potential out.

"It seems to me that the Warden is too chaotic to trust that he'll react well to bad news. At the same time, we'd like to get our hands on a means to boost your chaos energy output. As a related aside, I have to wonder how beneficial it is to have Markan and/or the Warden running roughshod over Warexia. The galaxy is so large, it's impossible to grasp all the ways in which they've manipulated outcomes. Who can say if Markan or the Warden is better or worse than the other. What we know is that they've both done bad things. The only logical output then is that they're both bad."

"What's your point, Lantz?" Matt asked.

"Only that it doesn't make sense to help the Warden destroy Markan."

"You're suggesting we stick to just trying to get home?" I asked.

"Not exactly. This isn't a binary choice. One or the other. We can also choose to aid both or neither. My vote is for neither."

"Which brings us full circle," Ben said. "Back to where I started this conversation."

"With one important difference," Lantz said. "What if we can stop them both?"

If there had been anything in my mouth, I would have spat it all over the co-pilot station. "Are you kidding? We're not anywhere near powerful or skilled enough to fight both of them."

"Maybe not at the same time," Lantz agreed. "Which is why Ben's idea to stay on the Warden's good side for now makes sense. But if we plan our next moves with the idea of possibly negating both their influences within Warexia, we might be able to put ourselves in a position to actually make it happen."

"We're still only one ship," Matt said. "One crew. Less than a dozen individuals. How are we going to shut down the two most powerful entities in this galaxy?"

"I don't know," Lantz admitted. "But figuring out how to get a siphon couldn't hurt."

"The Wardenship," Meg said. "If the Warden uses chaos energy as a power source, then the ship is sure to have one. If we can reverse engineer it—"

"How much do you want to bet that's why the Warden doesn't want us near his ship?" I said. "He knows he screwed up with Markan, and he's afraid of anyone else gaining that much power."

"It's a workable theory," Ben agreed. "Lantz, open the comms."

At first, I thought the Warden either might not notice he

had comms access or would choose not to use it immediately. Of course, it was a foolish thought.

A familiar laugh crackled across the flight deck, sending a shiver down my spine.

"Hello, my friends!" the Warden drawled. "It's been a while since we've chatted, hasn't it?"

"I just assumed you didn't want to talk to me," Ben said. "Since you made a point to contact Noah on Asterock."

I glanced back at Ben, who smirked in response. He had decided to play dumb about Lantz's security block.

"Yes…well…" the Warden stammered, taken off-guard by the statement. "I'm an equal opportunity master of the universe. I decided to grant Noah the honor of following up on the task. And how is that going, Noah?"

"It's going great," I replied. "I don't have you on video, though." I side-eyed Matt, who chuckled silently.

"Your systems must be malfunctioning," the Warden insisted. "No matter. Can you elaborate on the statement that things are going great? You've been in and out of hyperspace quite a bit recently."

"He means that we've completed your task," Ben said. "Markan is dead. It'll take some time for the syndicate to eat itself, but the head of the snake is cut off."

"Well, well, well!" the Warden replied excitedly. "That is unexpected and incredible news. Simply marvelous. To think you succeeded where so many others failed. I knew there was something special about you! My finest players in a long, long time. Amazing. Where did you find him? And how did you finish him off?"

"He was hiding from you," Ben said, "outside of Warexia's immediate boundaries, and using asteroids and chaos energy to keep himself hidden. We finished him off by blowing up his station with him on it."

"Incredible. How did you overcome his alleged access to chaos energy?"

"We infiltrated his group from inside, enlisted sympathetic allies, and...boom!" Matt answered.

"Boom!" the Warden repeated gleefully. "Very, very good."

"I was wondering," Ben said. "How did Markan get access to chaos energy? He had a ship powered by it that very nearly destroyed us."

"Really?" the Warden replied, acting surprised. "Markan was a very resourceful criminal. I'm sure one of his many connections assisted him with any methods he may have had to harness chaos energy."

"Well, we finished your task," Matt said. "Judging by your reaction, it seems like it was a pretty important one to you, too. So maybe you can help us get home now."

The Warden tsked. "Now, let's not get ahead of ourselves. There's still so much more for you to experience here in Warexia! You've barely spent any time here at all! Besides, I have another task for you. Something much easier and more entertaining than your last outing, I promise."

I barely suppressed a groan. Another task. Another delay. Another chance for the Warden to dangle the promise of home in front of us while keeping us firmly under his thumb.

Ben caught my eye, a silent warning in his gaze. Play along for now.

"We killed Markan for you," he said. "We should get something in return."

"Of course, of course," the Warden agreed. "I'm nothing if not magnanimous. Two boons have been distributed as a reward for your efforts."

"Thank you," Ben said.

With only four of us left who didn't have a boon, my odds were fifty-fifty. But what was my greatest desire, anyway? And how would the nanites manifest it?

"It is truly my pleasure," the Warden said. "Markan was a thorn in my side, and an incredibly dangerous presence within Warexia. His death and the coming collapse of his empire will spare many lives."

"Glad we could help," Ben said flatly.

"As for your next task," the Warden continued. "Your next mission, should you choose to accept it...and really, do you have a choice? ...is to travel to the vacation world of Ocypha. It's a lovely little resort planet, simply divine this time of year. Pristine beaches, crystalline waters, luxury accommodations...and a bit of a sea monster problem."

I blinked. "I'm sorry, did you say sea monster?"

"Oh yes," the Warden said cheerfully. "Nasty bugger the locals call Oblix. He's been terrorizing the tourists, capsizing boats, eating the occasional sunbather. You know, typical sea monster shenanigans. The Ocyphian Tourism Board is quite put out."

"Let me get this straight," Ben said slowly. "You want us to travel halfway across the galaxy...to deal with an unruly sea creature?"

"An unruly, carnivorous sea creature," the Warden corrected. "Do keep up, Captain. Oblix is no mere aquatic life form. He's 200 feet long, breathes fire, and has a particular fondness for blondes. I'd hate for you to underestimate him."

"A fire-breathing sea serpent," I said. "You can't be serious."

The Warden tsked. "Doubt me at your peril. Oblix is quite real, I assure you. And your mission is to stop his reign of terror by any means necessary. I'd prefer if you could capture him alive. He'll make a splendid addition to the Warden Wildlife Sanctuary. But I'll understand if you're forced to take more...permanent measures."

I shook my head in disbelief. "So that's it? We're monster hunters now?"

A dark chuckle rolled through the speakers. "Call it a working vacation. Think of it as a chance to unwind. I'm sure defeating Markan was no easy task."

"We're supposed to unwind while wrestling a kaiju?" Matt asked dryly.

"All in a day's work! Now, off you go. Ocypha awaits! Oh, and be careful not to get eaten. It would be a shame to lose you after you've come so far. Oh, and remember. No splitting up. I would hate to have to hurt any of you."

With that, the connection cut off, leaving us in stunned silence.

CHAPTER 3

"Wow," I said after a few heartbeats, turning to look at Ben. "We aren't actually going to Ocypha, are we?"

"Some of us are," Ben replied. "There's a sea monster eating tourists."

"Which the Warden should easily be able to deal with himself," I pointed out before holding up the disabler. "We don't need him anymore, remember?"

"No, but right now we still need to stay on his good side. Especially when Markan is sure to come after us."

"But you lied about Markan. You told the Warden he's dead."

"Right. Now the Warden will think that anything the syndicate does is ordered from whoever filled the power vacuum. He'll hit the syndicate harder than he might have before. And Markan won't openly challenge the Warden unless or until he's sure he can win. Meanwhile, we can do like Lantz suggested and put ourselves in a position to have multiple options, depending on how events unfold."

"You're playing with fire," I warned.

"I know. But we've been dancing to the Warden's tune since we arrived. It's about time we started playing by our own rules. With that said, I think it's time to split up. Most of us will head to Ocypha, but a small team will explore the Wardenship. The hop racer is only designed for one pilot, but it can carry two if they don't mind impersonating sardines.

Matt's brows drew together. "We can't split without using the disabler. And I assume using the disabler means losing our telephone enhancement, since that works through the nanites' comms, too. Whoever goes will be cut off from the rest of us."

"I know. On the flip side, the Warden won't know we've split up. We can finally visit the Wardenship without interference."

I turned the disabler over in my hand, considering. It was a huge risk. We had no way of knowing if the device would work as intended. If it didn't, if the Warden could somehow still sense when we used it...

"There's no guarantee this will work," I said, voicing my doubts. "If the Warden realizes he's lost contact with a couple members of the crew, he'll know something is up, which will ruin your entire plan of keeping him happy while we deal with the fallout from escaping Markan."

"I imagine we'll know pretty quickly if using the disabler draws the Warden's attention. He'll be back on our comms threatening us or hitting us with a shock or something to let us know his displeasure. Besides, getting to the Wardenship is still our priority. We have the means to circumvent the Warden's stall tactics. We have to use it."

"Only two of us to infiltrate Levain's station and uncover the Wardenship's secrets?" Matt pressed. "That's a heavy lift, Ben."

"It might be," he agreed. "Which is why we'll need to deepen Princess Goloran's involvement. She can provide secondary resources to help us get access to the ship."

"If Twama's any indication, we can't trust any of her resources."

"Did I hear someone say enemy spy?" Tyler asked, stepping through the flight deck doors as they whooshed open, with Ally at his heels. He paused, cautiously eyeing us. "Uh, what's going on? Why does everyone look so serious?"

Ben quickly filled them in on the plan. "No way," Ally said, shaking her head vehemently. "It's too dangerous. We should stick together."

"Normally I'd agree with you," Ben said. "But we're out of good options. If we want a shot at getting home, we need to get to that Wardenship. This isn't just our best chance of doing that. It's our only chance."

Tyler frowned, but I could see the acceptance settling over his features. He knew Ben was right, even if he didn't like it.

"Anyway," Ben continued. "We either need more help or a bigger second ship. Goloran is our best bet."

"So who's going?" Tyler asked. "I'm volunteering if you need one."

"I appreciate that," Ben said. "But I don't think you're the right choice to deal with Goloran, Tee."

"Why not?"

"You have an obvious crush on her. She'll eat you alive and spit out the bones while you're busy staring instead of negotiating."

"That's so not true!" Tyler complained.

"It's totally true," Ally countered. "You couldn't stop talking about her for a week after we left Cacitrum."

"That's just because she's rich, powerful, and beautiful."

"And old enough to be your mother," I said.

"I don't mind that."

"What about me?" Ally asked.

"Your boon is valuable, but I'm thinking we need someone with more technical skills."

"Lantz," Matt said immediately. "He's our software genius. If anyone can figure out how to fly that thing, it's him."

"Sure," Lantz said. "I mean, you should probably pay me for it since it's out of scope of our original agreement, but I'm game."

Ben hesitated. "I agree you're our best bet for hacking the Wardenship's systems, Lantz. But your skillset is also limited to software, and we may need hardware solutions as well. Besides, thanks to our fancy new comms unit, whoever goes can pick your brain remotely."

"True," Lantz agreed.

"I can do hardware," Karpov said.

"You won't fit in the hop racer," Matt replied.

"I can go," Meg offered. "I'm no Lantz, but I know my way around a hyperdrive. And I've doubled up in the racer before. There are benefits to being petite."

"I think either your or Leo are a good choice," Ben said. "We still need a second."

"What about you, Cap?" Tee asked.

"I best stay here with my ship and the sigibellum."

"I think Noah should go," Matt said.

My head snapped up. "What? Why me?"

"Actually, I think that's a great idea," Ben agreed. "You and Matt negotiated with the princess. She knows and trusts you."

"I wouldn't say she trusts me," I replied.

"She trusts you as much as she trusts any of us."

"Matt, why don't you go?" I asked. "It's your hop racer."

"I *could* go," Matt said.

"No," Ben replied, looking at me. "Noah, it has to be you."

I swallowed hard around the sudden lump in my throat. Ben's faith in me was humbling...and utterly terrifying.

"But why?" I persisted. "If I get cut off from the Warden..." I trailed off, unwilling to voice my selfish fears out loud.

Comprehension dawned in Tyler's eyes. "Are you worried about missing out on a boon?" he guessed. "Or just jealous because we'll be soaking in some sun on a resort planet while you're busy looking over some old fossil of a starship."

I ducked my head, face heating. When he put it like that, it sounded so petty. "I'd rather see the starship than a beach," I replied.

"Noah." Ally's hand landed on my shoulder, giving a comforting squeeze. "You might already have a boon and just don't know it yet. And even if you don't...this is so much bigger than that. This is our shot at getting home. At seeing our families again."

"Your families," I replied, still moping. A pang went through me at the thought of my parents. They were gone, lost to a stupid, senseless accident. But Tyler and Ally...they still had loved ones waiting for them. Loved ones who deserved to know the truth about what happened to us. Even so... "When do I get to be selfish?"

"You know, having a rocket fist isn't really that great," Tee said, trying to make me feel better.

"Neither is having the kill shot boon. And unlike T-Bone, I mean that."

From what Markan had said about how the boon was chosen and what Ally must have gone through to have it manifest the way it did, I believed her.

I met her gaze, resolve hardening in my chest. "You're right," I said. I looked at Ben. "But I still don't understand why you want me to go?"

"A few reasons," Ben replied. "Like I said, Goloran already knows you and doesn't dislike you. Two, you're a pilot and have studied the racer, so you already know how to fly it. Three, you were trained in deception, infiltration, and combat by Miss Asher."

"Only for two weeks."

"You already proved your worth there by rescuing me," Rena said, speaking up for the first time.

"You might need that training when you reach the station. Four, you're the closest thing to a second captain we have."

"Matt's co-captain, not me," I argued.

"But you've been my understudy since we got here. And, you're like a little brother to me."

That one made me smile. "You're like a big brother to me. You and Matt, both."

Tyler cleared his throat. "What am I? Bad sushi?"

"You're all like family to me," I said.

"Five, you have Archie, and it's the best protection you could ask for. Six, I have total faith in you," Ben finished. "I trust you to do this, and do it well."

My grin drifted wider, cheeks heating in response to the praise. "I won't let you down."

Ben's eyes shone with pride. "I know you won't. Levi, do we have a firm location yet?"

"Yes, Captain," Levi replied. We all turned to the front of the flight deck, where the Warexian star map appeared, our position marked by a blue robot head.

"Mark Ocypha and Asterock on the map," Ben prompted. The two planets appeared. Ocypha was a good distance away, Asterock a fair bit closer.

"Roughly estimating by the distance, I'd say it's four days to Asterock," Matt said. "Four weeks to Ocypha."

"Four weeks?" Ally cried.

"I know," Matt sympathized. "But at least we'll be kicking the ball forward instead of laterally now."

"I don't know if I can be cramped in the hop racer for four days," I said. "How will I go to the bathroom?"

"Didn't you read the manual?" Matt asked.

"I guess I didn't get that far."

"The racer suits have facilities for voiding. It's totally clean and dry, and the waste gets dumped out the back and vaporized."

"If we can find someone who can extract the data I uploaded, I can provide locations for all of my father's wormhole gates," Rena said. "That would make moving around Warexia faster and easier."

"Not if it means fighting our way through another gate station," Tyler said.

"It might mean that," Rena admitted.

"It might still prove useful," Ben said.

"Maybe we can find a data broker on Ocypha," Karpov said. "They should have the tools to do the extraction."

"That sounds like a plan," Ben said. He pointed to the disabler. "There's only one more thing to do."

CHAPTER 4

We gathered between the command station and pilot stations, tense and anxious. Ben held the nanite disabler in his hand, our entire future seeming to hinge on the effectiveness of the small device. Meg and I stood apart from the others. My hands trembled, my mouth dry as cotton.

"Are you ready?" he asked, his gaze flickering between Meg and me.

I swallowed hard. "As I'll ever be," I managed.

Meg nodded, a determined set to her jaw. "Let's do it."

Ben exhaled slowly. "Alright. Noah, you're up first."

I stepped forward, heart pounding. This was it. The moment of truth. If the disabler worked, I'd be free of the Warden's control. But if it didn't...

I didn't let myself finish that thought. "What do I do?"

"Your guess is as good as mine," Ben replied. "But the disabler only has one switch."

"Judging by the design, I assume you just need to turn it on and point it at us," Meg said.

Ben nodded. "Okay then, here goes nothing."

"Hopefully not nothing," Tyler commented behind him.

Ben positioned the disabler in front of me and activated

it. A shrill buzz filled my head for a half-second. Then, nothing.

"Did it work?" Ally asked.

"I...I think so," I guessed. "I heard a high-pitched buzz."

"Meg, tell us if you hear the same thing," Ben said, pointing the disabler at her. She stoically submitted to the procedure.

"Yes, I heard it too," she announced.

"Let's hope that's a good sign," Matt said. He glanced at Ben. "Now what?"

"Now...we wait." Ben set the disabler aside. "If the Warden realizes he's lost his connection to Noah and Meg, he'll probably try to punish them. Or all of us. At the very least, he'll likely contact us to find out if they might have died."

Seconds ticked by, each one feeling like an eternity. We all remained motionless, hardly daring to breathe. Waiting for the hammer to fall.

But it didn't. One minute passed, then two, then five. No pain. No incoming comms. Only silence.

I exchanged a disbelieving glance with Meg. "Is it...did it actually work?"

"It appears so," Ben said slowly, a note of wonderment in his voice.

Matt shook his head, a grin starting to split his face. "I can't believe it. That crazy bastard Markan actually did it. He found a way to neutralize the nanites without the Warden knowing."

"Noah, Meg, gather your gear and get to the hop racer," Ben said, his voice pressing. "I want you out of here and headed for Asterock immediately."

I nodded, already mentally cataloging what I would need for the mission beyond what I already had on me. Still dressed for our meeting with Markan, I already wore the nanofiber underlay, with a holomask in my pocket and an assortment of weapons both on my hip and tucked out of sight. I would need to change the jacket, though. It had been stained with Lavona's—

"Wait," I blurted, fresh shame piercing me. "I need to go to sickbay first."

Ben's brow furrowed. "Noah, we don't have time—"

"Please," I interrupted. "I have to see Lavona. I...I can't leave without saying goodbye." My voice cracked on the last word, betraying my churning emotions.

For a moment, Ben looked like he wanted to argue. But something in my face must have convinced him, because he finally sighed and nodded. "Alright. But make it quick. Every second counts."

"I will," I promised.

"I'll tag along with you," Tee said. I wasn't surprised. He and Lavona had become fast friends as well.

"Me. too," Ally said.

The three of us hurried from the flight deck. My heartbeat drummed in my ears as we boarded the elevator, a painful lump lodging in my throat. I couldn't bear the thought of leaving her behind without seeing her again. Not only to say goodbye. To say thank you. And to apologize.

The scene that greeted me in sickbay made my heart clench. Lavona lay still and pale on the autodoc, eyes closed. She looked so fragile, so broken. Not at all like the fierce warrior I had come to know.

Ixy glanced up from beside the autodoc, compound eyes fixing on me. "Noahsss," she hissed softly.

The sound of my name falling from her mandibles jolted me into motion. I approached slowly, gaze roving over Lavona's visible injuries. Fresh burns marred her flesh over her old wounds, while one of her arms was strapped across her chest, already encased in a brace. But the worst was the mask obscuring the lower half of her face, translucent tubes snaking from it to the machines clustered around her head, helping her to breathe.

"How is she?" I managed around the tightness in my throat.

Ixy's mandibles clacked. "Ssstabilized. Sssome burnsss, broken bonesss. But ssshe will recoversss."

A shaky breath left me, relief and gratitude mingling. Ally squeezed my shoulder, offering support.

I reached out hesitantly, brushing the back of Lavona's cheek with trembling fingers. Her skin felt cool and papery beneath my touch. Swallowing hard, I tried to find the words. There was so much I wanted to say, so much she needed to know. How grateful I was for her sacrifice. How sorry I was for abandoning her. How much her friendship meant to me.

But as I opened my mouth, Lavona's eyelids fluttered. A tiny, pained sound escaped her and I froze, breath catching. Slowly, those striking orange eyes blinked open, hazy and unfocused at first before sharpening on my face.

"N...Noah?" she rasped, the word barely audible through the oxygen mask.

"Hey," I whispered, fighting back the sting of tears as I dropped my hand to hers. I squeezed her fingers. "It's me."

Her brow furrowed. "What... what are you...?"

"I'm so sorry," I blurted. "I'm sorry for listening to you when you told me to run. I should have stayed. Should have fought with you..."

She shook her head weakly, wincing at the movement. "Don't be...stupid. You couldn't...help. You needed...to survive. Larev...he—"

"I know. He saved your life," I said, a single tear escaping and tracking down my cheek. "But he didn't make it."

"The rest of us did, thanks to you," Tee said, moving in beside me.

"Hey, Tee," Lavona said, eyes shifting. "Ally. Thank you…for coming…to see me."

"I came to see you because I'm leaving." I said, nearly choking on the words. "I hate to go with you like this."

"Where?" she asked.

"You grabbed the disabler for us. Ben used it on Meg and me. We're out of the Warden's reach now. We're going to take the hop racer to the Wardenship while you all go kill a sea monster."

Her face crinkled in confusion. "Sea monster?"

"It's a long story. But you have four weeks to get better so you can help Ben and Matt defeat it."

That earned a smile. "I better…heal faster…then. I'm glad you…we survived."

"Me, too," I agreed.

"Come back…in one piece…" Lavona mumbled, barely clinging to consciousness. "Thatsss…an order…"

"Yes, ma'am."

Her lips twitched one last time. Then her eyes slid fully closed, and she went still once more, chest rising and falling slowly with each breath.

For a moment, I simply stood there, watching her. Then I turned to Tee and Ally. "I need to go."

"We know," Ally answered. "Be safe out there, Katzuo." She wrapped me in a solid embrace.

"Yeah, man. Going home isn't worth you dying." He hugged me. too.

"Noahsss," Ixy said, messing up my hair with a pedi-palp. "Good lucksss."

"Thanks, Ixy," I replied. "If there's a way for us to get home, I'll find it. That's a promise."

CHAPTER 5

I stepped off the elevator onto the hangar deck, Meg beside me. Our new flight suits fit snugly over my civilian garb, so much so that I had to abandon my coat to keep it from being too tight around my chest. Colorful accents ran along the suits' arms and legs, standing out vividly against the otherwise dark fabric. Extra padding cushioned our rears, a thoughtful addition given how long we would be sitting. I tried not to dwell on the built-in waste filtration system. At least it promised to keep us clean and dry, even if it would be more than a little awkward to use. My only solace came from knowing that neither of us could hold our waste for that long. We were in it together.

Ben, Matt, Leo, and Lantz awaited us at the base of the stairs. The hop racer squatted nearby, its sleek, elongated shape both elegant and predatory. My stomach fluttered with nerves and anticipation at the sight of the craft.

"You look good," Matt said as we reached the bottom of the steps, a smile tugging at his mouth. Those suits fit you both well."

"They're surprisingly comfortable," I replied, plucking at the material. "Though I feel a bit like a superhero."

"Well, you're certainly about to embark on a heroic mission," Ben said. "Thank you again for volunteering, Meg. And thank you for agreeing to participate, Noah."

I nodded, resolve hardening in my chest. "Yeah, well, I couldn't risk you falling back to Tee."

"Remember, this isn't goodbye, sis," Leo said, stepping forward to clasp Meg's shoulder and kiss her cheek. "It's see you later." He offered her a helmet, his fingers lingering on hers as she accepted it.

"Don't be such a drama queen," Meg replied. "Of course I'll see you later. You don't have to make such a production out of it."

"Just make sure you come back in one piece, both of you," Lantz added.

"We will," I promised.

Matt handed me my helmet, meeting my gaze. "Be careful out there. And don't forget, we're only a call away if you need us."

"I won't," I replied. We clasped forearms, a gesture that conveyed more than words ever could. Then, with a final nod to the others, I turned and climbed into the hop racer's cockpit.

Matt followed, leaning in to ensure we could hook up the waste system and work the various controls. I'd read that part of the manual, which I saved on my personal access device. Even so, I didn't do anything to stop Matt from explaining. Despite his normally cool-as-ice demeanor, I could tell sending us off in his pride and joy made him nervous. "Throttle, stick, maneuvering thrusters," he said, indicating each in turn. "Nav computer is here. Most hop racers have voice-activated AI, but I find it too distracting and a crutch I don't need. She's real easy to fly. Practically reads your mind."

I settled into the pilot's seat, repeating the controls to

Matt to further ease his mind. "Throttle, stick, maneuvering thrusters, nav computer. Got it."

Matt clasped my shoulder, giving it a silent squeeze before hopping off the racer. Meg clambered up a moment later, pausing at the edge of the cockpit.

"Are you okay?" I asked, slightly nervous about having her sitting on my lap for the next four days. Not only because I'd never had a woman on my lap before, but even her diminutive size would become a heavy weight after over eighty hours. The only option would be to grin and bear it if I got uncomfortable halfway.

"Are you?" she replied, picking up on my hesitation.

"Yeah," I answered, tone lacking conviction. "I'll get used to it."

She nodded, carefully stepping on the seat between my legs before lowering herself onto my thighs. She angled her slight form sideways as best she could, putting more weight on the bulkhead behind her and providing me better access to the controls.

"Still okay?" she asked.

"You're lighter than I thought," I replied. "You?"

"Let's do this."

"Watch your head," I warned, reaching for the canopy control on the racer's dash. It closed with a soft snick, sealing us inside.

Drawing a steadying breath, I initiated the startup sequence. The hop racer hummed to life around us, displays flickering on. I watched in fascination as the pre-flight checks scrolled past, marveling at the speed and precision of the ship's systems. It really did seem to anticipate my needs, like an extension of my own body.

I activated the comms. "Head Case, this is Katzuo. Do you copy?"

"Loud and clear," Ally replied, her voice crackling

through my helmet. "You're clear for takeoff, Kat. Come back safe. Both of you."

"We will," I replied. "Here we go."

My hand closed around the stick, my other resting lightly on the throttle. I spared one last glance to the others gathered in the hangar, all of them clear on the other side of the Hunter mech. This was it. No more hesitation. It was time to forge our own path.

With the racer already pushed out of the corner and pointed at the open hangar door, I turned my head toward everyone seeing us off and gave them a two-finger salute before lifting off the deck and opening the throttle. Inertia pressed me back into the seat and Meg's shoulder into my chest as we shot out of the hangar and into the black, star-strewn expanse. Instantly, I was struck by the raw power thrumming through the ship. The racer's speed and agility were like nothing I had ever experienced. I could barely contain my spontaneous joy, the ship responding to my slightest touch as if hard-wired to my thoughts.

"Amazing, isn't it?" Meg asked, her helmet practically bumping against mine when she turned her head toward me, our eyes meeting through the visors.

"It totally is," I replied, sending the racer into a swooping dive before pulling up and barrel-rolling right in front of Head Case's face.

"Show-off," Ally said in response to the display.

"Just getting a feel for her."

"Enough playing around," Meg said after a few more maneuvers. "It's time to get down to business."

"Copy that," I replied. I activated the nav computer, entering Matt's coordinates for Asterock. It plotted almost immediately, the sheer speed of the racer's computer leaving me slack-jawed. It was a spry young teen compared to *old man* Head Case. "Course set."

I took a final look at the glittering jewel of Head Case

receding behind us, the urge to offer one last farewell tempered by a blending of excitement and fear over what came next. Matt's words echoed in my mind. We're only a call away. Our friends...our family...they had our backs, just as surely as Meg and I would watch out for each other. We could do this.

"You set?" I asked.

"Secure and ready," Meg confirmed.

I nodded. "Then let's get this show on the road." A huge grin split my face as I held my thumb over the hop trigger on the stick that would send the racer into hyperspace.

I punched it. The stars stretched and faded to black as we raced toward a future filled with both danger and promise.

There was no going back now.

CHAPTER 6

Between the confined space, the lack of meaningful sleep, and the inability to stretch our muscles, Meg and I were pretty miserable by the time we popped out of the final hyperspace leg near Asterock. Relief flooded through me as the connected hollowed-out planetoids grew larger in our view, their orbits busy with cargo ships, pleasure boats, and everything in between.

After four days cramped in the tiny cockpit, with barely enough room to remove our helmets and snack on food bars, we had both grown agitated and impatient. At least the flight suit biowaste system had worked as advertised. Otherwise, the trip would have been completely unbearable.

Not that Meg was a bad passenger. We'd had lots of time to talk along the way, since that was the only thing we could really do. I'd learned all about her and Leo's past, how they had wound up as part of Head Case's crew, her experiences dating Ben, save for the more private parts, and much more. I'd told her so much about my parents that she was probably sick of it, but even in her disintegrating mood, she'd humored me.

"Finally," Meg exhaled. "No offense, Noah. But I can't wait to get away from you."

"The feeling's mutual," I laughed, reaching for the comms. "Asterock Central Docking Control, this is the private star hopper Shelby Cobra requesting permission to dock."

"Shelby Cobra, we have you on our sensors," Control replied. "Please submit verification credentials for docking access."

Our only credentials were for Head Case, but Lantz had done something to the encoded algorithm that he swore would get us access. Apparently, he'd done something similar a few times before to earn extra quark. Even so, my voice trembled as I keyed in the data transmission. "Sending now."

I waited with held breath, grateful there was no video feed, so Control couldn't see how nervous I probably looked.

"Credentials received and accepted, Shelby. You are cleared to proceed to hangar bay nine, LZ74. Sending approach path and docking coordinates now."

I let my breath out, silently thanking Lantz. "Much appreciated, Central. Shelby Cobra inbound to hangar bay nine." I disconnected the comms, eyeing the HUD projected onto the cockpit glass, where augmented reality markers guided me toward the hangar bay. I shifted my attention to the sensor grid beneath it. "Any sign of Goloran's ship?"

"The density of activity makes individual ships hard to pick out," Meg replied. "That one looks promising." She pointed to a large, dark mass positioned ahead of us on the bottom level of central docking. "But wasn't Ben supposed to tell Goloran we were on our way?"

"He said he would try to pass on a subtle message, in case the Warden has her comms under surveillance," I replied. "I don't know how successful—" A rapid beeping from the comms interrupted me. "What is that?"

"Incoming hail," Meg said, leaning forward to flip the switch and answer the comms.

"This is the private star hopper Shelby Cobra," Meg said.

"Greetings, Shelby Cobra," a familiar voice replied. "I am Princess Goloran of Gothori. I believe we have a mutual acquaintance."

"Hey, Princess Goloran," I said, probably less formally than I should have. "It's Noah."

Her voice seemed to lighten pleasantly and unexpectedly. "Greetings, Noah. It is excellent to hear from you."

"Did our mutual acquaintance fill you in?" I asked.

"Indeed. I'm looking forward to a closer relationship. I also appreciate the faith and trust you've displayed in me. My apologies for placing Twama in your midst. It's a shame you couldn't bring her back with you. I should have liked to punish her personally."

"You'll still get your chance I'm sure," I replied. "Just not as soon as you might have liked."

"Again, indeed. What are your docking coordinates? I will have Kloth meet you when you arrive."

"Hangar bay nine, LZ74," I said.

"Very well. I will see you soon, Noah."

"I'm looking forward to it," I replied. Her comm disconnected.

"She seems nice," Meg said in an uncertain tone.

"She hasn't tried to kill us yet," I responded. "That's about as nice as we can hope for in this galaxy."

I followed the markers toward hangar bay nine, sticking tight to the coordinates to avoid drifting into the hollow cable-like tethers keeping the assorted planetoids attached. I also didn't want to accidentally side-swipe a larger vessel that would easily total the racer without even noticing the hit themselves.

Traffic only increased as we approached the hangar bay, though the size of the craft entering and exiting the open portal diminished considerably. Even so, it was my first time guiding any starship through such density, and it took some effort to maintain my calm. It took everything I had to remain steady on the stick as we crossed the threshold.

Our assigned landing zone illuminated on the HUD, making it easily recognizable. Activating anti-gravity controls and cutting the main thrusters, I eased around a launching shuttle and descended to the spot, gratefully touching down with a soft thump. Around us, the hangar buzzed with activity, an orderly chaos of mechanics bustling about and ships coming and going.

I popped the canopy, and Meg clambered out ahead of me. I wasn't far behind her, groaning as my stiff muscles and joints protested the sudden movement after four days crammed into the tiny cockpit.

"Let's never do that again," Meg suggested, bending at the waist while her back popped and cracked.

"Agreed," I replied, shaking my arms to increase the blood flow. "Should we stay in our flight suits or…"

"Leave them here," she replied, removing her helmet and placing it on the racer's wing. I did the same as she shook her head to let her hair flow freely, closing her eyes in relief as she sent it swinging in a halo around her pixie face. "Ahh…so much better."

I followed her lead as we stripped out of the flight suits, folded them neatly, and placed them back in the cockpit with our helmets before using the external controls to close and lock the canopy. By the time my boots returned to the deck, a uniformed alien had marched over, data pad in its three-fingered hand. "Landing fee is five hundred quark," he announced. "Payable immediately. Plus two hundred quark per day."

Fumbling for the paystick Matt had given me, I was just about to press it to the offered receiver when a large, clawed hand descended on the collector's shoulder.

"I will pay," a deep, familiar voice rumbled, using his pad to pass payment credentials to the worker.

"Very good," the worker replied, unconcerned with who paid for the spot. "Enjoy your stay on Asterock," he said before scurrying off.

"Good to see you again, Kloth," I said, greeting Princess Goloran's grithyak bodyguard with a nod.

He regarded us with piercing yellow eyes before his lips peeled away from gleaming fangs in what passed as a fleeting smile. Inclining his shaggy head in response, he was as mute as usual, his gaze shifting to Meg. He nodded a second time before turning and walking away, expecting us to follow.

"Charming fellow," Meg whispered under her breath as she and I both struggled to match his long strides.

I smirked in agreement but knew asking him to slow down would be a waste of breath. Besides, his left ear twitched, and I knew he'd heard her soft, unflattering remark. I doubted he cared since he continued his brisk pace through the crowded corridors, his imposing form easily parting the seas.

We boarded a tram at the bottom of central docking, riding it through the hollow tubes to what the pod's neutral AI voice announced as the VIP District, which didn't come as much of a surprise.

"So much for keeping a low profile," Meg remarked as the tram slowed to let us off.

"The princess definitely likes her comforts," I whispered as Kloth's ear twitched again.

Exiting the tram station, we soon emerged into the

bright lights and soaring chrome towers of a transparent-domed city built into the crevices and crags of a smaller-sized planetoid. Kloth led us past high-end shops selling everything from the latest in body mods to chrome-plated sport cruisers that made the hop racer's sleek design seem quaint by comparison. Well-heeled beings of various species strolled along the gleaming walkways, chatting and laughing.

My nerves spiked as we walked out in the open, remembering what Markan had said about having eyes and ears everywhere. Even Goloron's most trusted military engineer had fallen prey to the syndicate's promise of riches. It occurred to me that the princess might have chosen the VIP District for our meeting because these individuals didn't need quark from Markan. Then again, the main thing the rich all seemed to have in common was an unquenchable desire for more riches. Every being we passed on our way to the meet could potentially be a syndicate informer, and we would have no way of knowing.

If Kloth noticed my unease, he gave no indication. He simply forged ahead until we arrived at the entrance of a posh restaurant. As we approached, the front shimmered with a forcefield that parted like a curtain. Inside, the lighting was a dim, soothing blue, the walls softly pulsing with bioluminescence. Diners reclined on floating hover couches around tables that appeared to be made of living crystal, delicate fronds waving gently. The air smelled faintly of flowers and spice.

"This is unreal," I said to Meg, gawking at the interior design while Kloth guided us to a private booth at the establishment's rear. An opaque marbled forcefield faded to semi-translucent as it parted like a curtain to let us in, revealing Princess Goloran on the other side.

She rose from her seat, a genuine smile gracing her sculpted marble features. "Noah, it's wonderful to see you again." She paused, eyeing me with greater discernment. "You've changed."

"How so, Your Highness?" I asked.

"When last we met, you seemed like a child disciple following your master. Now, you appear to be a warrior in your own right."

My cheeks heated at the compliment. "Thank you, Your Highness. You haven't changed at all."

"I assume that's a good thing?" she asked.

"Of course," I replied.

The princess shifted her gaze. "And you must be Meg. A pleasure to meet you."

"You as well, Your Highness," Meg replied, trembling beneath Goloran's gaze. "I'm sorry, I'm a little nervous. I've never met a princess before."

"I may have a special title and a duty to the good of a planet, but I still eat, sleep, and breathe as you do." She motioned to the floating bench around the table. "Please, make yourselves comfortable. We have much to discuss."

I waited for Meg and Goloran to sit before joining them, adjacent to Meg and opposite the princess. My gaze briefly cut to Kloth, but Goloran waved a delicate hand. "Thank you Kloth, that will be all." The grithyak silently melted back through the forcefield, which regained its opaque hue.

Goloran leaned forward, lacing her fingers on the shimmering table. "Captain Murdock kept his request to a minimum to avoid the Warden's attention. I'm incredibly curious regarding the circumstances that have brought us together like this."

"I'd like to tell you everything," I said. "But I need to make sure you understand the gravity of the situation."

"Nothing that transpires between us both now and in the future will go beyond myself and Kloth. You have my word on my honor as Gothor's heir. Even my crew will have only as much knowledge as is necessary for them to complete their tasks. I understand the delicate nature of our partnership completely. Now, tell me everything that's happened."

Over the next hour, we filled her in on our exploits, from confronting Markan and Twama's betrayal to the revelations about chaos energy and the nanite disabler. It wasn't always comfortable to reveal so much, but Ben had made it clear that we needed allies, and she was our best immediate hope for aid. Besides, almost nothing I said was anything Markan didn't already know, and we were at least confident the princess wouldn't betray us to the Warden.

"This nanite disabler...do you have it with you?" Goloran asked, once we had finished our tale. "I'd very much like to see it."

Meg shook her head apologetically. "No. It's still back on Head Case. We may need to use it to disconnect from the Warden completely."

The princess considered that before nodding. "No matter." She sat back, steepling long fingers. "The vital thing is that you have the coordinates to Levain's secret station, and with it, the Wardenship itself."

"We do," I replied. "Up here." I tapped my temple. "I don't know if Ben mentioned this to you, but I intend to monitor your helm and enter the coordinates into your nav system myself."

Goloran's expression turned to stone, unhappy with the idea. "You still don't trust me, after all you've just revealed?"

"It's not you that we don't trust you, Your Highness," Meg said. "Even entering the coordinates ourselves won't guarantee their security. If your ship's network is compromised—"

"That would never happen," Goloran snapped.

"You might be surprised," I said. "You're familiar with Lantz?"

She rolled her eyes. "Of course. The contractor who thinks he's worth the moons and stars."

"He's pretty talented. He hacked the network of one of Markan's ships. So it can be done."

Goloran relaxed back into her seat. "Point taken. We shall need to be on alert when we reach the station in case we have visitors before our work is completed."

"If possible, we 'd like to move the Wardenship," Meg said. "Transport it somewhere safe as soon as feasible."

"A prudent course of action. Depending on size, we may be able to envelop it in Resolute's hyperspace field."

"Resolute is your personal flagship, I assume?" I said. She nodded in reply.

"If not, that's why I'm here," Meg said. "I'll do what I can to fix the hyperdrive. If it even has a hyperdrive."

"Very well," Goloran said. "Then the plan is set. I have been gathering resources for the mission, and my crew is already in place, including four units of my personal guard. They are some of the best trained warriors in the galaxy. You will meet Kloth in central docking, Level One, Arm One in three hours for departure. He'll escort you to Resolute."

"Just one thing," I said before she could finish dismissing us. "I promised Matt I wouldn't leave his hop racer behind. Meg can meet with Kloth. I'll transfer from the hangar bay to your ship once we clear Asterock."

Goloran seemed hesitant but ultimately agreed. "Very well. Since you have the coordinates, I suppose I have no choice but to agree to your terms."

"Great!" I said, sliding off the bench to my feet. Meg followed behind me. "It's always good to do business with you, Your Highness. We'll be in—"

My voice died in my throat as the restaurant exploded into chaos.

CHAPTER 7

As the restaurant erupted into pandemonium, my recently instilled combat instincts kicked into high gear. In one fluid motion, I dove back into Princess Goloran's booth, narrowly avoiding the hail of blaster fire peppering our position. Meg hit the floor beside me a heartbeat later, rolling into a crouch with her weapon already drawn.

The booth's forcefield shimmered and flared, absorbing the initial barrage of energy bolts. It wouldn't hold for long under such a concentrated assault. We needed to act fast or risk being pinned down and overwhelmed.

"Those have to be Markan's assassins," Meg snarled, risking a glance over the table's edge before ducking back down as fresh plasma scorched the air where her head had been. "At least a dozen, maybe more. They were posing as diners."

"So much for a low profile," I muttered darkly. I hazarded my peek at our attackers. My blood ran cold at the sight of multiple beings in nondescript clothing rising from their seats, an array of weapons clutched in clawed, scaled, or all-too-human hands. They fanned out in a loose semicircle, cutting off our escape routes and angling for clean shots around the rapidly failing forcefield. Meanwhile, the few innocent eaters crawled on their hands and knees for the front door.

"What about Asterock Security?" Meg asked.

"Markan probably owns them, too," I replied. "I wouldn't expect any help there."

A hiss drew my attention to Goloran. The princess held a small, sleek blaster in one hand and a hunting knife in the other—the same blade Matt had traded for her plasma dagger. The sight of it surprised me. I had thought she planned to keep it as a collectible, not carry it for protection. Her face was set in stone, fury and determination burning in her eyes.

"On my signal, focus fire on the left flank," she said tightly. "We punch through their line there and make for the exit."

I nodded, nerves twisting in my gut. "What about Kloth? Where is he?"

Goloran raised a finger as an ear-splitting roar shook the restaurant. I lifted my head over the table just in time to see Kloth come barreling into view like an enraged bull, fangs bared and claws extended. He slammed into the nearest assassin, sending the unlucky soul flying into a table in a crash of splintering crystal. Snarling, the massive grithyak fell upon his screaming victim, finishing him off.

The other attackers shouted alarm. Several spun to face the unexpected threat, unleashing a flurry of blasts at Kloth. He agilely escaped their barrage, using tables as cover as he circled the assassins before smashing into their midst with unstoppable momentum.

"Now!" Goloran cried.

Meg and I surged to our feet and burst out of the booth as the forcefield faded. Meg's blaster spat crimson light, quickly dropping an assassin, holes smoking in her chest.

The princess rolled out of cover, snap-firing at another foe. He crumpled with a gurgle, clutching his ruined throat.

I didn't have time to shoot. I had barely cleared the booth when a pair of masked killers closed in on me from my flank, plasma blades alight with deadly intent. I met their charge head-on, one hand up in a defensive stance while my gun hand swung toward them.

A sharp kick from one of the attackers knocked the blaster from my hands, leaving me backpedaling while I regained my balance. The second's blade scythed toward my eyes, and I swayed back as much as possible, feeling the heat of its passage singe my cheek. Planting my back foot and grabbing his extended wrist, I pivoted hard, using our collective momentum against him. He sailed over my hip with a startled cry, crashing headfirst into a floating bench with enough force that he didn't get up again.

I spun to meet his partner's follow-up strike, barely intercepting the incoming blade by catching the man's wrist. Even so, the heat of the plasma slowly sank into my forearm while I pushed back, surprising myself with my overall strength. Gritting my teeth, I managed to turn his wrist aside before lashing out with a palm strike to his chin. His head snapped back and I yanked the blade from slackening fingers. Reversing my grip in one smooth motion, I slammed the butt of the hilt into his temple. The assassin's eyes rolled back and he crumpled like a puppet with cut strings.

No time to celebrate the small victory.

More killers were already closing in, intent on avenging their fallen comrades. I tensed, ready to meet them, peripherally aware of Meg holding her own against another foe.

A barrage of plasma bolts seared past my ear, catching my would-be attackers. They tumbled backward as Goloran appeared at my side, her blaster's muzzle still wafting heat. The princess flourished her knife, lips peeled back in a feral smile.

"We need to get back to my ship," she panted. "If Markan is willing to be so bold to reach you, then nowhere on Asterock will be safe."

Exactly as I'd feared before leaving the hangar bay to meet her. Hindsight was twenty-twenty, but her insistence on leading us here so she could dine with other VIPs left me silently miffed.

"Agreed." I glanced at Meg, relieved to find her unharmed and standing over another prone form. "Meg, retreat!"

We ran, swinging around and even backpedaling to lay down cover fire. Kloth surged to meet us, his fur matted with blood, a savage light in his eyes. He alone had accounted for putting down half our attackers. The rest seemed far less eager to engage us after seeing his lethality at work.

We gained the exit with a scattering of hastily aimed shots. Spilling out into the street, I noticed a commotion further away, where Markan's promised reinforcements were trying to reach us.

"Tram station," Goloran urged. "Quickly!"

Kloth took the lead, powerful legs eating up the distance in ground-devouring leaps. The rest of us ran flat-out to keep up, the station rapidly growing larger ahead. More shouts and the zing of energy blasts erupted behind us. Stealing a frantic glance over one shoulder, I spotted additional armed figures spilling from side passages, joining the others in giving chase.

Reaching the station, we poured through the entrance toward the platform. Two station guards stepped out from behind the cover of support beams, their rifles shouldered, both weapons aimed at me. I fired wildly at one, my blasts peppering the beam and forcing him back behind it as confused riders screamed and searched for their own cover. The other guard succumbed to the combined fire of Meg and Goloran..

"Don't slow down!" Goloran cried as two more station guards opened fire from our flanks.

Archie moved beneath my clothes, crawling out to my shoulder and leaping away, shapeshifting to a maulvas before landing on the floor. I nearly did a double-take as he charged one of the guards. Now the size of a French bulldog, the Aleal had grown by at least fifty percent since leaving Head Case. It leaped onto the guard's chest, and before he had a chance to scream, Archie ripped his throat out in one jerk of its powerful jaws.

Pushing off the man's writhing body, Archie lunged at a second attacker, latching onto his lower leg and shaking him so hard none of the bolts he fired to dislodge Archie hit their target. Finally, the guard went down, his gun flying from his hands as he hit the floor and began kicking at Archie with his free foot. Archie hung on as tendrils snaked out from its sides and shot up to the man's groin, stabbing deep. I could almost feel the guard's pain.

"Archie!" I shouted. "Let's go!"

It responded immediately, releasing the assassin and sprinting across the floor, zig-zagging between plasma bolts on its way back to me. It leaped to my shoulder just as I skidded into the open doors of the waiting tram right behind Meg and Goloran. Hot on my heels, Kloth jumped in behind me.

"Come on, come on, come on," I repeated, waiting for what felt like a lifetime before the doors ground sluggishly shut and the tram began to move. That didn't stop Markan's killers from firing at the vehicle.. Shields unexpectedly absorbed the bolts in showers of sparks as the tram pulled out of the station. I leaned against the back of a seat, breathing a sigh of relief.

"They were waiting for us!" Meg hissed through labored breaths, shifting to a nearby seat. The tram had unloaded its passengers before our arrival, the entire car empty except for us.

Goloran shook her head, anger and worry warring across her face. "No one knew my whereabouts except for myself and Kloth. And I'll personally kill anyone who doubts his loyalty to me."

Kloth grunted in appreciation for her faith in him.

"Well, somebody told them where to find you," Meg insisted.

"All of those patrons were already in the restaurant when we arrived."

"Maybe you were supposed to survive this attack, but Noah and I weren't!"

Meg had barely gotten the words out before Kloth's large hand wrapped around her throat, using his other hand to pin her to her seat. Archie stirred on my shoulder, ready to defend her.

"Enough!" Goloran commanded. Kloth immediately let her go. "I will only say this one more time. My honor is more valuable than all the quark in Warexia, and will never be for sale."

"Twama must have told Markan of our involvement with you," I said. "He's likely had agents tailing you ever since. He also likely had assassins planted in every restaurant on the VIP asteroid."

"He can do that?" Meg asked.

"And a lot worse."

As if responding to my words, the tram shuddered and lurched, throwing us against the walls. A second impact rocked the car, metal shrieking in protest. Through the viewport, I caught a glimpse of an emblazoned black shuttle pacing us outside the transit tube, weapon mounts glowing red.

"You just had to say it," Meg groaned.

"Hang on!" I shouted.

The shuttle opened fire again, stitching lines of molten holes through the hollow cabling and into the tram's shields, shaking it inside the tunnel.

"We're easy targets in here," Goloran growled, more angry than afraid.

"At least we have shields," Meg replied, face pale.

A sudden, earsplitting bang sounded from the rear of the car. My head whipped around to see atmosphere venting from a jagged rent in the rear doors, the bent metal peeling away like foil. Frost crystalized instantly in the air, flash-freezing the inside of the breached compartment.

"The emergency bulkheads aren't dropping!" Meg cursed, staggering toward the front of the car. "We're losing pressure!"

Another barrage hammered into the tram's side, swaying us violently. I lost my footing and fell, rolling toward the hull breach. Scrabbling for purchase on the smooth deck, icy air clawed at my lungs as I fought to draw breath.

Meg's desperate shout rose over the roaring in my ears. She thrust her hand toward me, eyes wide with fear. Reaching for her, my fingers strained toward her outstretched grip as another blast struck home.

The tram shrieked and bucked, Meg's terrified face vanishing in a wash of sparks and smoke. I had one panicked instant to register my hurtling slide toward the hungry void. Before I could reach it, a clawed hand clamped around my wrist with crushing force.

Kloth hauled me through the air, his powerful form braced between seats as he held me aloft. His lips spread from yellowed fangs, tendons standing in sharp cords along his neck as he fought the pull of decompression.

It couldn't last. Even the grithyak's immense strength

rapidly failed against the vacuum trying to pull us out into space. My lungs burned, and my vision darkened to a narrow tunnel as anoxia set in. Meg and Goloran appeared as distant, writhing shapes fading into an encroaching haze. I knew they were trying to reach us, to pull us back from the brink, but their efforts seemed futile.

We were doomed.

With my fading senses, I almost missed the massive shadow rapidly rising alongside the tram cable. An angular, armored prow swelled impossibly large in our view, swallowing up the murderous shuttle pacing our dying tram. The attacking craft vanished as if swatted by a giant's hand, its broken remains spiraling into the infinite darkness.

"Got it!" Meg cried triumphantly as an emergency bulkhead cut off the last third of the tram, sealing the compartment and trapping the remaining air inside. I sucked in a great shuddering gasp, coughing harshly as my vision cleared.

Hazy shapes resolved into Kloth and Goloran kneeling over me, relief etched across their faces. The tram had come to a full stop inside the tunnel, and a glance out of the viewports revealed flashing lights of security vessels coming to our aid.

Thankfully, the large warship that had saved us remained adjacent on the opposite side, drifting ever closer to dock with the tram.

"How did they know we were in trouble?" I asked, voice strained.

"Kloth alerted them as soon as the trouble started," Goloran replied. "I may have underestimated Markan, but I'm no stranger to risk. A princess is always a valuable prize to certain sections of the galaxy."

"Well, we'd better hurry. I don't think Asterock Security is too interested in taking statements."

"Thankfully, the trams have emergency protocols," Meg said. "When they work, anyway. We came to a stop at an interlink point."

Before I could ask her what that meant, the craft shuddered lightly. A moment later, the doors opened. Several heavily armed Gothorian Marines in combat armor stood just outside, their weapons trained on us.

I gingerly pushed myself upright, quickly taking stock. Despite being battered and bruised, nothing seemed broken. My lungs ached with each breath, and based on the itchy sensation along one cheek, I figured my face was bruised and swollen.

On wobbling legs, I followed the princess from the savaged remains of the tram, across the interlock to the waiting marines.

"Matt is going to be pissed about me leaving his racer here," I commented when we stepped onto Resolute.

"I will replace your vessel if you fail to retrieve it later," Goloran promised. "Right now, reaching Levain's station is all that matters."

I nodded, resolve settling around my shoulders like Archie. She was right. Assassins and sabotage were only the beginning. We had kicked the hornet's nest by going after him on his home turf. It would require all of our combined ingenuity to outmaneuver him in this deadliest of games.

One thing was certain. The path ahead held only more danger. But we had come too far to turn back now. Everything we cared for might hinge on the success of this mission.

We had to reach the Wardenship.

Whatever the cost.

CHAPTER 8

My skin felt tight and tender as I gingerly touched the swollen flesh of my cheek, wincing at the fresh sting of pain. We followed behind Princess Goloran and Kloth through the sleek corridors of Resolute, my muscles protesting the abuse of our narrow escape.

The sick bay doors whisked open at our approach, revealing a sterile space filled with more advanced medical tech than Head Case had to offer. It also had cleaner bulkheads and nicer uniforms for the medical personnel, but otherwise wasn't that much different in appearance.

"Your Highness," a Gothori in a crisp white uniform said, rising smoothly to her feet to give the princess a respectful bow. "I wasn't expecting—"

"Don't worry yourself with decorum right now, Doctor Jashti," Goloran replied, waving off her concern. "We ran into some trouble planetside. Please see to our guest's injuries."

"Of course," Jashti replied. "Thankfully, all of our med bays are empty at the moment." She pointed to the first open bay, where a machine similar to Head Case's autodoc dominated the center of the room, its gleaming metal arms poised like a spider above the exam table. She gestured for me to approach. "Please, have a seat there."

I settled on the autodoc's seat with a barely suppressed groan, the adrenaline of our flight rapidly fading to leave every ache and pain I had in stark relief. I held still as the machine hummed to life above me, extending delicate scanner arms to play over my body. It was all I could do not to fidget under the tingling sweep of the beams.

After a moment, Doctor Jashti studied the holographic readout with a small frown. "Some minor contusions and lacerations," she reported, "but nothing requiring additional treatment. You'll be sore for a few days, but there's no serious damage."

I exhaled in relief, catching Meg's eye. "Guess I got lucky."

She snorted. "If that's what you want to call it."

Jashti returned with a small device that looked somewhat like a gun. "For the pain and inflammation," she explained, putting it to my neck. A warm tingle slithered down my spine. Almost immediately, a soothing numbness spread through my body, the jackhammer in my skull fading to a dull throb. "Thank you," I said sincerely.

Goloran stepped forward, relief evident on her sculpted features. "I'm glad you're relatively unharmed. We should get to the bridge. Time is of the essence."

I nodded, sliding off the autodoc's seat. As my boots hit the deck, a subtle vibration trembled through Resolute's hull, a sensation I immediately recognized. We had entered hyperspace.

"Looks like your crew had the same thought," I remarked.

Goloran smiled. "They know their duty. Come."

She led us through the ship, bypassing crew members

who snapped to attention as we passed. We arrived at the bridge in no time, the doors parting to reveal organized activity. Officers manned various stations, their faces a mix of concentration and unease. Because of the trouble we encountered on Asterock, they remained on high alert.

"Her Royal Highness, the Princess Goloran on the bridge!" a nearby Marine announced, snapping to attention. The rest of the bridge crew rose, turning her way and doing the same.

"As you were," Goloran said, advancing to the central command chair. A stern-looking Gothori woman glanced up from her status displays. Meg and I trailed right behind the princess.

"Your Highness, we jumped to hyperspace the moment we cleared Asterock."

"Well done, Commander Vaas," she replied. "And the enemy?"

"We destroyed the ship attacking the tram, along with a second smaller vessel that got a little too close. We took no damage."

"Excellent. How long will we remain in hyperspace?"

Vaas consulted her display. "Just under a minute, Your Highness."

"Noah, Meg, meet my first officer," Goloran introduced. "Commander Asha Vaas. Asha, this is Noah and Meg. They will assist us during our mission to the Wardenship."

I opened my mouth to correct her statement. She was supposed to be assisting us, not the other way around. An elbow from Meg cut me short. Now wasn't the time to split hairs.

"An honor," Vaas replied, though her tone and expression remained neutral. I got the sense she wasn't thrilled about outsiders being brought into the heart of Resolute's operations but was too disciplined to let it show.

"Likewise," I said.

"Do you think the individuals who attacked us will face any repercussions with Asterock authorities?" Meg asked while we waited for Resolute to finish its short jump.

"It seems hard to believe the syndicate can control the entire station," I replied. "Even if some of those authorities are on the take. If movies are anything to go by, someone will have to be the patsy and take the fall."

"Probably someone Kloth killed in the restaurant," Goloran agreed. "That way they don't lose any operatives."

"You have experience with this kind of thing?" I asked.

"The biggest difference between Markan and myself is that I try not to break galactic law to get things done. But even I have to bend or break the rules sometimes to achieve my goals. I'm certain any leader of a large group can say the same."

"Your Highness," Commander Vaas said before I could come up with a reply. "We are about to exit hyperspace."

Once again, I sensed the shift as we returned to sublight velocity. Almost immediately, a chime sounded from the comms station. "Your Highness, we're being hailed," the officer on duty reported, frowning at his console.

Goloran's brow furrowed. Whoever it was, they had likely been trying to contact the ship while it couldn't respond. "By whom?"

The officer hesitated. "The signal is encrypted, but the transit time suggests it is originating from Asterock."

One of Goloran's thin eyebrows went up. "I see." Goloran's eyes met mine, a silent question in their depths. I gave a tight nod. "Put it through," she ordered. "Audio only."

The screen dissolved into static before resolving into a voice I knew all too well.

"Princess Goloran," Miss Asher greeted, her tone dripping with mock cordiality. "I have to warn you that your choice of traveling companions leaves much to be desired."

Goloran's face remained impassive, betraying nothing. "I don't believe I know what you mean."

A dark chuckle rolled through the speakers. "Come now, Your Highness. Let's not play games. You know precisely of whom I speak. The would-be assassin you're currently harboring aboard your vessel."

"And who are you?" the princess demanded.

"My name is Helva Asher. I'm a representative for an organization that you should be very careful dealing with."

I flinched at the accusation, cold sweat prickling along my hairline. She knew. Of course, she knew. The syndicate had spies everywhere. Though it surprised me that she had come to Asterock herself and hadn't been in the restaurant.

Or had she? Having seen Kloth fight, maybe he had been a match for the Nycene.

Goloran's expression hardened. "I don't take kindly to baseless accusations. Nor do I appreciate your methods of doing business."

"Baseless?" he scoffed. "Hardly. The young man you plucked from the burning wreckage of the tram is a traitor to my organization. My former pupil. He betrayed his family, and needs to be punished. I want him turned over to me. Immediately."

Goloran straightened in her seat, practically vibrating with barely leashed fury. "How dare you. How dare you threaten me on my own ship, criminal. I am a princess of Gothori. I answer to no one save my King, and least of all the likes of you."

Silence stretched for a long beat. When Asher spoke again, her already meager pretense of civility had vanished. "I'll give you one chance, princess. One chance to reconsider your decision to meddle in business that doesn't concern you. We have no desire to make an example of the Gothori, but if you continue to shield the traitor, you will leave us no choice."

My heart pounded, panic leaving a sour taste on my tongue. This was it. Asher, and by extension Markan, had all the leverage here. His display of power on Asterock had shown he had the power and reach to upend Gothor, and the princess knew it. She would have no choice but to give me up to save her people, her planet.

I held my breath, not daring to move. Goloran remained motionless, eyes fixed forward, though she probably only saw red. I could practically hear the gears turning in her head as she weighed the risks and costs.

Slowly, Goloran leaned forward. "I don't respond well to threats, Helva. And I don't bargain with terrorists. Noah is under my protection. This conversation is over."

She made a sharp gesture, and the connection cut off, plunging the bridge into ringing silence. No one moved, hardly daring to breathe. I stared at Goloran, scarcely believing what had just happened. She had stood up to the syndicate, despite Asher's threat of war.

She had chosen me.

After a moment, Goloran turned to me, her face set in determined lines. "Noah. I believe you have coordinates for us?"

I nodded numbly, still reeling. "Y-yes. Yes, I do."

"Then please, take the helm. Time is wasting."

Shaking off my shock, I moved to the navigator's seat. The officer there shifted aside, allowing me access to the console. With trembling fingers, I input the coordinates I had long since memorized, the ones leading to Levain's hidden station and the Wardenship.

Behind me, I heard Goloran address her crew, her voice clear and unwavering. "All hands, prepare to jump. We have a mission to complete. I want this ship at high alert. Our list of enemies is getting longer, but we'll trim it back soon enough."

A chorus of "Yes, Your Highness!" rang out as the crew scrambled to obey.

I finished inputting the coordinates. The nav computer chirped, displaying our projected course.

"Six hours," I announced. "We're almost there."

Drawing a steadying breath, I backed away from the helm. The officer looked at Goloran. "Your Highness, shall I initiate the jump?"

"With haste," she replied.

The officer finished the sequence, and the stars blurred to black.

"Thank you, Your Highness." I said. "For refusing to turn me over to Miss Asher. I know that couldn't have been an easy decision."

She waved a hand dismissively. "Actually, it was an easy decision. It's like I said, I don't bargain with criminals. You can repay me by providing more detail about your relationship with that witch of a woman. It sounded like you jilted her quite badly."

"I guess she's taking my infiltration of the syndicate and subsequent turn pretty personally. She's probably mad she didn't see through the deception Ben and I exhibited." I allowed myself a sharp grin and a shrug. "What can I say... she's a sore loser."

Goloran chuckled. "We have a few hours. I will show you to your quarters, where you can clean up, rest, and refresh yourselves. I'll have food delivered as well."

"Thank you, Your Highness," Meg said. "We appreciate your hospitality."

"And I appreciate the opportunity to learn more about the Warden than anyone has in millennia. Hopefully, it will turn out to be as fruitful as I anticipate."

"Agreed," I said, lifting my eyes to the pitch black of hyperspace, to the unseeable future hurtling toward us. For better or worse, we had set events in motion that couldn't be undone. All we could do now was see this through and hope we came out the other side intact.

The Wardenship awaited us, a promise and a curse all in one. Would it be the key to everything we had been striving for, or a noose growing tighter around our necks with every passing second?

We would find out soon enough.

CHAPTER 9

I stared at the viewscreen in awe and trepidation as Resolute neared its destination. Jump variability being what it was, we'd come out of hyperspace nearly an hour away from the coordinates at sublight speeds, extending the time for my nerves to fray. Zoomed views had revealed the general nature of the station ahead of time.

It was shocking but not entirely surprising that Levain's secret construction completely hid its contents. Rather than a spindle or wheel shape, or a giant robot, or even asteroids linked together, Levain's station appeared as a huge but basic cube. It reminded me a little of Head Case in the way long sheets of likely thin metal had been riveted together to form the giant shell. Antennae and shield nodes bristled from the otherwise ordinary surface, hinting at sensors and comms despite the station boss' use of handwritten notes passed directly to Nyree to communicate with Levain. I also doubted the station had a commweb connection or any kind of external network capabilities. A small set of hangar bay doors stood out starkly against the monolithic structure, the only visible means of entry.

"Your Highness," Commander Vaas said. "Sensors are

picking up minimal energy output. Not even enough to fully power the shields. We could punch a screw through it without much effort."

"We didn't come to destroy the station," Goloran replied. "We came to explore it."

"Of course, Your Highness," he replied. "Based on the output, it is unlikely there is anyone inside."

"How do we know the Wardenship is even in there?" Meg asked. "This could all be an elaborate trick or misdirection. Or worse, a trap."

"Whose trap?" I replied. "The Warden doesn't need to trap us. Neither does Markan. They can come after us wherever we are. And Nyree had no reason to send us on a wild goose chase. If Levain has a Wardenship, it has to be in there."

Meg leaned forward, squinting at the display. "That makes sense. But there's no activity at all. No ships, no transmissions, barely any power output. Maybe whoever was there abandoned the place when they heard Levain was dead."

"How would they know Levain is gone, though? He only communicated with them through handwritten notes."

"Or so we've been led to believe," Meg countered, playing devil's advocate.

"Even if it seems uninhabited, that doesn't mean it is," Goloran intervened. "Remember, Levain's primary legal business was building bots. We only met because I was on Cacitrum to purchase his machines. It's possible the station is fully automated, occupied by robots instead of organics."

"Good point," I said.

"We'll send a drone in first to investigate." She turned to her tactical officer. "Launch a recon probe. I want sensor readings from the interior, and a better look at what we're dealing with."

"Yes, Your Highness," the officer replied crisply, fingers waving across a control surface only he could see through sleek goggles. "The drone is dispatched."

"Put its feed on the secondary viewscreen."

We all turned our attention to the feed as the drone streaked out into space, heading toward the distant station. Maneuvering thrusters flared, propelling the small craft toward the looming cube. It looked insignificant against the vast, featureless expanse, a fragile mote of metal and circuits.

As the drone drew closer, its scanners searched for any new hint of activity. But the station remained dead and unresponsive, an impassive block of silence and shadow. I shifted uneasily, anxiety and excitement playing tug of war in my gut.

Mere meters from the hangar doors, the drone paused. For a moment, it hovered there, sensors straining. Searching. The quiet on the bridge was oppressive, the tension palpable.

A precision laser lanced out from the drone. It burned through the doors' thick metal with unsettling ease, the edges of the new opening glowing molten in the darkness. My heart pounded, my throat dry as I watched the drone enter.

The interior feed flashed onto the screen, and my breath caught. The hangar stretched out before us, cavernous and empty—too empty. There were no starships, shuttles, towering Wardenships, maintenance bots, or anything else. An eerie stillness pervaded the space, further setting my nerves on edge.

We barely had time to process the absence before the feed dissolved into static. Beside me, Meg gave out a startled curse.

"What happened?" Goloran demanded.

Her tactical officer's fingers waved like Archie's tendrils

as he tried to reestablish the link. "Unknown, Your Highness. We've lost contact with the drone." He shook his head, clearly baffled. "The last sensor report showed no anomalous readings. No movement, energy spikes, or anything else out of the ordinary."

"Did we get anything before the drone went dead?" Meg asked.

"Not much," the officer replied. "Scans indicate the hangar is protected by a stable forcefield, and oxygen levels are within tolerable range."

Goloran steepled her fingers in front of her chest, clearly weighing her options. "Prepare a second drone. Let's see if we can glean anything else before we commit to a physical incursion."

The second probe met the same fate as the first. It passed through the breach in the hangar doors without incident, only to wink out seconds later. No warning, no explanation. Just an unnerving absence where there should have been answers.

I exchanged an uneasy glance with Meg. "Maybe you were right. Maybe it is a trap."

"Probably not specifically for us, but for anyone who might happen to stumble across the place," she replied.

"Agreed," Goloran said, jaw tight. "We never expected this to be easy. And we haven't come this far to turn back now." She turned to her first officer. "Commander Vaas, assemble a unit of Marines. I want them suited up and ready to deploy in five minutes."

Vaas snapped a tight salute. "Right away, Your Highness."

I shifted restlessly. "Your Highness, with all due respect, I'm not sure sending your forces onto that station without more information about what to expect is our best move."

"I could send the rest of my drones to vanish over the

threshold," she replied harshly. "That's not what I would consider an efficient use of resources."

"Do you have any other tools that might be able to see into the station?"

Goloran looked to Vaas for a response. He shook his head. "Resolute's sensors are unable to pierce the outer shell."

"Shielded from prying eyes," Goloran said. "We have no other choice but to deploy Marines."

"I should go with them," I said.

"No," Goloran replied. "It's one thing for me to risk my own subordinates. I won't risk your safety needlessly."

"I understand you're trying to protect us," I pressed, "and I appreciate that. But this is our mission. It's my responsibility to see it through."

The princess' eyes narrowed. "You doubt my intentions."

"No," I said quickly. "I trust you. You could easily toss us both in the brig on a whim." I met her gaze steadily, willing her to believe me. "I'm just asking that no one boards the Wardenship without us. Please."

For a long, taut moment, Goloran simply stared at me, searching my face. Then, slowly, she inclined her head. "You have my word. No one will set foot on that ship before you."

Relief swept through me. "Thank you, Your Highness."

We watched in tense silence as a shuttle loaded with armored Marines detached from Resolute's hangar. It swiftly crossed the distance to the station, making a more substantial hole in the hangar doors before slipping inside. Like before, we lost contact as soon as it crossed the threshold.

"Kilo Unit, this is Resolute," Vaas said. "Report status."

Silence.

A muscle jumped in Goloran's jaw. "Kilo Unit, respond."

More silence. The seconds crawled by, each one more agonizing than the last.

Just as I was certain something catastrophic had befallen our scouts, a hiss of white noise sputtered from the comm speakers. I flinched as a voice emerged from the static.

"...tain Hyn, reporting in." The Marine commander's face flickered onto the main screen, his marbled features tight with strain. Behind him, I could make out the interior of the shuttle, consoles dark and emergency lights painting everything in shades of red. "Apologies for the delay. We...ah...ran into a bit of trouble on entry."

Goloran leaned forward intently. "Explain."

Hyn grimaced. "The moment we passed into the hangar, the shuttle lost all power. We crashed into the rear bulkhead. Think we crushed our drones when we hit. As you can see..." he gestured to the eerily lit cabin. "...we're on backup systems now."

Meg frowned. "An EMP?"

"Unlikely," I murmured. "Resolute's sensors would have picked up the pulse through the hole we opened. This is...something else."

Vaas' voice crackled over the comms. "Captain, what's your team's status?"

"A few bumps and bruises," Hyn replied, "but we're combat ready. Whatever blew the electronics didn't have enough juice to get through two layers of heavy shielding and take out our personal power supplies."

As he spoke, four more video feeds winked to life on the secondary display, resolving into the helmet cams of the other Marines. They had already departed the crippled shuttle, fanning out on the hangar's forward bulkhead with weapons at the ready. Their boots made soft clomping noises as they moved across the hangar deck.

"Do you see any signs of activity?" Goloran asked, a thread of tension underlying her words.

"Negative, Your Highness," Hyn replied, exiting the shuttle behind his unit. They waited for him before advancing to the nearest hatch, where one hit the door control. The blast door slowly moved aside, barely receiving enough power to open automatically.

I held my breath as I watched them pass through the hatch, the beams of their rifle-mounted lights scything through the darkness to reveal a long, nondescript passageway. Exposed wiring dangled overhead while hoses occupied the corners of the deck.

"Looks like they built the place in a hurry," Meg said. "They didn't bother with solid piping or conduits."

The Marines trekked deeper into the station, navigating through passageways bereft of signs of any recent activity. The station's interior quickly became a labyrinthine of featureless corridors, silent and still as a tomb. No movement. No hint of the promised ship. Nothing.

Captain Hyn led his Marines deeper into the maze of corridors. Their helmet-mounted lights created shifting pools of illumination in the oppressive darkness, the beams dancing across featureless metal walls and ominous shadows. Every step echoed too loudly in the stillness, a staccato rhythm of barely controlled dread.

"Kilo Unit, report." Vaas' voice crackled over the comms, shattering the eerie quiet.

"Negative contacts," Hyn replied, his voice a low rasp. "No sign of hostiles. Or anything else." Despite his steady tone, I caught the flicker of unease in his gaze. This place was getting to him. Getting to all of them. It was downright spooky.

They pressed on, boots ringing on the decking, lights probing the darkness. Despite their simple construction, the corridors twisted and turned, doubling back on themselves in dizzying patterns. A maze designed to confuse and disorient. To trap the unwary in an endless circle of metal and shadow. Levain hadn't wanted to make it too easy to reach the prize.

If the prize existed.

Cold sweat beaded on my forehead, my heart's constant thudding becoming painful. My muscles ached from tension. My mind practically screamed for something to happen. Anything that would offer release.

Hyn rounded another corner and froze.

"Captain?" Vaas called, alarm bleeding into her voice. "Captain Hyn, what do you see?"

For a moment, the Marine didn't respond. He stood there, rifle lowered, staring at something beyond his helmet cam's view. Something that had struck him dumb. Then slowly, he raised a hand and pointed. "There," he breathed. "Through the viewport. Is that...?" He trailed off, but he didn't need to finish. As he took a hesitant step closer, his helmet cam zoomed in on the sight before him.

"The Wardenship," I whispered, my blood turning to ice in my veins. It wasn't identical to the one that had confronted us when we arrived in Warexia. Its bulbous, bubbling, dragon-scale shell seemed more primitive, an earlier iteration perhaps. Its overall design made it as undeniable as anything else.

We had found it. Finally.

"Captain Hyn," Goloran said. "Hold position. We will join you on the station shortly."

But something was wrong. Even as relief and stunned joy surged through me, I could feel the claws of dread sinking deep into my gut. I didn't move either, because Hyn wasn't responding. He wasn't moving, reporting more on the find, or ordering his team to secure the area. He wasn't doing anything at all.

He just stood there, staring at the ship. His light flickered.

And then, in the strobing flashes of the malfunctioning

light, I saw them. Shapes, moving in the darkness between Hyn and the ship. They darted between the shadows with a speed both mesmerizing and utterly terrifying.

The lights of the other Marines began to strobe wildly, the beams swinging in dizzying arcs as they spun to confront this new threat. Shouts of confusion and fear erupted over the comms.

"Hyn, report!" Vaas demanded.

Instead, the sharp retort of weapons fire filled the air as the Marines opened up on the unseen attackers. It was chaos, utter panic as muzzle flashes illuminated frantic, disjointed snippets of the carnage. Armored figures struggled against writhing shadows sweeping through the passageways, followed by the wrenching sounds of rending metal and then screams sharp with pain and terror. They were the death cries of hardened warriors torn asunder by an enemy they could barely comprehend.

I watched in mute horror as Hyn's rifle spun crazily, light strobing once, twice...and then shattering into a burst of sparks as something struck it with incredible force. His scream rose above the rest, a raw, animal sound of pure agony before abruptly cutting off. He dropped to the deck, his feed leaving us looking at the overhead wiring, the lens spiderwebbed with cracks.

All around, the other helmet cams captured only the barest impressions of the carnage. The enemy moved too quickly to track, blurs of shadow that danced between the strobing lights.

None of the Marines seemed to land a hit. Their shots went wide, the panicked full-auto fire punching through thin bulkheads without making contact with their attackers. They were firing blind, the enemy never more than half-seen horrors lunging from the gloom.

And then, choked screams faded into final breaths. The

gunfire petered out. Lights flickered as they dimmed.Finally, one by one, the helmet cams winked out.

The bridge remained still, all of us frozen in horror. Goloran stood like a statue, face bloodless, eyes fixed sightlessly on the dark screen where the Marine feeds had been. Her hands gripped the edge of the tactical console with crushing force.

I slumped back in my chair, numb with shock. This couldn't be happening. Those Marines...Captain Hyn...it had all occurred so quickly. One minute they were there, strong and vital. The next...

Meg made a soft, choked sound. I glanced over to see her staring at the darkened screen with wide, haunted eyes, tears tracing unheeded down her pale cheeks. I knew my own face likely mirrored hers, an amalgamation of disbelief and terror.

Because we had seen...something. Something fast and brutal. Something that could wipe out a unit of hardened soldiers in the space between heartbeats.

And it stood between us and the Wardenship.

CHAPTER 10

Goloran's voice, when she finally spoke, emerged rough and strained. "This mission is over. We're leaving."

Her words jolted me from my stunned daze. I turned to stare at her, not quite believing what I'd heard. "What? No. We can't just give up!"

She fixed me with a flat, empty gaze. "You saw what happened. Whatever is on that station, we're not equipped to face it. I won't send any more of my people to their deaths."

"But the Wardenship is there! After all I've gone through to get here… We've come too far to turn back now."

"Did you not see the same feed I did?" she snapped, a flicker of anguish breaking through her icy facade. "An entire unit of my best soldiers, wiped out in seconds. We wouldn't stand a chance."

I pushed to my feet, desperation lending strength to my words despite the vein of horror and fear threatening to keep me quiet and allow Goloran to turn tail and run. I didn't want to die, and right now, going in there sure seemed like an effort in futility, but this was too important. Despite what Tyler had said, this might be worth dying for.

"We have to find a way! This is our one shot at getting information that might help us get home. That might help us stand up to both the Warden and Markan. That ship is likely the key to everything!"

"Maybe," Goloran retorted, "but how many lives would you have me throw away over a possibility?"

"Please," I tried again, forcing myself to meet her gaze. "I know you're scared. I am too. But we can't let fear stop us. Not when we're this close."

She shook her head, unmoved. "I'm sorry, Noah. But this mission is over. We're returning to Gothor immediately. I'll inform Captain Murdock that I'm taking you home with me."

I couldn't let it end like this. An idea struck, equal parts reckless and determined. I stepped closer, holding her eyes intently.

"One," I said.

"One what?" she replied.

"How many more lives should you throw away for the possibility? Only one more. Mine," I said, clapping my palm to my chest.

"What?" Meg and Goloran gasped in unison.

"You saw what's out there!" Meg exclaimed. "Noah, it's suicide!"

"I have to try," I insisted, my resolve hardening. "That ship is our only lead. Without it, Tyler and Ally might never make it back to Earth. You, Leo, Ben, Matt…you'll never get back to the Spiral. I have to do this. For them. For you."

"If you're going, then I'm going with you," Meg insisted.

I shook my head. "No. I need to do this alone. It may not be as much of a suicide mission as you think. My nano-fiber underlay can cloak me, and the holomask has night vision. I can hopefully stay hidden, and see in the dark. I can scout the area, find out what those things are, and see if there's a

way to either destroy them or somehow get around them."
I turned back to Goloran. "Just give me a shuttle. If I fail,
you've only lost me."

The princess stared at me for a long, tense moment. I
could practically see the gears turning behind her eyes as
she weighed my request. Finally, she exhaled a sharp
breath.

"I'm not your princess. Your life is your own. If you
want to risk it on this, then against my better judgment, I
will provide you with transportation."

Relief surged through me, chased by a thrill of fear.
"Thank you. I won't let you down."

"Do not make me regret this, Noah. Too much hangs in
the balance."

"I agree. That's why I have to go."

She turned to Meg. "Go with Noah. Help him prepare.
And see if you can establish any sort of video link with his
suit. I want eyes on him at all times."

"Yes, Your Highness," Meg replied.

"I'm already wearing the suit," I said. I reached into my
coat pocket, retrieving the holomask and holding it out to
Meg. "I don't think you can get a video feed through this,
and carrying an external camera will risk the cloaking capabilities."

Meg examined the holomask, shaking her head in disbelief. "I'd need a microscope to even guess at this thing's
capabilities. But whoever made it...this thing is way more
advanced than anything in the Spiral."

"Markan made it," I said. "On top of being a Gilded,
he's an inventor. He's also a thousand years old, so he's had
some time to learn some things. Unfortunately, he never
learned how to be anything but an asshole."

Meg turned to Goloran. "I'm sorry; there's nothing I can
do with this. Not without weeks to study it."

"I understand," she replied, looking thoughtful. Whatever was going through her head, she didn't share. A sudden thought struck me then.

"Your Highness, can I ask another favor?"

"You can ask."

"I'd like to borrow your knife. The one Matt traded to you. It's low tech, which seems like it might be more effective against whatever is on that station."

Goloran retrieved the blade from a thigh sheath beneath her long gown and handed over the knife without further comment.

"Thank you," I said, securing it to my belt. "I'll transfer it to a pouch in the underlay when we get to the hangar. Otherwise, I'm ready to go."

"Are you certain about this?" Goloran asked.

A large part of my brain tried to scream that I was anything but certain. I overrode it, nodding my head. It didn't matter how scared I was, I had to go through with this.

"Very well. Commander Vaas, make the arrangements."

"Yes, Your Highness," she replied.

"Noah, Meg, follow me."

We made our way to the hangar, where a small shuttle was in the final stages of preparation, already warmed up and moved closer to the bay doors. I was surprised when Kloth emerged from the vessel, bowing to the princess.

"Kloth will accompany you," Goloran announced. "I won't send you in completely alone, and I desire an active feed during your ingress." I opened my mouth to argue, but she cut me off with an upraised hand. "This is non-negotiable. Kloth will keep his distance so as not to give away your presence or position. He will engage only if you are in grave peril. Grithyak have naturally good night vision, plus he is an elite warrior and may be your only lifeline in there."

I still wanted to refuse. To insist on shouldering this

burden myself. But the steel in Goloran's eyes brooked no argument. And if I was being honest, the thought of Kloth watching my back felt reassuring.

I blew out a breath. "Alright. Together then." I handed Matt's knife to Meg to hold while I removed my coat, shirt, pants, and everything else that wasn't the underlay, leaving me in a skintight bodysuit that I would have been embarrassed to be seen in a few weeks earlier. It seemed so unimportant right now. Putting my free hand out, Meg passed me back the knife, and I tucked it into a slim opening in the underlay made for carrying equipment "That's it then," I said. "I have comms. I'll let you know how things are going as soon as I can."

Goloran put a hand on my shoulder. "Be careful, Noah. And good hunting."

"Thank you," I replied.

Meg threw her arms around me the moment Goloran removed her hand. "Be safe," she said, holding me tight. " You better come back. I'll be waiting for you."

"I'll do my best, Meg," I replied, returning her hug. "But if I don't make it b—"

"No," she ground out, her hands moving to grasp my wrists as she drew back and scowled at me. "You'll make it back. I have faith in you."

"Thanks, Meg," I said, giving her a brief smile before advancing to where Kloth waited at the shuttle's open hatch. The grithyak bowed to the princess one last time, and we boarded the shuttle. Stepping inside, I noticed an array of basic blades arranged in bandoliers spread across one of the shuttle's bench seats.

"Maybe I should have asked *you* for a knife instead," I commented. Of course, Kloth didn't respond. He stared at me until I moved onto the flight deck and settled into the pilot's chair. He continued looming behind me as Commander Vaas' voice came out of hidden speakers.

"Shuttle Fren, you are cleared for launch," she said.

"Copy, Commander," I replied, lifting off the deck and opening the throttle. The shuttle shot out of the hangar, my heartbeat synced with its acceleration toward the station.

I angled our approach vector, aiming through the hole the first shuttle had burned into the hangar door.

"Hang on," I told Kloth as we neared the opening. "The moment we pass through, we'll lose power. Gotta land this thing fast."

The bodyguard merely grunted, bracing himself. I took a final steadying breath, hands tightening on the controls. I had one shot. I had to make it count.

We streaked toward the breach. The instant we crossed the threshold, the shuttle gave a sickening lurch, every system winking out like a snuffed candle. Prepared, I already had the back skids angled down to take the brunt of the shuttle's weight off the nose skid when we hit. Backup systems quickly came online, not enough to provide flight control, but enough to activate the maglocks as we collided with the deck.

Metal screeched and groaned as the maglocks sent us spinning across the hangar in a shower of sparks until finally, we came to a sudden stop. For a moment I simply sat there, heart galloping, breath ragged in my ears. We'd made it. Step one complete.

Now, the real work began.

I turned to Kloth, meeting his unflinching gaze. No fear showed in his flinty yellow eyes. Only a grim determination that mirrored my own. Moving to the shuttle's back cabin, I took a moment to put on the holomask, setting the underlay to initiate cloaking. We popped the hatch and climbed out onto the hangar deck, senses straining for any hint of the horrors that lurked deeper within.

My suit's HUD glowed before my eyes. Looking down at my hands, I was pleased by the way I could see right through them, with only a faint outline visible at the edges. Night vision already active, my environs jumped into sharp relief. No movement. No signs of life, human or otherwise. Just Kloth at my side and the silent bulk of our downed shuttle at our backs.

Even so, fear churned in my gut, terror threatening my resolve. The feeds of Hyn's unit being slaughtered played over and over in my mind. Every instinct screamed at me to turn back, to flee this metal coffin before it claimed me, too.

But I couldn't. Not with so much at stake. Tyler, Ally, the memory of my parents... I owed it to them to see this through. To find out what dark secrets this place guarded and perhaps if one of them could get us home.

Sinking into a low crouch, I began creeping into the gloom, the grithyak a shadow trailing silently some distance behind.

Even if I didn't make it, I would at least die knowing I'd done all I could to help us return to where we belonged.

But I didn't really want to die doing it.

CHAPTER 11

I crept through the darkened corridors of the station, heart pounding, every sense straining for any hint of danger. The silence pressed in on me, a tangible weight broken only by the barely audible scuff of my padded feet on the deck. Even with my cloaking engaged, I felt exposed. Vulnerable.

Rounding a corner, I froze. There, sprawled across the passageway, lay the bodies of Hyn's Marines. A wave of nausea churned in my gut at the sight of them, armor rent and bloody. I swallowed hard, fighting down the urge to retch. Seeing death on a viewscreen was one thing. Confronting it in person was something else entirely.

If I hadn't already known Kloth shadowed me at a distance, I never would have guessed he was there. He moved like a ghost, soundless and unseen. Only the prickling sensation between my shoulder blades, the constant feeling I was being watched, assured me he remained close at hand.

Carefully, I picked my way forward, giving the fallen a wide berth. Ahead, I could just make out the edge of the viewport where Hyn had spotted the Wardenship. My pulse kicked up a notch. So close. We were so close to unlocking the secrets of that ship. I just had to get past whatever horrors lurked between here and there.

Archie shifted restlessly beneath the nano-fiber under-lay, sensing my unease. I sent a soothing thought to the Aleal. I needed to stay focused.

But Archie wasn't in the mood to be placated. It squirmed free of the suit entirely, dropping to the deck in the form of a small maulvas. I sent an urgent thought toward it, but it didn't react, so I started reaching out to keep it from doing anything too reckless. We couldn't afford to break stealth.

That's when I noticed the walls.

At first glance, they appeared as normal bulkheads. A little more pitted and worn than the rest of the station, but nothing overtly strange.

Except the surface seemed to ripple and undulate when viewed from the corner of my eye. A texture that crawled and skittered, there and gone between blinks.

Unease sent a chill down my spine. Slowly, I leaned in for a closer look, my brow furrowed in confusion. What was I looking at?

And then I saw them. Hundreds of them clinging motionless to the bulkheads. They looked like large cock-roaches or scarabs, their sharp, segmented bodies a flat metal, revealing them as machines. They covered nearly every inch of the bulkheads, packed so tightly together for as far as I could see they almost seemed to merge into a single grotesque mass. Seeing they were bots and not monsters momentarily lifted some of my unease until I reconsidered how easily they had cut down Goloran's Marines. Maybe not the terrifying beings I'd envisioned and feared, but still just as dangerous.

My gaze flicked to Archie, my gut clenching. The Aleal had slipped between the dormant machines without issue, its inky form nearly invisible against the shadows. It waved a tendril at me as if telling me to advance because everything was fine.

No part of me felt like anything about this was fine. Still, right now, the machines seemed dormant. There were too many to try to destroy them all or clear a path through them, despite what I had initially hoped. I had to trust the underlay's cloaking and infrared blocking to allow me to pass through them undetected.

Shifting my weight slowly, I crept forward. One step. Two. All my attention remained locked on the machines, searching for any hint of activation. Hunting for even the slightest sign they'd sensed my intrusion.

A barely perceptible flicker of red blossomed to malevolent life on the nearest construct. Infrared for a pinhole camera eye at the top edge of the small machine.

I froze, ice flooding my veins. I was pretty confident it couldn't see me. It would finish its sweep, and the light would go out, satisfied that the corridor remained clear.

Meanwhile, Archie had already reached the far side of the passageway without incident, waving its tendrils urgently.

I didn't dare move while the tiny Eye of Sauron remained fixed. I kept waiting for it to blink out and my path to clear.

It didn't.

Instead, more of the red beacons blinked into existence along the bulkheads, duplicating rapidly. Glancing down, I saw the syndicate's stealth suit working as designed. It mirrored the corridor perfectly, rendering me invisible while blocking my heat signature completely.

Somehow, they knew I was here but didn't know Archie had already snuck past. It couldn't be that they didn't care about the Aleal's presence. It didn't have a heat signature either, but it remained visible in the soft, resultant glow of the many eyes. What was the difference between Archie and me, according to the machines' programming?

I realized with sinking dread that it could hear me—my booming pulse, my tense breath—the tenets of most organic life, but not all. Archie didn't breathe in a traditional sense. Its colony accepted necessary molecules from its surroundings directly and individually, and its processes occurred on a microscopic scale that the machine hadn't been designed to register.

That was my working theory, anyway. And the outcome remained the same. Despite the stealth suit, I couldn't get through.

Slowly, so slowly, I took the first step back and then another. The machines remained affixed to the bulkheads, seemingly content to bar my path rather than pursue it. I took it as a small but important victory that I'd managed to identify at least what had attacked Hyn and his unit while avoiding their fate.

As soon as I'd cleared their immediate vicinity, I turned and hurried back the way I'd come. I needed a Plan B. Archie rejoined me before I'd gotten too far, scampering along the deck like man's best friend and coming to heel beside me. I looked down at him several times, certain he'd grown a little more in the few minutes we'd spent in the passageway.

"Kloth," I whispered harshly into the darkness once I'd backed far enough away from the machines to feel safe. "We have to find another way through."

The grithyak materialized from the shadows ahead, approaching from less than twenty feet away and leaving me amazed at his natural stealth. When he arrived, he stared at me silently, waiting for me to explain.

I opened one of the pouches in my stealth suit to retrieve my robot-head-shaped comms and tapped on it. "Meg, do you copy?" I whispered breathlessly.

"I copy," Meg replied. "What's wrong?"

I locked eyes with Kloth. "Is Goloran with you?"

"I'm here," she said, voice slightly more distant. "What's happening?"

"The good news, if you want to call it that, is I've identified what killed Hyn and his unit. There are hundreds of small robots that look like insects clustered along the bulkheads leading to the ship. I tried to sneak past them, but I think they're attuned to biological signatures. Heartbeats, respiration, that sort of thing. Archie waltzed right past them without a problem."

Silence reigned over the comms for a long moment. I could practically hear the wheels turning in the others' minds as they digested this new intel.

"If they're machines," Meg said, "then there has to be some way to shut them down. Otherwise nobody would ever be able to access the Wardenship."

"She's right," Goloran agreed. "A failsafe, or a central control system. Or even a special transmitter that would identify you as a friendly. Something to allow authorized personnel through."

"You need to find the station's control room. There has to be a way to bypass the defenses from there."

"Maybe. What if there are more of those bugs between here and the control room?" I asked.

"How smart is your pet?" Goloran asked. "Can it work independently?"

"Archie isn't a pet. It's a friend. And yes, it's smarter than I am. It just can't speak. We'll find the control room and see if we can find a way to shut down those bugs."

"Be careful, Noah," the princess said. "And keep us updated."

"Affirmative." I cut the link, glancing at Kloth.

The grithyak remained stone-faced as always.

"Sounds like we need to find the control room," I said. He responded with a barely perceptible nod.

With that, we forged through the gloom of the abandoned station, searching for any hint of the command center or any other space that looked like it might help us deactivate the sentries guarding the Wardenship. Time was lost as we prowled the corridors, opening every hatch and following every passageway. The station remained barren, not only of life but supplies, equipment, and sundries that might suggest anyone had been here in the past or planned to be here in the future. I knew someone had occupied the station at some point because they had sent messages back to Levain. So where were they? Why had they left?

My dark musings over the idea that they might have forgotten their ID badge one day and had inadvertently been shredded by the defenses almost had me smiling. Of course, if that had been the case, their decomposed body would have been in the corridor with Hyn and his Marines.

Which brought me back to the original question. Why was the station so deserted? Levain had managed to capture a Wardenship, and then after the station was finished, he apparently had left it to rot. No crew, no personnel, just empty halls and dormant machines standing guard over untapped secrets. It made no sense.

Kloth's sudden hiss snapped me from my spiraling thoughts. I followed his unflinching stare to a nondescript hatch just ahead. It looked like any other door we'd passed, except it bore additional biometric security measures— what looked like a retinal scanner, in combination with a keycode entry.

This had to be it. I flashed Kloth a tight grin. "Jackpot."

Approaching the panel, I ran my fingers across the smooth surface. Kloth touched my shoulder, eyeing me questioningly when I looked back.

"This shouldn't be a problem," I told him. Reaching into

the hidden pouch of my underlay, I retrieved one of the small security cracking devices we had recovered from the SpecOps module on Nakata. Placing it against the control panel, I counted the seconds as it adhered to the smooth surface, tiny lights flickering along its edges as it started its infiltration program.

I'd reached seven when the device flashed green. The hatch swished open with a pneumatic hiss, revealing the darkened interior.

Immediately, two pairs of crimson optics faded into being directly ahead of us, revealing a pair of humanoid robot defenders who apparently hadn't taken kindly to our unannounced entry. They began raising gun-hands toward us.

Kloth reacted instantly, a throaty roar erupting as he leaped to meet the constructs. Razor claws unsheathed from his fingertips, the wicked talons raking across metal and digging in with brutal efficiency.

I didn't have the luxury of going for my blaster. The robots were already too close, their gun-hands swiveling to track me with deadly intent. Instead, I surged forward to close the distance between them and me. Their ranged advantage would be negated if I could get inside their guard.

The nearest robot reacted with unsettling speed, its free hand lashing out to snatch my neck in its crushing grip. Cutting off my air, it hauled me off my feet with terrifying strength and slammed me against the bulkhead. Pain flared through my shoulder and ribs.

In my peripheral vision, Kloth fared only slightly better. His claws screeched across the other robot's armored chassis, tearing a gash down its torso. Sparks and fluid spewed, but the machine barely slowed. Its fist slammed into the grithyak's gut, forcing him to backpedal into the shadows, out of view.

That and the fact that I couldn't breathe were the least of my worries. The gun-hand of the robot holding me by the throat swept toward my head, and I knew a moment's hesitation meant a plasma bolt through the skull. I groped frantically at the pouch in my stealth suit, where another of Miss Asher's favorite toys—a sort-of EMP device—was hidden.

As my fingers closed around it, Archie slammed into the robot's gun-hand, and the plasma bolt meant for my head seared past my holomask, slamming into the bulkhead. Black spots danced in my vision as I pulled the device from my pocket, shoved it against the bot's chest, and pressed the charge button. The device made a soft thudding sound as it sent a powerful pulse into the robot. The machine sputtered once before completely losing power, my mission only half-accomplished.

The robot's pneumatic fingers remained locked tight around my throat, constricting my airway. I struggled to breathe, finally panicking when all I could do was wheeze. I knew I didn't have the strength to pry its mechanical fingers apart, but I reached for them anyway, pulling in vain at them with everything I had. Behind me, I could hear Kloth still struggling as hard as I was to land a killing blow to his own opponent.

Archie again came to my rescue. Leaping onto my shoulder in his maulvas form, it melted into gelatin and sank between the robot's fingers, pushing them apart. As the bot's grip on me loosened, I ripped its hand loose and dropped to one knee, finally able to gasp for air.

I whipped around at the crack of rending metal, just in time to see Kloth toss his opponent's gun-hand into the shadows, the robot's body still spraying sparks and fluids. The grithyak roared in bestial triumph, driving the robot to the ground and pounding it with his fists until the light finally faded from its optics.

Archie returned to my side, back in maulvas form. "Thanks, bud," I rasped, my throat raw as the Aleal rubbed its head against my leg. "I think I owe you for about a hundred saves now."

I met Kloth's eyes across our fallen foes, a look of weary camaraderie passing between us.

"Nice moves," I offered, my voice just beginning to sound normal.

He chuffed, a predatory sound equal parts dismissive and approving before nodding his head toward the cleared passageway, urging me forward.

I certainly wasn't going to turn back now.

CHAPTER 12

With the robotic sentries destroyed, we remained alert to the likelihood of encountering more as we proceeded cautiously into the inner sections of the station. The areas we passed through now—abandoned workstations, empty bunks, even a small kitchen with a thin layer of dust on the counters—held obvious signs of past habitation. It seemed this deeply embedded space had once housed a skeleton crew, though they were long gone.

We had just finished opening a hatch into a storage compartment stocked with cleaning supplies when the metallic clang of robotic feet alerted us to incoming contacts. With a choice to fight or flee, I would have chosen to duck into the compartment to wait them out.

Kloth had a different idea.

He let out a wild roar and vanished around the corner before I could stop him, forcing me to follow. By the time I reached the corridor, Kloth had already removed the head of one bot and turned to engage another.

Archie sprinted from my side to join the fray, darting ahead and jumping at one of the bots, shape-changing in mid-air into a hardened spike. The bot, confused by the nature of the attack, froze in place, allowing the Aleal to spear it through the head. It lost power, standing limp as Archie extracted itself.

I wasn't idle either. My EMP device still in hand, I lunged forward and jammed it against the robot engaging Kloth. It too stopped moving, arms dropping to its sides as its power supply shorted out.

It must have had time to call for backup. We barely had a moment to catch our breath before another trio of sentries bore down on our position and opened fire. Diving behind the dead sentries, we returned blaster and plasma fire.

"Archie!" It turned, raising two tendrils as if to ask what I wanted. It caught the EMP device I tossed, pulling it into its gelatin mass. "You know what to do with it."

It waved a tendril and darted toward the bots, bounding this way and that to avoid their fire. Kloth hit something vital on one, creating a shower of sparks and smoke as it collapsed to the deck. Archie reached the remaining two, lashing out with a tendril to attach the EMP to one of them before flowing up the leg of the second one, finding a path inside the robot at its knee joint. Whatever it did in there stopped the bot mid-stride, and it toppled to the deck with an echoing clang.

"I think we're getting the hang of this," I said as Archie popped out of the bot's hip joint and returned to my side. Kloth responded with an approving grunt.

We encountered two more groups of sentries as we ventured deeper into the station. We dispatched each with increasing efficiency, finally arriving at a heavy blast door deep in the heart of the station. A control panel embedded in the bulkhead beside it meant we needed a new level of clearance to enter.

"This has to be it," I said. "The command center."

Kloth grunted in agreement. I retrieved the cracking device and affixed it to the panel, watching with bated breath as it worked to subvert the defenses. I didn't know how complex the software behind the security hardware would need to be to stymy Markan's tech, but if any door might resist the cracking device, I figured this one stood the best chance. Time stretched, tension coiling ever tighter in my chest. I didn't want to have to come up with a Plan C if this didn't work.

A soft chime sounded, and the device flashed green, the blast door cracking open. I met Kloth's gaze, relief and trepidation mingling. "Archie," I said softly. "Scout it out."

The Aleal crept forward, slipping through the gap into the control room. Almost immediately, a plasma bolt flashed and sizzled against the inside of the door.

"Archie!" My heart seized. I whipped around the door frame and stopped short. The Aleal crouched before a scorch mark on the deck, its maulvas teeth bared and a quarter-inch diameter bolt-hole through its chest. As I watched, the hole filled in with gelatin, the wound vanishing before my eyes and its mass smoothing over as if a hole had never been there. Archie's maulvas had shrunk slightly but otherwise looked no worse for wear.

Beyond Archie, a plasma pistol gripped in one shaking hand, stood a small Hemid. His eyes were wide, the pupils huge in a scarlet face filled with shock, confusion, and fear at the translucent mini-wolf.

Behind me, Kloth growled, surging forward to attack. I quickly threw out my arm to stop him, pointing my blaster toward the overhead.

"Archie, Kloth, stand down," I ordered. I wasn't sure Goloran's bodyguard would listen until he eased off. Archie remained fixed in place, waiting in case I changed my mind. "Easy there," I told the Hemid, his eyes shifting from Archie to me. "We're not here to hurt you."

I could almost see the wheels turning behind his over-sized forehead. His arm began to move, his pistol swinging my way. Kloth suddenly ducked under my arm and grabbed the Hemid's wrist, twisting the gun from his grip and slamming him to the deck. Looming large over him, he raised his clawed hand for a killing blow.

"Kloth, wait!" I cried. "We need him."

Kloth looked back at me, his eyes narrowed in confusion until the Hemid yelped, feet kicking at the big grithyak's leg. Kloth's features dropped back into a scowl as he returned his attention to the Hemid, grabbing the little fire-brand up off the deck and giving him a hard shake.

"Bastard!" the Hemid spat, straining against Kloth's iron hold. "Whoever you are…" He looked back and forth between us. "…you don't belong here. And when Levain finds out about this, you're going to wish you were never born."

"Levain is dead," I told the Hemid bluntly.

His struggling stilled. His face slackened in shock. "Wh-what? No… you're lying!"

"Zariv's bots ambushed him and put about three dozen holes in him. I was there when it happened."

"I don't believe you," the Hemid insisted.

"You have no reason to," I replied, "except, how do you think I found my way here? I've been to Levain's penthouse. I found the handwritten notes you exchanged. I know his daughter, Nyree, was the messenger, and that she probably hasn't been here in at least three months."

"You know Nyree?" he said, calming a little. "Where is she?"

"Unfortunately, she's dead, too. I didn't kill her," I quickly added. "Zariv did, right before I killed him. She gave me the coordinates to the station."

"That…that all seems so impossible."

"Yet, here I am."

The Hemid considered what I had said. Finally, he relaxed in Kloth's hold. "I can't think of how you would know all of this if you weren't telling the truth. Only Levain, Nyree, and myself knew about the messages."

"Kloth, let him go," I said.

The grithyak looked back at me, hesitant until I narrowed my eyes in a glaring challenge. Thankfully, he respected me enough to release the Hemid, letting him fall on his butt and back away.

"What's your name?" I asked as the Hemid returned to his feet, his eyes fixed on Archie while the Aleal returned to my side.

"Wh…what is that thing?" he asked.

"Its name is Archie. It's my friend."

"Friend? I shot it, and it didn't even bleed."

"It doesn't have blood," I replied, stating the obvious. "Now, tell me your name."

He worked his jaw for a long moment, calculations visibly racing behind his eyes. Finally, he croaked, "Faarl. I'm Faarl."

"Faarl," I repeated. "I'm Noah. We're not your enemies."

"But you aren't my allies, either, are you?"

"That depends on you," I answered. "How long have you been here? From the look of things, I'm guessing it's been a while."

The Hemid looked away, shoulders slumping. "Too long," he muttered. "Levain was supposed to send a research team to examine the ship a year ago. But they never arrived." His mouth twisted bitterly. "I've been alone here ever since. Just me and the machines."

"No one else?" I pressed. "No one has tried to board the Wardenship?"

Faarl barked a humorless laugh. "Even the poor bastards that towed that thing in haven't been on board. No one has. Levain forbade anyone from attempting it." He shook his head. "He said it wasn't safe. He needed to find the right experts."

I digested that, wheels turning. "Of course," I said, nearly laughing out loud. Levain wouldn't trust anyone to board the Wardenship without him being here.

"Of course, what?" Faarl questioned.

Levain wasn't an engineer himself. He was smart enough to know he needed people to decipher the Wardenship's mysteries. "Levain went looking for high-end scientists and engineers to help him with the ship. Only the Warden probably got to them first, and they refused to sign on. You were left stranded here while the Warden plotted to have Levain killed." I paused, still considering everything I knew about Levain and the Warden. "Only, I don't think the Warden realized Levain wanted them for help with the ship. He probably thought the specialists were coming to help him with the tech that let him travel to Earth. But who knows, maybe he wanted them for both."

"Earth?" Faarl asked, still not following me.

"The Warden manipulated things so that Levain and Zariv both wound up dead, along with their two-timing, double-crossing, double-agent Jaffie." His name still tasted vile coming out of my mouth. "That's why those specialists never arrived here. Whether the Warden dissuaded them or had them killed is a question for another day."

"I don't understand," Faarl said.

"Kloth, you get what I'm saying, don't you?" I asked.

He shook his head. No clue.

"Archie?"

Archie waved a sad tendril. It also didn't know what I was getting at.

"Nevermind," I said, slightly deflated as I returned my attention to Faarl, holding his gaze. "You've been here a long time, alone and forgotten. I understand your hostility. But with Levain gone, continuing to follow his directives is pointless, don't you think?"

"What do you suggest," Faarl asked.

"Help us help you," I answered. "Help us reach the Wardenship. In return, you have my word that we'll take you with us when we go. No more solitude. No more waiting for a master who will never come."

Faarl wavered, indecision and desperate hope warring across his crimson features. I could only imagine the toll his long isolation had taken.

"You're really going to board the ship?" he asked.

"We're going to try," I answered honestly. "Will you help us?"

For a long, tense moment, Faarl simply stared at me, searching my face. Then, slowly, he closed his eyes and exhaled a shuddering breath. When he opened them again, a new light flickered in their depths. The light of newfound purpose.

"I've always wanted to see what's on that thing, and Levain can't threaten me if he's dead. So, sure. Why not? I'll help you."

CHAPTER 13

I stepped away from Faarl, retrieving my comm badge from the pouch in my underlay. "Meg, Princess Goloran, do you copy?"

"Noah!" Meg's relieved voice replied a moment later. "I'm happy to hear from you. What's your status?"

"Banged up, but alive," I replied. "We made it to the station's command center."

"Is Kloth well?" Goloran cut in with a surprising display of concern.

I glanced at Kloth, who nodded despite the blood matting his fur. "Also banged up. He could use a medic, but he'll never admit it."

"Then he is well enough to continue," she answered, hiding her feelings toward the grithyak once more. "Have you disabled the defenses?"

I glanced at Faarl, working diligently at a console, pointedly ignoring my conversation. "Not yet, but we're working on it. We encountered a Hemid named Faarl. He was part of Levain's crew."

A pause, then Goloran's voice again, sharp with suspicion. "Can he be trusted?"

"I believe so. He's been alone here for months, ever since Levain stopped sending supplies or relief crews. He's agreed to help us access the Wardenship."

Meg blew out a relieved breath. "That's the best news I've heard all day. What's the plan now?"

"Faarl is shutting down the remaining security measures. The guard bots, the drones, the hangar defenses, all of it. You should be clear to dock and join us shortly."

"Understood," Goloran replied crisply. "We'll prep shuttles immediately. I'll be bringing a unit of Marines to recover our fallen, and my engineers to assist with the Wardenship. And Ashti to look you and Kloth over."

"Good idea," I agreed. "We'll meet you in the hangar."

But whatever else she intended to say was swallowed by a sudden rumble from deeper within the station. The deck shuddered beneath my feet, the vibrations growing stronger by the second.

Kloth was on Faarl instantly, ready to cut his throat for betrayal.

"W...wait," Faarl cried. "I restored full station power. That's just the primary reactors initializing. They've been offline for some time, at Levain's orders. I'm also fully disengaging the hangar bay doors so your companions don't need to continue shooting their way in." He laughed nervously.

Understanding clicked, and I nodded. "Kloth, let him go. We'll see you soon, Your Highness." Kloth released Faarl and backed away.

"We'll be there shortly," Goloran replied before Meg disconnected.

I returned the badge to my pocket and looked up to find the Hemid watching me, his craggy face unreadable.

"It must be nice," he said quietly, "having allies who care what happens to you."

His words hit like a punch to the gut. He knew Levain

didn't care about him. "Why did you agree to come here?" I asked.

"I didn't have a choice. Once you're under Levain's employment, you do what you're told. If you want to keep breathing, you don't say no."

"You never thought about leaving when nobody came?"

"Of course, but did you see any other vessels in the hangar?"

"No," I replied, realizing that he probably would have left if he'd had the means. Levain had stranded him out here in the middle of nowhere. "Well, Levain is gone, and we're here now."

"Right." Faarl visibly shook himself, turning back to his work. "I've shut off the station defenses. You have a straight shot to the Wardenship."

"Well done, and thank you," I replied, and meant it. "We should head down to the hangar."

Faarl rose from his seat, something rekindled in his formerly haggard features. Something that looked a lot like hope. "After you."

With Archie still in maulvas form and sticking close to my right side, we quit the control room and retraced our steps through now silent corridors. The lack of threats, of metallic foes lurking in the shadows to ambush us, left me in endorphin-fed relief, my prior tension replaced with hopeful anticipation.

Goloran organized her forces quickly, the shuttles already visible as they approached the hangar bay through the protective forcefield. By the time they settled into the cavernous space, the four of us waited for them near the entrance..

Immediately, they began disgorging Marines and engineers, who organized in columns on opposite sides of the deck. Princess Goloran strode out last, bearing regal and commanding even here, far from her home world. Behind her, Doctor Ashti pulled what appeared to be a portable autodoc, the machine hovering a few inches off the deck.

Meg flanked the doctor, looking uncomfortable in the midst of the landing party. A wide grin spread across her pixie face when her eyes landed on me. "Noah!" She broke away from the doctor's side, urgency quickening her steps until she took in the rents in my underlay and the orange blood drying on Kloth's fur. Her smile immediately disappeared. "You two look like hell."

"But I feel great," I replied sincerely. "We did it!"

"We did!" she agreed excitedly. "I can't wait to get a look at the Wardenship."

Goloran joined us as Meg finished introducing herself to Faarl. She didn't share her pleasantries, eyeing the Hemid with obvious distrust."You are Levain's man," she said, a statement, not a question.

To his credit, Faarl didn't flinch beneath her laser regard. He dipped his head in a formal bow, the gesture somewhat marred by his ragged uniform and haunted eyes.

"I was," he replied carefully. "But if Levain is gone as you say..." A spark of defiance entered his gaze as it lifted to the princess. "...I'm not his man anymore. My loyalty is to myself foremost. But I already agreed to help you gain access to the Wardenship, with the understanding you'll help me in return."

Goloran studied him for a long moment, the weight of her appraisal near tangible. Then, slowly, she inclined her head a bare fraction. "Of course," she allowed. "I expect this transaction to be profitable for all of us."

It wasn't exactly trust, but it was a start.

"Kloth, stand still while I scan you," Doctor Ashti said as she attempted to run a device along the grithyak's bloody fur. He seemed uncomfortable with the attention, trying to wave her off as if he were unharmed.

"Kloth, remain still," Goloran barked. The grithyak

froze at once, allowing Ashti to work. "You have a number of lacerations and burns," the doctor reported once she finished her scan. "But nothing serious." She turned to Goloran. "I recommend returning him to Resolute for full treatment."

Kloth grunted in displeasure.

"Can it wait?" Goloran asked.

"I can patch him up here, Your Highness, but we'll need to repeat the process once we're back on board the ship."

Goloran considered. "Kloth, you're dismissed. Return to the shuttle and await transport back to Resolute."

I thought the grithyak would argue. Instead, he bowed his head and retreated to one of the shuttles.

"Noah, what of your injuries?" Goloran asked.

"One of the guard bots choked me, but Archie came to my rescue. Again. My throat's sore, but I'm fine."

"Let's just take a quick look," Ashti said, scanning my throat before nodding. "Just some light swelling and bruising."

"Should we go then to see what we've got?" I asked.

"Indeed," Goloran replied, satisfied with the doctor's report. "Captain Loravan," she snapped, getting the attention of the Marine unit's leader.

"Yes, Your Highness," Loravan replied.

"Your mission is one of recovery. Provide Captain Hyn and his Marines with the respectful attention they deserve."

"Of course, Your Highness." She turned away from Goloran, her voice barely audible through her helmet comms as she gathered the Marines and led them past us, deeper into the station to recover the other Marines' bodies.

"Doctor Ashti, you're to wait in the shuttle with Kloth," Goloran said.

"Yes, Your Highness," she replied, bowing before following Kloth to the shuttle.

"Shall we?" Goloran said, motioning for Meg and me to

move in with her behind the Marine unit as we retraced our steps through the corridors. We paused while the Marines collected their fallen, gently placing them in body bags before securing a Gothori flag over each of the bags.

Simply witnessing the respectful procedure left me close to tears. Even stone-faced Goloran softened at the display, clearly pained by the loss of her troops. Once all of the fallen were properly covered, we waited as the princess went to each to say what appeared to be a short prayer in a language the Warden's pill, for whatever reason, didn't translate. It wasn't long before we were on our way again, leaving the Marines to escort the dead back to the ship.

The ratlike drones seemed far less deadly now that the station's lights were at full brightness. They remained massed against the bulkheads, small silver shapes gathered in the hundreds. I noticed now that each had two pairs of folded gossamer wings, like a dragonfly, tucked against their bodies. A few of the wings were dirty with dried Marine blood, suggesting the seemingly fragile extensions were sharper and more sturdy than they looked. As close as I had come to feeling their sting, a shiver skittered down my spine as we passed them by.

Reaching the end of the passageway, we all paused at the transparency to look down at the Wardenship, resting silently in its enclosure. In many ways, it resembled the ship that had intercepted Head Case soon after we emerged from the rift. In other ways, it appeared to be a different animal altogether. Or rather, a less evolved version of the same animal.

Where the first Wardenship was composed of dozens of bulbous protrusions as if someone had melted a few hundred spheres into dragon scales, this ship was much more angular, joined by polygons instead of scales. It didn't have the same shimmering sheen of the other Wardenship, and this ship was at most two-thirds the size of the first if not half the size.

Like the other Wardenship, there was no indication of thrusters or any sign of external propulsion, weapons, or shield generators. There were no window ports and nothing that suggested cameras or any other means of external view. And while the first Wardenship had felt intimidating and powerful, this one seemed surprisingly mundane. Although, maybe that had come more from my inexperience during our first encounter. I've learned and grown up so much since then.

"Is it powered up?" Meg asked, standing on tiptoes to get a better viewing angle of the ship.

"It has been offline since it was discovered," Faarl replied.

"Then why is it floating?"

I hadn't noticed that up until now. The ship hovered nearly a foot off the deck despite the artificial gravity on the station.

"One of many mysteries," Faarl answered.

"How do we get down there to enter it?" Goloran questioned.

"There's an elevator this way," Faarl replied. "Follow me."

He guided us along the viewing area to an elevator. Our main group boarded first, leaving the Gothori techs and engineers to wait. On reaching the lower deck, the doors opened to a small atrium ahead of an airlock.

"We'll need to pass through the sanitization chambers beyond that door to access the ship," Faarl said, shrugging out of his coat. "We'll need to remove our clothing here, pass through the sanitizer, and put on clean suits before entering the main chamber."

"Don't be ridiculous," Goloran snapped. "Open the seal."

"But…you may contaminate the Wardenship."

"It belongs to us now. And it's a risk I'm willing to take. Noah?"

I nodded. "Me, too."

"Then it's settled. Open the seal."

Faarl didn't look happy, but he also didn't argue as he put his coat back on. He let the control panel beside the door scan his face before pulling a lever to open the hatch. It whisked aside, allowing us to enter.

"Normally, sanitizing aerosols would come out of the vents along the bulkheads," Faarl explained as we passed through. "The process removes one hundred percent of debris on the skin, from dust to bacteria."

"Better than a shower," Meg commented.

"Not as relaxing," I countered.

"True."

The moment Faarl opened the next door, alarm klaxons blared, sensors picking up potential contamination. He quieted them quickly, and we crossed to the final sealed hatch. Opening that one left us standing at the edge of a raised platform leading to a barely visible seam in the underside of the Wardenship's hull. From this distance, I could see that the polygons weren't as jagged as the scales on the other ship. Instead, they appeared to be composed of an inky black metal that seemed to be on the verge of melting into a liquid.

"Amazing," Meg commented. "I can't wait to analyze the hull's composition."

"I've never seen anything like it," Goloran added.

"I've never been this close before," Faarl mentioned. "It is quite remarkable. Seeing it like this now, being so close to going inside, it almost makes it worth the solitude. Almost."

We crossed the platform, pausing again a few feet from the side of the ship. "How do we open the hatch?" I asked, looking at Faarl.

He shook his head. "I don't know. I don't know if anyone knows."

We all looked at one another. It was almost funny that none of us had considered we wouldn't be able to get inside. Actually, it wasn't funny at all. My excitement quickly deflated, replaced by frustration.

"I suppose that's our first order of business," Goloran decided, turning back toward the sanitization chamber, where the first group of techs were approaching. "I'll have my engineers set up their equipment to solve the puzzle."

"After all this time, I guess we can wait a little longer," Meg said, disappointed.

I stared at the hatch, sighing heavily. "Yeah. Guess so." Still, after all we had gone through to get here, I wanted to at least touch the ship before I let Goloran's techs take over.

I stepped forward, half-expecting Goloran to order me to stop. She didn't. I could feel all eyes on my back as I closed the gap and reached out, my fingers hovering a hair's breadth from the strange metal.

Rather than let me touch it, with the barest whisper the hatch irised open. I snatched my hand back in surprise as a gust of cool, stale air sighed from within, ruffling my hair. It carried the weight of time, the mustiness of untold centuries adrift between the stars.

No one spoke. No one moved. As one, we stared into the opening as invisible lighting activated along rounded bulkheads as if to guide me deeper inside, the mysteries of the Wardenship laid bare before us at last.

"Well, that was easy," Meg said behind me. "What did you do?"

I turned back to look at the others, grinning wildly. "I have no idea. It just opened when I tried to touch it."

"Should we go in?" Faarl asked.

"No," Goloran said, surprising me again. "Noah, step away from the hatch."

"What? Why?" I asked.

"Please," she pressed. That she asked instead of ordering motivated me to back away. Almost immediately, the hatch slid closed. "Meg, try to open the hatch."

"I get it," I said, understanding dawning. Since we didn't understand why the hatch had opened, she wanted to experiment.

Meg slipped past me, approaching the closed hatch and reaching out. Her hand brushed the metal, and she pulled it back as if she had been burned.

"It's so cold," she said, rubbing her fingers.

"It didn't open for you," Goloran said. "Faarl?"

The Hemid repeated the test, with the same results as Meg. Then Goloran tried to open the hatch herself. Again, it remained sealed.

"What the heck?" I asked, chilled by the outcome.

"At first, I thought it might be because of the Warden's pill," Meg said. "But if that were the case, it should have opened for me, too."

"No," Goloran said. "There's something else at play here. Whatever the reason, it appears almost as though it wants Noah on board."

Our eyes met, my whole body shaking. The most frightening thing I had ever heard anyone say was that my parents were both dead.

Goloran's terrifying words were a close second.

CHAPTER 14

"What do you mean, it wants me on board?" I asked, my entire body tingling with trepidation.

"Precisely what it sounds like," Princess Goloran replied. "It responded to you the moment you reached for it. It didn't respond to any of us."

"She has a point," Meg agreed.

"Maybe it's just a coincidence," I argued. "Or maybe it's because of the stealth suit or the holomask. Or Archie."

"Back away and let Archie try," Meg suggested.

"Okay," I agreed. The hatch closed when I retreated. It remained that way after Archie tapped a tendril to it. And, of course, it opened again when I neared. "Damn it."

"Why do you act like it's a bad thing?" Faarl asked. "We would have no way to get inside otherwise."

"You have to admit," Meg said, "the Warden gave you special treatment from the moment we arrived in Warexia. He singled you out."

"Yeah, to pick on," I replied. "He refused to give me a boon."

Meg shrugged. "He may have finally given you a boon."

"There's zero proof of that. I'm the same Noah I was before we came here."

"Except you can enter a Wardenship," Goloran said. "Perhaps that is the boon."

"Maybe you're right," I agreed. "That would at least make a tiny bit of sense."

"Why would the Warden give you a boon to let you onto his ship?"

"The nanites respond to your greatest desire. Maybe mine is to get my friends home."

"Is it?" Faarl said.

"I...it might be. I honestly don't know."

"Well, the ship is open to us, regardless of how it happened," Goloran said. "It would be foolish to waste this opportunity."

"I can't argue with that." I turned back to the open hatch, looking down the sterile passageway. The bulkheads were stark white and glossy, with warm white light diffusing through an overhead membrane. I took a couple of deep breaths to calm my nerves before stepping over the threshold. When I wasn't instantly vaporized, I took a few more steps before looking over my shoulder. "Well. Are you coming?"

"We're right behind you," Goloran said. Behind her, the techs and engineers started unloading hover carts laden with equipment.

We ventured deep into the Wardenship, the stark white corridors stretching before us like an endless labyrinth. The air was cool and musty, sealed for who-knows-how-long. Our footsteps echoed loudly in the eerie stillness, the only sound inside this Jony Ive-designed tomb. I wondered if we'd find any bodies here.

Meg walked to my left, her eyes wide with wonder as she took in every detail. I could practically see the gears turning behind her gaze, her brilliant engineering mind already working to unravel the ship's mysteries. Goloran and Faarl followed close behind, the princess' face an inscrutable mask while the Hemid fidgeted nervously. Archie stayed close on my right, maintaining its maulvas form. While the evidence of our fighting against the station bots ringed my neck, the Aleal showed no signs of wear and tear, even after being shot virtually point-blank.

We passed through corridor after featureless corridor, the glossy bulkheads broken only by the occasional sealed hatch or darkened alcove. Some passages terminated abruptly in dead ends, the deck just in front of the terminal bulkheads marked by strange discs. We were only partly surprised to find them inscribed with Sigiltech. Meg paused to examine one, brow furrowing.

"These almost look like mini-sigibellums," she mused, tracing a finger above the intricate patterns of swirling lines and glyphs. The discs were about three feet in diameter, the sigiltech etched into the metal in concentric rings. An aura seemed to emanate from them, an almost imperceptible thrum of power.

"It's probably better not to touch them," I cautioned, eyeing the discs warily. "We have no idea what they do."

She nodded, stepping back. "Right. If I had to venture a guess, I would say they're transporter pads. That would explain why they're at the dead ends of the passageways."

"That makes sense," I agreed. "But let's not jump to conclusions until we have more information. The Warden likes to play games. These might be here to misdirect. What if they transport us out into space or something?"

Meg nodded. Knowing the Warden, the possibility couldn't be completely discounted.

We pressed on, avoiding the strange discs as we delved deeper into the ship. After several more minutes of wandering, we encountered a series of hatches lining one wall. Exchanging a glance with the others, I reached out and touched the nearest one. It slid open with a soft hiss, revealing a small, dimly lit space beyond.

Stepping inside, I found myself in what appeared to be a barracks of some kind. Rows of individual chambers lined the bulkheads, each one a smooth, oblong pod about nine feet long. They reminded me of sleek, high-tech coffins, their transparent canopies allowing a view of the padded interior. A control panel, covered in unfamiliar symbols, was set into the base of each pod.

"These resemble hibernation units," Goloran observed, running a hand along one of the canopies. "But who used them? And what happened to them?"

Meg had moved to a seam in the bulkhead at the far end of the compartment. After examining it, she pressed in on the edge, backing up and grinning when the panel slid aside, revealing familiar uniforms and weaponry behind it. "Look familiar?" she asked me over her shoulder.

"Prall," I replied. "The Warden's slaves. The uniforms and guns are here, but none of them are."

"What do you think happened to them?" Faarl asked.

"Nothing good, I'm sure," I replied. The Hemid blanched in response.

"There's nothing useful in here," Goloran said. "We should move on. There is a lot of ship left to explore."

"Agreed," I said as Meg closed the closet panel.

We found officer's quarters next, small individual rooms containing a single hibernation pod and a small closet each. The uniforms told the same story as before.

In the same area, we discovered a head and even a galley. The equipment was designed for prall physiology, with larger handles and controls to accommodate their powerful frames. Instead of water showers, the head contained a large, transparent sealed pod with vents top and bottom, suggesting sanitation like in the chambers we had bypassed outside the ship.

"I had thought the prall were mindless clones, fully controlled by the Warden," I said, surprised by the living quarters for the aliens. "But here they appear to be regular crew members who eat, sleep, and crap."

"This Wardenship seems much older than the one we encountered," Meg replied. "Maybe the Warden's relationship with the prall evolved over time."

"Or devolved if it cost the prall their autonomy," Goloran said.

Moving from the head to the galley, I made a startling find.

"Check this out," I called, waving the others over to a boxy machine set into one bulkhead. "Where have we seen this before?"

Meg leaned in, eyes narrowing. "Is that...an assembler? Like the one on Head Case?"

"Sure looks like it," I confirmed. The similarities were uncanny.

"Do you think it responds to Asshole?" Meg joked.

"I doubt it," I replied. "But what are the odds the Warden would have the same technology? Your Highness, do you have assemblers in Warexia?"

"What does an assembler do exactly?" the princess replied.

"It breaks down raw materials into individual molecules and uses those molecules to reconstitute whatever you ask it for. As long as it knows how to make it."

"We have nothing like that here," Goloran confirmed. "It sounds incredible."

"We have one on Head Case. I'm surprised they don't exist here since you're ahead of us on technology in so many ways."

"Perhaps the Warden sees such devices as a threat," she suggested. "The ability to make anything you desire in a box seems dangerous."

"I guess in the wrong hands, it could be," I agreed. "Though it seems the Warden used it to feed his prall, just like we use Asshole to feed ourselves."

We spent the next hour finishing our sweep of the deck. We'd found no other way to access other levels of the ship. No elevators, no stairwells.

"I think you were right about the Sigiltech discs," I told Meg. "They must be used to move between the decks."

"I wonder if they work," she replied. "The ship somehow has power after all this time, but we know Sigiltech uses a lot more juice here than in the spiral."

"Except the Warden has machines that pull chaos energy in to use as a power supply," I replied. "If it's active, the discs should be, too."

"We haven't found the power source yet."

"It probably isn't on this deck." I noticed we were approaching one of the dead ends. "There's only one way to find out if it works." I started toward it.

"Wait!" Meg cried with enough force to bring me to a quick stop. "What if you were right about it transporting you out into space? Or even a compartment without oxygen? You should let Archie go first."

"What do you say, bud?" I asked, glancing at Archie. The Aleal nodded its maulvas head and padded down the corridor to the disc. It looked back at me before stepping onto it and vanishing in a rainbow flash of color.

"Wow, I didn't expect that," Meg said, awestruck by the display.

I stared at the disc, waiting for Archie to return. I knew it would take a lot to hurt the Aleal, but I still worried about it for the twelve seconds it took to reappear on the disc in a reverse of the flash of light.

"Archie! What's the status?"

It responded by nodding, stepping off the disc and stepping back on, vanishing a second time.

"I guess we should follow it," I said, leading the way. The instant my boots touched the metal, the world dissolved into a swirl of light and color. Vertigo gripped me, and I squeezed my eyes shut against the unexpected dizziness. When I opened them again, I stood in a different corridor, only identifiable because Archie stood alone just ahead of me. There was no sign yet of Meg, Goloran, or Faarl.

I barely had time to orient myself and step off the disc before the air behind me shimmered, disgorging Meg and then Goloran. Faarl appeared a few seconds later, the Hemid looking decidedly pale.

"This technology is incredible," Goloran said. "If we can harness it for ourselves…"

"There's a finite amount of chaos energy that can be drawn into Warexia," I said. "It works great for the Warden and Markan to a lesser extent, but it won't scale."

Goloran scowled at the bad news. "Still, there must be something of value to discover here."

"Let's find out," I replied with a smile.

We forged onward, excitement mounting with each new discovery. In one room, we found banks of towering cylindrical pods filled with bubbling orange liquid. Tubes and wires snaked from each pod to a central control station, its screens dark and lifeless.

"Cloning tanks," Meg breathed, eyes wide. She pointed to a pod with a half-formed prall suspended inside, its skin slick and glistening. Muscles and bone were clearly visible beneath its translucent flesh, still knitting together. "You were right after all, Noah. The Wardenship does grow its crew."

"But not as mindless slaves," I replied. "I guess that came later."

In another bay, we stumbled across a similar setup, except all of the pods were empty.

"What do you think the Warden grew in these?" Faarl asked, checking each one.

"If I had to guess," I answered. "More Wardens."

Faarl looked like he wanted to puke. I didn't blame him. The whole scene churned my senses in a bad way, too. We already knew the Warden cloned himself. That didn't make it any less disconcerting.

I was glad to move on from that part of the ship.

Nearly two hours later, reaching what I believed to be the ship's center, we discovered what appeared to be the engine room. Easily thirty feet in diameter, a massive metal sphere dominated the space. Floating free of the deck, its surface was etched with intricate sigils. Cables as thick as my arm emerged from the sphere's top and bottom. The six coming out of the bottom connected to towering black obelisks that ringed the room, while the single top cable vanished into the overhead. I had no idea where it led.

"That's the reactor," Meg said, her voice hushed with awe. "I imagine those sigils are designed to pull in chaos energy."

I examined the sigils on the sphere more closely. I hadn't gotten much chance to look at Markan's generator in such detail, but the sigils did seem vaguely familiar. "It doesn't seem to be active," I pointed out.

"Perhaps these obelisks contain the energy," Faarl theorized, pointing at one of them. "Look at the way they're linked to the core. But their symbols aren't the same. My guess is the obelisks still have some residual charge, even if the main reactor is offline."

Meg looked like she wanted to start dismantling the entire setup to unravel its secrets. But we had to stay focused. There would be time for in-depth study later. I hoped.

We continued exploring, moving through the Wardenship with a singular purpose—locate everything of interest first, then decide what to study in greater depth.

As it turned out, the cable connected to the top of the reactor led to a device etched with sigils and resembling a massive gyroscope. I could only assume it was the ship's propulsion.

And then there were the Warden's quarters, which we discovered on the deck below the reactor. While I might have expected something ornate and ostentatious, especially given his personality, his living space was instead a spartan room with little more than a plain slab that served as a bed. If the minimalist digs were anything to go by, it was no wonder the Warden went out of his way hunting for entertainment.

After nearly four hours, exhaustion began taking its toll. But we had one last discovery to make.

The bridge.

It wasn't a bridge so much as a cockpit, with a single seat surrounded by a flat control surface that had to be touch responsive. A curved surround enveloped the seat.Seeing it, I almost felt sorry for the Warden. He could make limitless copies of himself, but by all indications, he was very much alone.

"I think we've seen everything of value," Goloran said, viewing the flight deck.

"We haven't found the hangar yet," Meg replied.

"How do you know there is a hangar?"

"I guess there might not be. But I'm still hopeful. We also haven't found the ship's datastore, though it might not have a compartment of its own."

"Well, we've dallied long enough. It's time to bring my techs in to examine everything more closely. There is so much to learn."

"That's fine with me," Meg agreed. "I can't wait to get a closer look at the reactor. Noah?"

I barely heard her as I stood there, staring at the control seat, an inexplicable pull drawing me to the station. This was the heart of the Wardenship, the seat of its power. All its secrets, all its terrible potential...

"Noah?" I heard Meg say again, though her voice sounded like it passed through the mud before reaching me. Before I could stop myself, I slipped into the control seat.

And my world erupted into searing agony.

A thousand knives shredded my mind, fire searing through my blood. I was distantly aware of my hoarse screams, of hands grasping at me, trying to pull me free. But it was too late. I was drowning, the pain dragging me down into oblivion.

And through it all, a familiar voice.

"You don't belong here."

My heart pounded like it would explode out of my chest, my entire body instantly cold.

"Dad?" I replied, certain I was hallucinating.

Darkness took me.

CHAPTER 15

I jolted upright with a scream lodged in my throat, head pounding. Disoriented, I blinked against the glare of harsh white lights, taking in the sterile confines of a med bay. I was pinned to the autodoc, restrained while I was unconscious. Based on the surroundings, I had to be back on Resolute.

"Noah! Oh thank the stars." Meg's face swam into view, pale and pinched with worry. She laid a gentle hand on my shoulder, easing me to relax.

"W-what...happened?" I croaked, mouth dry as old parchment.

"The chair," she said, shuddering. "It...it did something to you. Electrocuted you, or zapped your brain, or...or something." She trailed off, swallowing hard. "We barely got you out in time."

I squeezed my eyes shut, trying to marshal my spinning thoughts. The Wardenship. The command chair. That voice...

I lifted a shaking hand to clutch at hers, desperate. "Meg... did you hear it? Right before I blacked out?"

She frowned. "Hear what?"

"The voice," I insisted, pulse climbing. "Did you hear it? Please tell me you heard it."

"I'm sorry, Noah. I didn't hear anything except your strained breathing while you convulsed in the seat. If Goloran and I hadn't pulled you out...I don't know what would have happened to you. You might have died."

"Thank you for saving me then." I let my head fall against the padding, staring at the overhead. "It was my father, Meg. I heard my father's voice."

"What did he say?"

"You aren't supposed to be here."

"Well, considering that seat tried to kill you, he was right." She kept a reassuring hand on my shoulder. "I'm sure it was just your mind trying to deal with the stress it was under."

I could accept that. "But stress from what? Do you know what actually happened to me?"

"Overstimulation," Doctor Ashti said, entering the med bay. "At least, that's what the report from the autodoc says. From what I've been able to surmise, with the help of the techs on the Wardenship, is that when you sat in the command seat, you activated its interface. Which apparently is a direct neural connection."

"Direct neural? You mean—"

"The station transmitted a combined data flow from the ship to your mind."

"Like a firehose," Meg said. "Your brain couldn't handle the volume."

"So it went into self-defense mode. If you heard a voice, it was likely part of that defense. Something it found familiar and comforting."

I relaxed further as I came out of my stupor. "That makes sense," I replied. "I didn't realize the chair would be so dangerous."

"No offense, Noah, but it was stupid to sit in it like that," Meg said.

"I know. I just...I felt it calling to me. Mentally, I couldn't resist it."

"What's done is done," Meg said. "Just don't ever do that again."

Movement near my legs drew my attention. A tendril snaked up from beneath the blanket covering me. It found my hand and wrapped around it. "Archie," I said. "I'm okay now, bud."

"It wouldn't let us pull it away from you," Ashti said.

"Thanks for looking out for me, Arch."

Another tendril appeared, waggling in relief.

"So, I'm back on Resolute," I said after a few heartbeats of silence. "How long was I unconscious?"

"Four hours," Meg replied.

"Goloran's techs are all set up?"

"Mostly."

"Did you find the hangar yet?"

She laughed and nodded. "Captain Lorovan's unit finished the recon of the ship. They found it."

"Anything cool inside?"

"Small, single-person shuttles," Meg answered. "Which is interesting on its own. Did the Warden use them by making multiple copies of himself at a time? But then why did we only find one set of quarters separate from the barracks? And even more intriguing, why was one of the shuttles missing?" She grew excited as she posed the questions, an engineer ever searching for answers.

"Do you have any theories?" I asked, setting her loose.

"I do! My best guess is the Warden had the potential to make copies and use them simultaneously, but in the case of this specific Wardenship, he didn't. I think the single Warden who ran this ship abandoned it. That's why the shuttle is missing."

"Where do you think he went?"

Meg shrugged. "I don't know, but I'm hoping once we can figure out how to access the ship's logs we can suss out an answer. Or at least some clues."

"How can I help?" I asked.

"You can help by resting," Ashti replied before Meg could answer. "Your readings are still fluctuating more than I'd like. Some of your neural pathways were damaged, and your brain needs time to correct the misconnections. If you tried to stand now, at best you'd see spots of color in front of your eyes. At worst, you'd get dizzy and collapse."

"The most exciting thing that's happened since we got here and doesn't involve being shot at, and I'm sidelined?" I said, disappointment replacing my curious calm.

"Only for a little while longer," Ashti said. "You'll be discharged as soon as the autodoc registers consistent brainwave activity."

"Fine," I agreed, as if I had a choice. "Do you mind giving me a few minutes alone with my teammate?"

"Of course," Ashti said. She retreated from the bay, closing the hatch behind her.

"Goloran is sharing everything she learns with you?" I asked once she had gone.

"So far," Meg replied.

"Any indications that she might stop?"

"No. You still don't trust her?"

"I trust her more than anyone else who was born in Warexia, excluding Lantz and Lava. But she has a duty to her planet that will override any loyalty she has to us. If she finds something she can use as leverage and she's the only one who knows it…"

Meg nodded. "You're wise beyond your years to consider it."

"I've just played a lot of strategic video games," I

answered. "And I was the planner for the Stinking Badgers. My e-sports team."

"With Tyler and Ally, right?"

"Yeah." I closed my eyes, remembering our last match. We'd lost, but who cared? "I'd give anything to go back to life before my parents died." I opened my eyes to look at her. "No offense."

"I understand. This has been difficult for all of us. Maybe less for me, because I always have Leo, but I'd still rather be back in the Spiral." She paused thoughtfully. "I'm not sure how we can force Goloran to share every byte of information she extracts."

"We can't. At least not with her knowledge."

"You're suggesting we hack her equipment?"

"Whatever information she picks up will have to be stored here on Resolute. We only need to get into the ship's main datastore. Whatever she puts in, we pull out."

"That's a slippery proposition and might not be worth the risk. Even if the princess did keep some secrets from us, she's a valuable ally."

"Maybe you're right," I agreed. "Maybe I'm not thinking clearly. I wish Tee and Ally were here. And Ben, Matt. Everyone."

"Me, too," Meg agreed. "At least we have one another." Archie waggled a tendril over my sheet. "And you too, Archie," Meg added.

"Well, I'm sure you'd rather be exploring the Wardenship than hanging out here with me," I said. "Though I do appreciate your company and concern. I'm fine now. I'll rest under doctor's orders, and join you as soon as she sets me loose. I've got Archie watching over me in the meantime."

Meg smiled. I could see the relief and excitement in her body language. "I'm glad you're okay. You have your comm badge if you need me."

"I'll be fine," I repeated.

"Feel better, Noah. I'll catch up with you later." She squeezed my shoulder and left the med bay.

I exhaled a weary breath, doing my best to relax and let my mind work out its kinks. Easier said than done. Sitting still left me too much time to process, thoughts returning to my father's voice. Meg's reasoning was sound logic, but there was enough incongruity to introduce doubt.

Could it be possible my father was really the Warden? Or rather, a Warden? He certainly hadn't looked like the little, curly-haired fop who kept harassing us, but this Wardenship didn't look just like that Wardenship either. And we had only met one Warden. Was it possible the Warden for each ship had a different appearance? I would need to ask Princess Goloran if she knew.

Beyond that, I knew Dad was German and had come to the United States to go to school. I'd never met my grand-parents. They'd died before I was born. But I'd seen pictures of them.

Of course, for a Warden, pictures would be trivial to fake.

I shook my head. There was no way Dad could be a Warden. Except the ship responded to my presence. It only opened up for me. But...even if there was a remote possibil-ity, how did he know about Earth, and how had he gotten there? What had caused him to leave his life as a Warden behind?

And, was the accident that had killed him and Mom really an accident? I'd always felt like there was some connection between everything that had happened from the moment Jaffie slammed his SUV into our car. I thought it centered around chaos energy and Sigiltech. But what if there was more to it than that? What if Levain had sent Jaffie to find the missing Warden and kill him?

"I wish you could speak to me, Archie," I said, looking

down at the Aleal. "You have Jaffie's memories. You know why he was on Earth, don't you?"

Archie stirred beneath the sheet, pulling his mass out into the open on my chest, tendrils reaching out to stroke my cheeks. I could have asked it about Jaffie earlier, but I never wanted to go there. I didn't want to relive that moment or reopen those wounds. It wouldn't bring them back, and Jaffie was gone, so what did it matter?

Only, it mattered now.

"Did he hit us on purpose?" I asked. "Was my father his target?"

I held my breath, my whole body shaking while I waited for Archie to respond. It hesitated, and I wondered if the colony had overwritten those memories with new experience, instructions on how to shape itself like a maulvas, or something else entirely.

Archie's tendrils retreated from my face, one hanging tentatively over my head. When it bobbed up and down in affirmation, it did so with intense remorse.

I squeezed my eyes shut, still barely understanding all of the implications or meaning as the pain rushed back. Tears streamed from my closed lids, my heart wrenching.

Cold realization stopped my thinking in its tracks. My eyes snapped open, and I stared at Archie. "He didn't intend to kill him, did he? He came to Earth to retrieve him. Somehow, Levain found out who and what he was, and that he was the only one who could open the ship."

Archie again bobbed his tendril in agreement.

"The Warden told him, didn't he?"

Archie's tendril waggled. No, that wasn't right.

"Not the Warden," I said. "Markan."

This time, Archie agreed.

"And if Markan was helping Levain with his find, then…" I trailed off, sudden panic kickstarting my heart, my hand reaching down to dig my comms out of my pocket. "Meg!" I practically shouted into it. "Where are you?"

"I just reached the station on a shuttle," she replied. "What's wrong?"

"Where's Faarl?"

"I don't know, why?"

I could have growled I was so angry with myself for trusting that damn Hemid. Would I ever learn?

"We need to get out of here!" I cried. "Markan knows about the Wardenship. And thanks to Faarl, he knows I can open it."

"What? Noah, Doctor Ashti said what you went through would leave you confused for a while. She—"

"I'm not confused!" I insisted. "It all makes sense. It all fits. My father was the Warden on this ship. That's why it responded to me."

"Noah, you need to calm down," Meg said. "Take a moment to think."

I did take a moment to think, but not about whether or not the command seat had made me crazy. Every passing second only left me more certain I was right. Every shifting neuron in my brain assembled a bigger picture.

"The black ship," I said. "The one that attacked us in Earth's orbit."

"What about it?"

"Archie, was Jaffie on that ship?" I asked.

Archie's tendril bobbed. He was.

"Noah?" Meg asked when I didn't respond right away.

"They used the ship to get to Earth. Markan said himself, even if he could go back to the Spiral he wouldn't. Maybe he figured out a way, but he has no interest. Instead, he wants to bring the Warden down and replace him. Which means he wants the secrets of the Wardenship as much as we do. The Warden thought it all began and ended with Levain, Jaffie, and Zariv because he couldn't keep track of Markan. He doesn't know he was involved. That ship, wherever it is, is our ticket home!"

"Noah, I'm on my way back to you. Please, call for Doctor Ashti. There's a button on the side of the autodoc. You sound delirious."

"No. I know what I'm talking about! The ship didn't fog my brain, it made everything clear. Think about it! Jaffie wasn't working for Levain or Zariv. He was working for Markan the entire time! Everything else was misdirection and manipulation."

"Then why didn't Markan capture you when we were on his station? Why did he try to kill us?"

Her questions stopped me in my tracks. "I...I don't know. Maybe Jaffie never had a chance to tell him about Head Case. About us. Maybe he didn't know who I was."

"Plausible, but not probable."

I froze into silence, unable to find another fit for that puzzle piece. It had to go somewhere, but Meg was right. How could Markan not know about Head Case when the black ship had known to fire on us?

For that matter, how would the black ship's pilot know that Ben would open a rift to escape, or that the Warden would intercept us and drag us to Warexia?

Warning klaxons suddenly blared, my fears realized too soon. We were out of time.

The enemy had arrived.

CHAPTER 16

I turned to Archie, frightened, desperate, and angry. "Archie, quick! Get these restraints off me! We need to get to the bridge!"

The Aleal stretched across my body, its sinuous tendrils manipulating the soft straps holding me to the autodoc. With unerring agility, it set me free, and I scrambled off the chair, nearly collapsing the moment my feet hit the deck. A wave of dizziness crashed over me, and I stumbled, reaching out just in time to slap my palms against the bulkhead, breaking my fall.

The med bay spun around me. I couldn't tell what part of the movement came from my scrambled neurons and what part came from the ship shuddering under weapons fire.

"Meg! We're under attack!" I cried as I moved out of my compartment into sickbay proper, Archie still beside me in its maulvas form.

"I know. I'm on my way back to the shuttle."

That was a relief. I was sure Goloran already knew, too. Commander Vaas would have informed her the moment the attackers appeared on sensors.

Archie and I had almost reached the exit when Doctor Ashti emerged from a side hatch, our eyes meeting. "Noah, you shouldn't be up!" she said, crossing the room to force me back to the autodoc.

"I'm fine," I replied, thrusting a hand out to stop her.

"Then why are you out here holding up the bulkhead?"

"I'm not sitting in sick bay while the ship is under attack," I growled. "I can help."

"You can barely stand!" she snapped back. "Come on... She dropped her arms, reaching out as she started toward me. "...let me help you—"

"No!" I insisted, pushing off the bulkhead. "They're here for the Wardenship, and for me." There were two of her, but at least they remained relatively stable as she stopped again, dropping her hand and huffing in frustration.

"For you?" she replied, looking confused. "That doesn't—

I used the opportunity to break for the exit, passing through the opening hatch and into the corridor before she could stop me. Still getting my balance, I crashed into the opposite bulkhead, angry with my inability to walk straight.

"Noah!" Ashti called out, coming through the hatch to help me again.

I didn't give her the chance, practically throwing myself down the corridor, my dizziness settling as I progressed. Finally, it allowed me to move away from the bulkhead and start dodging crew members as I made for the bridge, Archie loping behind me. My lungs burned with the effort, but I pushed myself faster. Every second counted.

"Meg? Where are you now?" I asked.

"We just landed in the hangar," she replied. "According to the pilot, Goloran and Faarl are right behind me."

The deck shuddered violently beneath my feet as Resolute absorbed a definite hit. The force of the impact sent me staggering once more into a bulkhead. I caught myself with a grunt, the breath leaving my lungs in a rush. The situation was deteriorating faster than I'd feared.

Archie and I rounded a corner at a sprint, nearly colliding with a trio of Marines rushing to their battle stations. Barely drawing a glance as they rushed past, we moved aside just in time to avoid being steamrolled. Grateful I remembered the path from sickbay to the bridge, we continued to the nearest elevator and ascended to the bridge.

Bursting through the doors, I was greeted by a scene of controlled chaos. Officers manned their stations with intense determination, their faces cast in stark relief by the glow of their displays. Shouts and urgent reports filled the air, nearly drowned out by the incessant blaring of warning klaxons.

A nightmarish vision unfolded on the main viewscreen. A half-dozen ships with the outward appearance of large cargo vessels bore down on our position. Their revealed gun batteries exposed them as members of Markan's hidden fleet. Energy bolts lanced out from the arrays, searing across the void to batter at Resolute's straining shields. The impacts sent shudders through the deck, the vibrations traveling up my legs and body.

Starfighters, sleek and deadly as birds of prey, streaked between the larger ships. Resolute's starfighter squadrons rose to meet them. They twisted and rolled in dizzying swirls, their movements a lethal dance as the two forces clashed in a storm of activity too frantic to track all the engagements.

I watched a Gothori fighter whip through a dizzying series of evasive maneuvers, narrowly avoiding a barrage of cannon fire. The pilot juked and spun, the craft a blur of motion, before the pilot lined up a shot at their pursuer. A lance of searing light connected the two ships a heartbeat later, the enemy fighter disintegrating in a silent ball of fire.

The small victory was short-lived. As the Gothori pilot peeled away, seeking a new target, a trio of enemy craft fell upon it. Energy bolts stitched the void, the Gothori fighter reeling under the onslaught. Smoke and flame gouted from its ruptured hull, the pilot struggling to maintain control.

It was a losing battle.

With a final, gut-wrenching twist, the crippled fighter spun out of the fight, trailing a plume of debris. Its reactor going critical, it vanished in a blinding flash of light.

Across the viewport, the scene repeated itself in a dozen variations. Gothori fighters clashed with Markan's forces, the two sides tangling in a web of destruction. For every enemy craft destroyed, it seemed two more took its place, the tide of battle slowly but inexorably turning against us.

"Status report!" Commander Vaas barked from the command chair, her voice cutting through the cacophony like a blade.

"Shields at sixty percent and falling," the tactical officer replied, his fingers flying across his console. The lights of the bridge flickered, casting his face in stark shadows. "They're focused on our engines and hyperdrive, trying to disable us."

Vaas turned, her gaze falling on me. Her eyes widened fractionally, surprised to see me there. "Noah, hold onto something!"

I lunged for the back of a nearby chair, my fingers wrapping around the cool metal just as another barrage struck, the deck pitching beneath my feet. I held on tight, the force of the impact threatening to tear me from my precarious perch. Archie, in his gel form, wrapped around my leg and held on until the effects of the impact receded.

"It's Markan," I said. "He's come for the Wardenship."

Vaas shot me a confused look, her brow furrowing. "Who is Markan?"

I shook my head, frustration welling up inside me. There was no time to explain now or lay out the tangled web that had led us to this moment. On the viewscreen, I watched as our fighters fought valiantly against the overwhelming odds, their efforts nothing short of heroic. But it wasn't enough. Markan's ships pressed their advantage, ruthlessly hammering at Resolute's faltering shields.

Princess Goloran's voice on the comms cut through the chaos like a knife. "Vaas, I'm en route. Prepare for immediate departure."

"We can't leave the Wardenship!" I shouted, the words tumbling from my lips in a rush. After everything we'd been through and all our sacrifices, the thought of abandoning our prize now was almost physically painful.

"Noah?" Goloran replied. "What are you doing on the bridge? You should be in sickbay."

"I want to help."

"You can help by staying out of everyone's way." Her tone softened. "It pains me to abandon the ship as well, but we have no choice. We're outmatched here. Badly. If we stay, we'll be captured or killed."

I wanted to argue, to rail against the injustice of it all. We'd come so far and risked so much. Of course, Goloran was right. Markan had us dead to rights. If we stayed, if we tried to fight, it would be nothing short of suicide.

"Your Highness, you need to restrain Faarl. I was wrong. I thought we could trust him. We can't."

To her credit, Goloran didn't question me. "Understood."

The distance from the station to Resolute was short, but that didn't make the minute it took for Goloran's shuttle to cross the space between them any less intense. I hovered near the center of the bridge, tracking her progress on the sensor grid, my breath catching every time an enemy starfighter ventured near, but her shuttle pilot was skilled, his movements fluid and sure. The craft maintained its evasive tactics all the way back home, always just a hairsbreadth ahead of the enemy.

"Commander Vaas," Goloran said over the comms. "I'm aboard. Get us out of here!"

Vaas turned to her helmsman, her voice ringing out across the bridge. "Full retreat! Maximum thrust!"

Resolute surged forward, inertia tugging on me as the powerful thrusters strained to push us clear of the enemy formation. We still needed to clear the area before going to hyperspace. Markan's ships, already in motion, quickly matched our changing vector, starfighters picking off Gothori ships trying to return to the hangar.

"Commander!" the sensor officer cried, her voice tight with barely restrained panic. "They're launching boarding shuttles!"

"How many?" Vaas demanded, her gaze snapping to the tactical display.

"Six, Commander! They're accelerating fast."

Vaas' face hardened, her eyes flashing with cold determination. "Shoot them down!"

"We're trying, Commander," the tactical officer said. "They're slippery bastards."

"Target destroyed," one of the weapon's operators announced.

"Target destroyed," another said.

"We have contact on the hull," the sensor officer reported. "Two contacts. Three."

"All hands, prepare to repel boarders!" Vaas cried through the comms, announcing the locations of the enemy ships. "Deck Nine, juncture forty-one, Deck Twelve, Juncture Thirty-three, Deck Nineteen, Juncture Thirty-eight."

"Where is that?" I asked. "I can fight."

"Starboard," the nearest bridge crew answered. "Juncture Thirty-three is closest. Port side, leave the bridge, make a right and go straight back."

"Got it," I replied, already sprinting for the door and trusting Archie to keep up. If we could get there in time, maybe we could stop them from establishing a foothold.

I ran flat-out through the corridors, my lungs burning with the effort, my legs pumping like pistons. At least my head had settled, the dizziness fading as my adrenaline flowed.

Markan's larger warships were still targeting the thrusters to set Resolute adrift and hoping to make us easier pickings. The deck shook. I stumbled, the lights flickering overhead as I caught myself against a bulkhead, the cold metal stinging my palms. I pushed off, forcing my legs to keep moving.

I couldn't stop now.

I raced around a corner and skidded to a stop, immediately finding myself in big trouble. A hulking orc in black armor towered over two dead Gothori Marines, his plasma rifle still smoking in his massive hands. Behind him, more of Markan's armed troops pushed through a ragged breach in the hull.

I retreated to the corner, realizing too late how badly I'd underestimated the situation. Ashti and Meg were right. I wasn't thinking clearly at all.

The orc spun to face me with supernatural speed, his weapon swinging to aim at me. I saw my death in his cold, dark orbs as his finger tightened on the trigger.

Time seemed to slow suddenly, each heartbeat an eternity until Archie shot forward in a blur of fluid motion. Its form elongated in mid-leap. Sharpening to become a hardened, barbed spike, it drove itself through the orc's faceplate with a sickening crunch, the point erupting from the back of its helmet. Archie rode him down as he toppled, tendrils writhing in glee as the orc's rifle clattered to the deck.

The rest of the boarding party opened fire on me. Plasma bolts stitched the bulkheads, the air crackling with their passage. I scrambled back around the corner just as a bolt sizzled past my ear.

I pulled my blaster and leaned out around the corner to squeeze off a few shots before ducking back again. My pea shooter didn't stand a chance against their hardened armor, their return fire was so relentless my only option was to turn tail and run back the way I'd come.

Returning to its maulvas form, Archie rounded the corner behind me, catching up to me as I swept around a bank of three snack machines and squatted down to peek around them, my blaster ready. The pounding of boots on the deck grew louder as Markan's orcs approached the corner.

"Get ready, Archie. The first one's yours."

The orcs charged around the corner and barreled up the passageway toward our hiding place. On the leader in an instant, Archie's maulvas teeth sank into his calf, biting right through armor, flesh, tendon, and bone alike. The orc screamed as his leg gave out. Archie had already shifted into its gelatinous form by the time he hit the deck and raced up the orc's body. Latching onto his throat. Its dagger-like teeth sank deep, its see-through body disappearing into the orc's yielding flesh.

I was ready when the next orc, obviously thinking we'd fled down the passageway, barreled around the corner in hot pursuit. At the last second, I stuck my leg out from behind the snack machine and sent him sprawling almost directly on top of the dead orc. Archie popped out from the first orc's mangled throat, quickly finishing off the second one.

I scooped up one of the dropped plasma rifles—a

serious upgrade from my simple blaster—my hands shaking as I aimed the weapon toward the corner. The remainder of the boarding party had wised up, their pounding boots slowing before they reached the corner.

I slapped my comm badge to activate it. "Meg!" I cried. "I need help. Deck Twelve, Juncture Thirty-three."

"Hang on, Noah!" Goloran replied over Meg's comm. "Captain Lorovan is already on her way."

"ETA?" I replied, a measure of relief surging through me. "There are too many for me to handle." But at least they had halted their advance, their footfalls silent now as they remained out of sight, obviously considering their next move.

"You shouldn't even be there," Goloran snapped back, her voice colored with frustration and a clear hint of admiration. "ETA thirty seconds. Until then, you're all that's between Markan's orcs and defeat. They cannot be allowed to reach the flight deck or the engines."

Archie perked up from its place on top of the second orc. The sight of its gelatin body hued with the enemy's blood would have horrified anyone else, but all I felt was gratitude for my deadly little friend. I couldn't track how many times it had already saved my life.

Rising, I stepped forward, quietly moving to the corner to risk a peek around it. Nearly two dozen black armored soldiers lined the corridor but had turned in the opposite direction. As I watched, they started marching toward the engines, which Goloran had just implored me not to let them reach.

But how was I supposed to delay them until reinforcements arrived?

I glanced down at Archie. "What do you say, bud?" The Aleal raised an inquisitive tendril, so I pointed down the passageway. "We need to keep them busy for a bit longer."

Archie stretched multiple tendrils out from its body, all

bristling with barbs, reminding me of a displacer beast from Dungeons and Dragons. Then the Aleal went to work while I watched in awe.

Charging the unsuspecting enemy, Archie sank into their trailing ranks, spinning and lashing out with all its diamond-sharp tendrils. Orc after orc went down in a melee of strangled screams, drawing the attention of those at the head of the column.

I steadied my rifle and moved out from cover, carefully firing single bolts to avoid hitting Archie. My aim still wasn't great—most of my bolts bounced off the deck and bulkheads—Archie and I at least gave the orcs something to think about until the thunder of booted feet announced Lorovan's arrival.

"Archie!" I shouted, backing out of the way as the Gothori warriors swept into both ends of the corridor. "Fall back!"

Lorovan's troopers closed in on the enemy boarders with ruthless efficiency. Catching them in a withering cross-fire, the fight was over in seconds. The last few orcs threw down their weapons, hands raised in surrender..

I nodded to the Marine Captain as she approached me. "Thanks for the assist," I managed, my knees feeling a little rubbery under me as what felt like sea waves surged through my stomach.

"Anytime," she replied. She glanced at Archie, who padded back toward us, cool as a cat in his maulvas guise.

"What about the other boarding parties?" I asked her.

"Already taken care of," she replied. "This juncture was the least defended. If you hadn't been here…" She pointed the way I had come. "The bridge is a direct shot that way. The engines, a fairly close haul the other way. They would have reached one or both."

"I'm glad I could help," I said, though I hadn't done

much other than bring Archie to the fight. "What about the prisoners?"

"We'll take them to the brig for later questioning," she replied, touching my shoulder. "You look pale. You should go back to sickbay." She moved past me, signaling to her unit. They hauled the captives past me, once more leaving Archie and I alone in the corridor.

I looked down at Archie, sitting on his maulvas haunches and leaning against my leg. "Good work, buddy," I murmured, stroking its blood-tinged, gelatin fur before laying my hand over my queasy stomach. "I owe you. Again." Archie rippled slightly, a faint sense of smug satisfaction radiating from its alien consciousness. "I think I should probably head back to sickbay like Lorovan suggested."

Archie's tendril wagged in agreement. I smiled and turned to leave, sensing the shift in momentum that signaled Resolute had made it to hyperspace. Exhaling with relief, I knew how lucky I was that my cognitive impairment hadn't cost me, or anyone else, their lives.

Markan's ambush had failed.

We'd escaped.

But I knew this was far from over. Markan knew about the Wardenship, and more importantly, he now knew that I could help him gain entry into it. That knowledge made me and everyone around me a target.

"We need to figure this out, buddy," I said softly. "My father, Jaffie, Markan, the Wardenship...all of it. And we need to do it fast."

CHAPTER 17

I made my way through the corridors of Resolute, aiming
for sickbay with Archie padding beside me. My thoughts, a
mix of relief over our narrow escape and unease over the
mysteries still unsolved, churned in my mind right along
with my nausea. I was so lost in thought that I almost ran
headlong into Princess Goloran as she rounded a corner,
Kloth and Meg flanking her. With one hand on the bulkhead and one on my stomach, I stumbled to a halt, blinking
in surprise.

"Noah," Goloran said, her voice tight. "We need to talk.
Now."

I glanced at Meg, who gave me a slight, apologetic
shrug. "I was just heading back to sickbay," I began. "I don't
feel so—"

"Change of plans," Goloran cut me off. "Follow me." Her
tone left no room for argument.

I sighed but fell into step behind them as we made our
way to one of Resolute's conference spaces. As soon as the
door sealed behind us, Goloran rounded on me, her eyes
flashing. "What were you thinking?" she demanded. "You

were told to stay in sickbay. You could have gotten yourself killed!"

I bristled at her tone, my temper flaring. "I was trying to help! We were under attack, in case you didn't notice. I couldn't just lie there while Markan's goons swarmed the ship."

"You were in no condition to fight," Goloran snapped. "You're still recovering from whatever the Wardenship did to you. According to Doctor Ashti, your cognitive functioning, especially your judgment, is highly impaired."

I opened my mouth to argue, but the words died on my tongue. As much as I hated to admit it, she had a point. My actions on the bridge, charging off to confront the boarders alone, hadn't been my most brilliant move.

Goloran must have seen the realization in my face because her expression softened. She sighed, some of the tension leaving her shoulders as she sank into the seat at the head of the conference table. Blinking several times, she finally looked up at me. "I know you meant well. But we can't afford any more reckless heroics. The stakes are too high."

She leveled me with a severe look. I could sense her mind working behind her gaze, weighing variables and options.

"Maybe they're higher than I ever guessed when I approached you on Cacitrum. I need you to explain, in detail, these suspicions you shared with Meg. About Markan, Levain, your parents...all of it."

I glanced at Meg again. She gave me an encouraging nod. "If you don't mind, I'd like to sit down." She waved her hand at the chair nearest me. Meg pulled it out for me and then sat down next to me.

Drawing a deep breath, I launched into my theory, laying out the tangled web of connections as best I could. Markan's involvement with Levain. Jaffie's true loyalties.

My crazy hunch that my father had been the Warden of the abandoned ship.

As I spoke, Goloran listened intently, her brow furrowed. Meg chimed in occasionally, adding details I'd missed. But even as I laid it all out, doubt continued to creep in at the edges of my mind.

"It's the only thing that makes sense," I finished, though my voice lacked some of my earlier conviction.

Goloran was silent for a long moment, her fingers steepled beneath her chin. When she finally spoke, her voice was carefully measured. "Noah... I understand your reasoning. But you have to admit, there are still a lot of holes in this theory of yours."

"I know," I admitted, frustration welling up inside me. "Like the black ship that attacked us in Earth's orbit. I don't know how that factors in."

Goloran didn't answer right away. Her mind continued working, adding my story to her algorithm. When her lips curled downward slightly, I knew she was about to deliver bad news.

"I need to be honest with you," she said, eyes dancing from me to Meg and back. "With you both. We're dealing with too many unknowns. And frankly, I'm not comfortable staking the safety of my people on any of this."

"So what are you saying?" I asked.

Goloran sighed. "I'm saying that I made a mistake getting involved in this. If I had known I was stepping into the middle of some secret war between the Warden and Markan..."

"But we found the Wardenship!" I protested. "That has to count for something. We can't just give up now."

"We found it and immediately had to abandon the station. Markan's syndicate has the ship now. Getting it back would be…"

She didn't need to finish her thought. After everything

we'd been through, all the danger and sacrifice, to think of our prize in Markan's hands...

"We not only abandoned the ship, you left it wide open for him," I cried. "He's already powerful enough. Do you have any idea what he'll be able to do with—"

"I didn't leave it open," Goloran replied, remaining impressively calm in the face of my outburst. "We removed the device wedging it open on our way out. If he wants to get into the ship, he'll need to tear a hole through it, which I doubt he'll do."

It was a small comfort, but I'd take what I could get at this point.

"What about the data your team collected?" I asked Goloran, grasping for any other shred of good news. "Did they manage to learn anything useful before we had to evacuate?"

The princess nodded slowly. "We got detailed scans of some of the key systems—the reactor, the cloning chambers, the propulsion. It's not much, but it's a start. My engineers are already working to analyze it."

"How long will that take?" I pressed.

"Weeks, maybe months," Goloran admitted. "This is beyond anything we've seen before. Cracking its secrets won't be easy."

I slumped back in my seat, suddenly so tired that all I wanted to do was lay my head down on the conference table and sleep. The adrenaline of the battle was fading, and the exhaustion of my ordeal was catching up with me. "So what now?" I asked quietly.

"Now, we regroup," Goloran said. "We're on our way to Gothor as we—"

"What? No!" I sat up straight, alarm surging through me. "We can't go to Gothor. We need to get to Ocypha, to meet up with Ben and the others."

"Out of the question," Goloran said firmly. "In case you

haven't noticed, we just narrowly escaped disaster. My priority now is the safety of my people. I need to return to Gothor, to make preparations in case this conflict escalates."

"But my friends—"

"Will have to fend for themselves," she cut me off. "At least for now. I'm sorry Noah, but my mind is made up on this. We're going to Gothor."

I wanted to argue, to rage against the unfairness of it all. But I could see in her eyes that it would be futile. Goloran had made her decision. And as much as I hated it, I could understand her reasoning. She had her own people to think about. Her own responsibilities.

"You must realize," she continued. "The only thing I've gained from all of this is a powerful enemy who's not only threatened my home, but proven he has the power to make good on those threats."

I blanched at the thought, recalling what Lavona had told me of Markan's atrocities on Viconia. If he could create the same instability on Gothor, it would be a disaster for the Gothori.

"For whatever it's worth, I'm sorry," I replied.

"I believe you," Goloran said.

"So are you planning to just abandon us on Gothor?" Meg asked.

"Abandon? No. Of course, not. This isn't your fault. When we reach Gothor, we will arrange for you to escape from the palace and steal a starship suitable for your needs. Once you're gone, I will seek out the syndicate and offer my apologies, in hopes I can prevent retaliation."

"How can you just give in like that?" I asked. "How can you even stomach the idea?"

"Not easily, I assure you. But my foremost responsibility is to the security of my people. I've put them in grave danger, and I need to get them out of it. Being a leader means doing things you don't want to do much more often than things you do want."

I could tell by her face how distasteful the whole situation had become for her. There was no sense acting like a spoiled brat and complaining when she had already sacrificed so much to try to help us.

"I understand," I said. "And we're grateful for all the aid you've provided, and will provide. How long will we be in hyperspace?"

"Two weeks."

"Well, I don't want to just sit on my hands for the next two weeks. There has to be something I can do to help figure things out."

"There is," Goloran said, surprising me. "You can march yourself straight to sickbay and let the doctor finish treating you. You're no good to anyone if you collapse from exhaustion or cause permanent damage to yourself."

"That's not really what I had in mind."

"Don't make me have Kloth drag you there."

The grithyak perked up at the mention of his name, fixing me with his inscrutable yellow eyes. I had no doubt he would follow through on Goloran's threat if given the chance.

I held up my hands in surrender. "Alright, alright. I'm going."

"Good." Goloran softened slightly. "Get some rest. We'll talk more later, once we've had a chance to catch our breath and think things through a bit more."

I nodded, pushing myself to my feet. When the room swayed, I slapped my palm back down on the table to catch myself. Meg laid a steadying hand on my elbow, concern etched into her features.

"Come on," she said gently. "I'll walk with you."

"Your Highness," I said, bowing my head to the princess. Together, with Kloth trailing behind like a particularly menacing shadow, we made our way out of the conference room and into the corridor.

As we walked, my thoughts drifted back to the Wardenship and its secrets. I couldn't shake the feeling that the answers I sought were just out of reach. My father's voice echoed in my memory, an inexplicable beacon in the darkness.

You aren't supposed to be here.

But I *was* here. And one way or another, I was going to unravel this mystery. No matter what it took.

We arrived at sickbay to find Doctor Ashti waiting for us, her arms crossed and a severe expression on her face. I had a feeling I was in for another lecture, and I mentally braced myself.

"What part of being restricted to the autodoc was unclear?" she asked as I stepped through the door.

"The entire part, apparently," Meg muttered under her breath.

I shot her a dirty look but couldn't exactly argue. "Doctor Ashti, I—"

"Save it," she cut me off, holding up a hand. "I don't want to hear excuses. I want you back on that autodoc bed, now. We need to make sure you didn't create an even bigger problem for yourself with your reckless bravado."

I sighed, knowing when I was beaten. Trudging into the medbay, I hoisted myself onto the autodoc and laid back, trying to ignore the dizziness as I did.

Ashti busied herself with the controls, muttering under her breath as she adjusted settings and checked readouts. I caught the mumbled words "stubborn" and "idiot" and decided it was probably better not to listen too closely, much less say anything.

Meg hovered nearby, watching the proceedings with concern and amusement. Apparently satisfied that I wasn't going to make a break for it, Kloth had planted himself by the door like a surly sentinel.

As the autodoc started to hum and whir around me, I felt my eyelids droop. The day's events caught up to me, the exhaustion settling deep into my bones.

"Sleep," Ashti instructed, her voice softening a touch. "You need time to heal."

I wanted to protest, to insist that I couldn't afford to waste time napping while so much remained unresolved. But my body had other ideas.

As I drifted off, my thoughts turned again to the Wardenship and the tantalizing secrets it contained. With bone-deep certainty, I knew that the key to everything—my past, future, and the fate of those I held dear—lay within that enigmatic ship.

And now it was completely out of my reach.

I drifted into fragmented, disjointed dreams. Snatches of memory and imagination tangled together in a confusing web. I saw the Wardenship, its halls pulsing with strange energy. Levain's face, contorted in a scheming sneer. Markan, his eyes burning with fervor and ambition. And my father... always my father, his voice an anchor in the chaos.

"Noah," he seemed to call from a distance. "Noah..."

"Dad?" The word escaped me as a raw croak, my throat dry and scratchy. My eyelids fluttered open, the sterile white of the sickbay gradually coming into focus.

For a moment, I simply laid there, blinking against the bright lights. Confusion muddled my thoughts as I tried to separate my dream from reality.

"Noah? Are you awake?"

Meg's face appeared above me, her brows drawn together in concern. I managed a nod, attempting to sit up. She hurried to help me, adjusting the autodoc so I could sit comfortably.

"How long was I out?" I asked, my voice rough from disuse. I noticed Kloth was gone, and I didn't know where Archie was.

"You've been asleep for about twelve hours," she replied. "Doctor Ashti said your brain needed the rest to heal."

I grimaced, rubbing a hand over my stubbled face. Twelve hours. Half a day, lost to unconsciousness while the galaxy continued to spiral into whatever Markan had planned.

"I can't afford to lay around," I said, my frustration bubbling over. "We need to—"

"What you need," Ashti's sharp voice cut in as she strode into view, "is to follow my instructions. Your neural scans are improving, but you're not out of the woods yet."

I opened my mouth to argue, but something in her expression made me reconsider. I'd seen that look before, on my mother's face when I was being particularly obstinate. It was the look that said "I know what's best, and you'll do as I say or else."

Wisely, I closed my mouth.

Ashti gave me a curt nod, satisfied with my compliance. She ran through a series of checks while I tried not to fidget.

As she worked, my gaze drifted to Meg. She had remained by my side, a steady presence in the whirlwind of activity. I felt a rush of gratitude for her friendship, her unwavering support. "Thank you," I said quietly after Ashti stepped away for a moment. "For being here."

Meg smiled, reaching out to squeeze my hand. "Of course. We're in this together, whatever the outcome."

I returned her smile, some of the tension easing from my shoulders. She was right. Whatever challenges lay ahead, whatever mysteries we had to unravel, we would face them as a team.

As family.

"All right," Ashti announced, drawing my attention back to her. "Your vitals are stable and your neural activity is within acceptable parameters. I'm clearing you for light duty, emphasis on light." She fixed me with a stern look. "You are to take it easy and report back to me at the first sign of any unusual symptoms. Am I clear?"

"Crystal," I assured her, already itching to get moving. "Thank you, Doctor."

She waved off my gratitude. "I'm just doing my job. Now, go on. Get out of here."

I didn't need to be told twice. I slid off the autodoc, pleased that the room remained stable. Archie moved to my side, appearing from wherever it had sequestered itself. He'd lost his blood hue and also grown a little more. Actually, a lot more. In terms of size, he had graduated from French Bulldog to the English version. I didn't think I'd be carrying him around anymore.

Meg and I made our way out of sickbay, Archie following along. My steps grew more confident with each passing moment, all while my mind raced ahead, grappling with the challenges that confronted us.

We needed a way to uncover the truth about my father, the Wardenship and its connection to Earth. We needed to find a way to stop Markan from replacing the Warden as the biggest threat to Warexia.

But first, we needed information. And I had a sinking feeling the only way to get it was to confront the one being I least wanted to interact with.

I needed to talk to the Warden.

CHAPTER 18

Of course, speaking to the Warden while in hyperspace was impossible. And even once we reached Gothor, I didn't know how I would contact him, especially since we'd disabled my nanites' comms array. I also had a feeling Ben wouldn't be happy with me making contact with the Warden alone. No matter what method I found to contact him, it would reveal our use of the disabler, and who knew how he might react once he knew we could cut him off.

And who knew how he would react once I told him about Markan, who was supposed to be dead?

The more I thought about it, the more I questioned whether or not going to the Warden was a good idea. I did my best to float the concept to Meg and Princess Goloran and of course, got two different answers. Meg wasn't in favor, at least not without consulting Ben and Matt. She said they had experience dealing with high-powered mega-lomaniacs, so they could offer a more thoughtful take. Meanwhile, Goloran seemed to be in favor despite her earlier comments about the Warden. I didn't blame her. She had a lot more to lose if Markan remained unchecked.

Having two weeks to think about everything—from

what I'd learned to connecting all the pieces to how to do something about it—didn't make things any easier. In a lot of ways, it made the whole situation harder. Since Ashti wouldn't let me do much more than light calisthenics and as much reading as I wanted, my only options for keeping myself occupied were rumination or playing Aktak, a cross between Go and Chess, with Archie. The game might have been fun with anyone else. Archie kicked my butt every time we played.

The little booger also continued growing to the extent that I couldn't call him a little booger anymore. Its English Bulldog had become Golden Retriever, and he tended to remain in the maulvas form more often than not, though at times, it would sprout tendrils to interact, like with the Aktak pieces. It made sense that the more cells it had in its colony, the faster they could split and increase its size, but it was still startling to come back from a meeting with Goloran or Meg about discoveries from the imaging the techs had done only to find the Aleal a few pounds larger. I could only wonder how much longer it would be before it reached maturity and what size it would be when it did. From talking to Ben and Matt about Aleal in general, I knew it would gain the ability to take on a human form at some point and then the ability to speak. I also wondered how soon that might be or if it would decide it preferred the appearance of a vicious dog.

Thankfully, my episode with the Wardenship's command chair didn't create any lasting effects. My dizziness had disappeared, my brain fog cleared, and my energy and appetite had returned. When I sensed Resolute dropping out of hyperspace, I was pretty much back to my usual health.

I thought I would be excited to finally arrive at Princess Goloran's homeworld, but no sooner had the sensation of leaving the compression field pass than butterflies knotted my stomach. The moment of truth for everything I'd mentally obsessed over for the last two weeks became imminent.

Meg and I had already gone over some of the details of what would happen next with Goloran. A short stay at the palace, followed by a choreographed escape in a jump-capable starship, destination: Ocypha. We'd meet up with Ben and the others, review what we'd learned, and figure out what to do.

Simple enough, until it wasn't.

"Noah," Meg said, her tone chipper over the comms. "Princess Goloran wants us to meet her in the hangar."

While I'd spent the time in hyperspace worrying about the future, she'd been in geek heaven. After spending hours a day poring over the three-dimensional imaging, she'd helped Goloran's techs create blueprints and schematics while also breaking out the sigils on each device in hopes Ben might be able to decipher at least a few.

"Copy that," I replied, glancing over at Archie. He was in the middle of returning the Aktak pieces to their starting positions for another round. After I'd given up, the Aleal had started playing against itself. With any other entity, it might have seemed pointless. But watching it play, I got the impression it utilized the different essences it had captured to guide its moves. It looked odd, but Archie didn't care. "Hey bud, time to go."

Archie lifted its maulvas head in my direction and nodded almost humanly before rising to its feet.

"Did you win?" I asked jokingly. Arch growled softly back at me as if suggesting I wasn't funny.

When we arrived at the hangar, Meg and Princess Goloran were already waiting by the shuttle, Kloth an inscrutable presence at their side. With my bag slung over one shoulder and Archie padding beside me, I crossed the deck to join them.

"Are you ready?" Goloran asked as I approached, her sculpted features unreadable.

I nodded, trying to ignore the flutter of nerves in my gut. "As I'll ever be."

We boarded the shuttle, strapping in as the pilot initiated the launch sequence. Within moments, we were soaring away from Resolute's gleaming hull, angling down towards the curved horizon of Gothor.

As we descended, I leaned forward, eager for my first glimpse of the Gothori homeworld. I wasn't sure what I expected—towering cities perhaps, or vast swathes of verdant green—but as the shuttle skimmed lower, my original expectations were quickly crushed by reality.

Gothor was nearly barren. A world of red rock and shifting sand, broken only by a narrow band of greenery and small blue pools in a ring around the equator. Nine parts a forbidding landscape of cracked earth and jagged peaks and one part apparent paradise, I struggled to hide my overall dismay.

"Not what you were expecting?" Meg asked from beside me, noting my surprised expression.

I shook my head slowly. "No. I guess I thought it would be more..."

"Hospitable?" she finished wryly. "Yeah, me too."

As we drew closer to the surface, I saw signs of civilization—clusters of low, domed structures—that nearly blended into the ruddy landscape. They seemed to be made of the same red earth as if they'd sprouted organically from the ground itself.

"Those are Gothori citizen dwellings," Goloran explained, following my gaze. "They're constructed from a temperature regulating clay mixture. Given the climate of our habitable zone, we've had to adapt our architecture to suit our environment."

The shuttle banked, angling towards a massive plateau

rising from the barren plains. The sprawling structure atop it had to be the Gothori Royal Palace. It was a strange organic fusion of styles reminiscent of ancient Middle Eastern and medieval European architecture. Smooth domes and arches flowed into soaring spires and buttressed castle walls, the whole of which was formed from the same clay as the lesser dwellings around it. Its stone base made it look as if it had grown organically out of the rock.

We touched down on a landing pad jutting from the palace's flanks, the shuttle's engines stirring up clouds of fine red dust. As we disembarked, the searing heat enveloped me like a physical force, the thin air shimmering with the intensity of the alien sun.

A small party awaited us at the edge of the pad, led by a stately couple flanked by a contingent of grithyak guards. The king was tall and broad-shouldered, his craggy features aged and weathered. He wore a high-collared tunic of deep purple, the fabric shot through with threads of gleaming gold that caught the light.

Beside him, the queen stood straight and regal, her willowy form draped in flowing robes of shimmering orange that rippled with every movement. Younger than the king, her face was a study in cool, distant beauty, with high, sharp cheekbones and eyes glittered like obsidian chips.

"Mother, Father," Goloran greeted as we approached, dipping into a formal bow. "May I present Noah, Archie, and Meg, my honored guests."

The royal couple inclined their heads in acknowledgment, but there was a tightness around their eyes, a slight strain in their polite smiles that set my nerves on edge. Something was off, an undercurrent of tension thrumming beneath the surface of this meeting.

Meg caught my eye, a flicker of unease passing between us. She sensed it, too.

"Welcome to Gothor," the king said, his voice a rich baritone. "We trust your journey was not too arduous?"

"Not at all, Your Majesties," I replied, trying to match his formal tone. "We're honored by your hospitality."

The queen's arctic gaze swept over us, imperious and assessing. "We hope your stay with us will be...productive." More than a simple pleasantry, I suddenly felt uneasy that the queen's words carried a weight other than their surface meaning. The queen's next words did nothing to assuage those concerns. "Darling, I hate to be a poor host, but I'm afraid it can't be helped. We need to speak with you *immediately*."

"This can't wait?" Goloran asked.

"No," the king answered. "I'm afraid this is a matter of..." He gave the queen a sharp look. "...great importance."

"Very well," Goloran replied. "Kloth, please show our guests to their quarters." She glanced at Meg and me. "It appears I need to catch up with my parents. Rest assured, every comfort will be provided while you wait for my return."

The grithyak grunted his acknowledgment, gesturing for us to follow.

"It was good to meet Your Majesties," I said, bowing slightly toward them in my best approximation of what I had seen on television.

"Indeed," the queen replied stiffly, their only offer of response before Kloth led us away. As we set off across the sun-baked courtyard, I glanced back to see Goloran deep in conversation with her parents, their expressions and gestures tense. I didn't want to make assumptions, but the odds were good they were talking about Meg and me.

Our rooms were in a wing of the palace that seemed reserved for visiting dignitaries. The walls were adorned with intricate tapestries depicting what I assumed to be

Gothori history and mythology, the colors vibrant against the pale stone. Despite the heat outside, the interior remained cool and comfortable.

Kloth stopped at a pair of opposing rooms, their privacy defended only by opaque curtains that waved gently in the air conditioning's soft breeze. He motioned Meg to one side and me to the other, glaring at us impatiently until we left the corridor. I was faintly aware of his claws clacking along the clay tile floor as he left us.

A quick survey of the room revealed simple yet colorful appointments, much of it made from thin materials that either allowed the air to flow through or helped increase its movement. A fan made of large feathers turned gently overhead, while a comfortable sofa-like hammock dangled beneath it on golden ropes. Rooms off the main space revealed a bathroom with an exposed water delivery mechanism and a second hammock with an overstuffed pillow at one end and a light blanket spread over it.

When I returned to the main area, Archie was on his back, thoroughly relaxed on the hanging sofa, enjoying the breeze from the fan on its belly. Meg stood just inside the entry curtain, looking concerned.

"You felt it, too?" I asked.

"How could I miss it?" she replied. "I'd need a plasma cutter to get through that tension."

"Something tells me we should make a run for it right now, instead of waiting on the princess."

"If I thought we had any way of getting out of here, I might agree. But we've trusted her this far."

I nodded. "Yeah. Her parents might do us dirty, but I don't think she will."

Of course, that didn't make waiting any easier. I started pacing, restless energy thrumming through my limbs. It felt like hours before the curtain pushed aside, Goloran entering without preamble. She swept the curtains firmly closed behind her.

"What's going on?" I asked without preamble, my unease sharpening into genuine fear at the look on her face. "Your mother already made a deal with Markan, didn't she?"

Her hands clenched into fists at her sides. Her voice shook with barely suppressed fury and something that might have been fear. "Yes. His emissaries are here in the palace. I just spoke to them. I excused myself and ran here to warn you. You need to leave immediately!"

CHAPTER 19

Archie stirred in response to the princess' statement, sliding off the sofa to heel beside me.

"Here," Goloran thrust her personal access device into my hand. "I planned to transfer all this to a different device later, but there's no time. It has a map of the palace and surrounding area to the spaceport, and access keys for the ship I selected for you. It's called Burnock. A Gothori fire-bird. It will get you to Ochnya."

"Thank you," I said, gripping the pad more tightly.

"Wait," Meg cried. "What about the research? The sigils? We're supposed to just leave everything with you?"

"Of course not," she replied. "All of the work is on my pad. If I can, I'll destroy the rest before Markan can get his hands on it. I'm sorry it came to this. My mother is adamant. If it were in my power, I would do more to help. But Markan took the options out of my hands before I could speak to my parents. Good luck out there."

She turned to go, but before she could take more than a step, the curtain moved aside and a pair of servants in brightly colored pants and tunics entered carrying food and drinks.

"Y…Your Highness," the female on the left stammered, quickly bowing her head. "I…I didn't expect to see you here."

"Good," Goloran replied. "I was never here. Do you understand?"

"Yes, Your Highness," the servant answered.

The doorway curtain rippled closed behind Princess Goloran, leaving Meg and me alone with the servants. I watched closely as the servants began setting up a low table, arranging an assortment of unfamiliar foods and drinks with practiced efficiency.

Something about the female servant's precise movements caught my eye—the way her fingers curled around the pitcher, pressing tight against the handle, as she poured. It triggered a prickle of suspicion at the base of my skull. Had she perhaps pressed a button on the handle, releasing some kind of poison or sleep agent? I held my tongue, not wanting to jump to conclusions.

The servant straightened, fixing me with a polite smile as she offered a plate laden with what appeared to be some sort of pastries. "Cookie, sir?"

I hesitated, looking her in the eye. I didn't see any deception there, but still…Miss Asher had taught Lavona and me to always remain hyper-vigilant, especially in known hostile territory. With that in mind, I reached out as if to take the proffered treat, but at the last second, I redirected my hand to her wrist. My fingers found the telltale ridges of a disguised control surface, a pattern I recognized immediately. In an instant, I tapped the sequence to deactivate her nanofiber disguise. The servant's eyes widened in surprise as her features rippled and distorted. Even though the assassin wore a holomask, I knew instinctively and by the shape of the head beneath the cover who Markan had sent for me.

"Asher," I growled, my grip tightening. "I knew there was something off about you."

The Nycene assassin's lips curled in a sneer. "You always were an astute student." Then she moved, her hand a blur of speed and deadly intent as she twisted from my grip.

I reacted instinctively as her fist whistled past my ear. I lashed out with a return kick, catching her in the midsection and sending her staggering back. But Asher was inhumanly fast, and she recovered almost instantly, coming at me in a flurry of precise, brutal strikes.

Across the room, I heard Meg cry out in surprise as the other servant lunged at her, his disguise melting away to reveal another assassin. I had no time to worry about Meg. Archie leaped to her defense instead. Its maulvas form rippled and shifted, razor-sharp tendrils whipping out to slash at her attacker's face and eyes.

Asher's blows were fast and furious. I dipped and wove, barely avoiding her onslaught until a sharp pain exploded in my ribs, her strike driving much of the breath from my lungs.

Desperate, I launched myself forward, latching onto her arm. Grappling with her, we crashed into the table, clay dishes and glasses flew, shattering around us as they hit the tiled floor. I nearly slipped on scattered food but managed to turn her back to my chest and snake an arm around her throat. Squeezing with all my strength, Asher snarled, reaching back to gouge my face with her nails, drawing bloody welts.

A guttural scream told me Archie had found its target. I cast a fleeting look at the assassin attacking Meg just as he stumbled back, clutching at the ruin of his eye, but that was all I saw as Asher slammed her elbow into my solar plexus. I heard Meg's blaster go off as Asher tore free of my hold, whirling to face me.

"You've improved, Katzuo," she spat, her eyes blazing with rage and respect. "But not enough."

She came at me again, low and fast. I braced myself, but she juked at the last second, pivoting behind me with blinding speed. Like a steel band, her arm wrapped tight around my throat.

As I gasped for air, my fingers trying in vain to dislodge her hold, I realized Meg had missed the second assassin with her first shot. She fired again, her blaster set on spray. Four sizzling rounds center mass dropped him to the floor. She swung her blaster toward Asher, Archie ready to pounce if she missed her shot.

"Wait!" Asher cried, holding me protectively in front of her as she turned me to face them. "I'm only here for this traitorous scum." Growling softly, Archie bunched itself to pounce. "I said stand down, Aleal!" Asher snapped.

"You can't kill Noah," Meg said. "You need him."

"I need myself even more," Asher replied. "I'll do whatever is necessary."

"Meg…shoot…her," I wheezed through my constricted throat.

Asher's grip tightened. "Be silent, Katzuo. I trained you better than that. You're wasting air."

I tried to plead with Meg using just my eyes. But she held her fire, playing right into Asher's hands.

"That's a good girl," Asher said. "Now, I'm going to take Katzuo and be on my way. If either of you make a move to stop me, I promise I'll kill him before I kill you."

She dragged me toward the curtain. Meg and Archie remained stone still, poised to strike, their attention trained on her, both waiting for me to find some way out of her chokehold. But she had taught me the hold, and I knew there was no way to defeat it. The whole fight had been unfair, perception time moving faster for Asher than any of us. That I had landed a few blows was nothing short of a miracle.

Asher pushed the curtain aside with her foot, and suddenly, the pressure on my throat was gone. I gasped as sweet air flooded my starved lungs. I spun around just in time to see Kloth throw Asher against the adjacent wall. The assassin screamed—a high, terrible sound quickly cut off as the grithyak's claws sank into her throat. When he pulled them back, ripping her throat out, Asher collapsed to the floor, the light of life leaving her eyes.

"Kloth!" I cried. Never happier to see the furry bodyguard, I grinned, running over to clasp his thick biceps. "What are you doing here?"

"Smelled wrong," he replied, referring to the two assassins.

"Were you just waiting out there the entire time?"

Kloth remained poker-faced, which to me meant yes.

A sickening crack drew my attention back to Asher, and I cringed as Archie sank a tentacle into her skull, drawing in her essence.

"We don't have time for this, bud," I said as Meg appeared at my side, winded and bruised but alive. She glanced down at Asher's bloody form with a mix of revulsion and relief. Distant shouts echoed from the corridors beyond. It had to be Gothori royal guards, drawn by the commotion. They would be here in moments.

My eyes remained fixed on Archie. He'd given me an idea. I crouched beside Asher, quickly searching the pouches on her stealth suit.

"Noah, we need to go," Meg said. "Now."

"Kloth, are you coming?" I asked.

He shook his head. "My place is here."

"Do you think you can slow them down a little? Buy us some time?"

He glared at me a moment before nodding. Turning away, he quickly vanished around the corner.

"What are you doing?" Meg asked as I recovered Asher's pad and moved to her stealth suit, withdrawing a thin wire from mine to connect the two.

"Copying whatever holographic scans she's made," I replied. "So I can disguise myself as one of them. Preferably, the one who entered the spaceport."

Meg smiled. "So you can leave as her? That'll make it easier to get out of here."

"If you were a bit taller, we could stick you in Asher's suit."

"A bit? She's gigantic."

"No, you're tiny."

"Not to me, I'm not. She's gigantic."

I finished copying her data and yanked the cable from her suit. "I've got the scans, her pad, and Goloran's pad," I said. "Let's get the hell out of here."

Whether finished with digesting her brain tissue or not, Archie retracted his tentacle and changed back into maulvas form. The sound of boots, louder now at the far end of the corridor, grabbed my attention.

"Remember, don't hurt them," I said, pulling my blaster as a pair of guards surged around the corner. I joined Meg, laying down cover fire that allowed us to clear the corner at the other end of the passageway without hitting anyone on either side.

The hunt was on, the enemy closing in. But we were still standing, still fighting.

And I wouldn't stop fighting. Not until this was finished, once and for all.

CHAPTER 20

Meg and I burst out of the palace like rats running from a sinking ship, Archie loping at our heels. The intense heat of the Gothori sun slammed into us like a physical wall, momentarily stealing my breath. But there was no time to adjust. Shouts and pounding footsteps echoed behind us, the palace guards hot on our trail.

"This way!" I called, consulting the map on Goloran's pad. I veered left towards a narrow servants' passage winding between the palace's outer buildings. Meg and Archie followed without hesitation, trusting my sense of direction.

We plunged into the shadowy corridor, our breathing harsh in the suddenly cool air. The passage joined with others, leading to different parts of the palace's outbuildings. With the map as our guiding star, we managed to advance on the marker Goloran had placed along an apparent river, one of two pins on the map.

Suddenly, a squad of palace guards emerged from a side passage, weapons drawn. There was no time to think, only to react. I charged forward, ducking under the first guard's stun baton swing. My fist connected with his jaw, and he dropped like a stone.

Meg held her own beside me, her blows precise and economical as she wove between two guards. An elbow to the groin and then a kick to the jaw of one, and then a neatly done throw of the other left them both unconscious on the ground.

Archie surged past us, tendrils sprouting from his haunches as he neared the remaining two guards. Frightened by the slavering, red-hued maulvas, they fired wildly, plasma bolts sizzling erratically through the air. The Aleal dodged them all, its tendrils wrapping around their weapons, yanking them from their hands. Meg and I finished off the two guards sprawling with a well-placed combination of kicks and punches.

In only a few moments, it was over. The guards lay sprawled in the corridor, unconscious. We paused just long enough to catch our breath.

"We can't stay here," Meg panted. "More will be coming."

I nodded, already moving. "The map shows a way out, to the river. From there we can…"

Another nearby shout, another group of approaching guards silenced me. They were catching up to us. Maybe they'd even guessed where we were going.

We raced between outbuildings, making a beeline for the river with the shouts of the palace guards echoing behind us. Meg and Archie kept pace beside me, our footsteps ringing against the stone.

We burst into the blinding Gothori sun again, squinting against the glare. There, stretching out before us, was the river. A sluggish ribbon of water, it was so clear the sun made the red clay at its bottom look like blood. Moored along its banks, a handful of boats bobbed gently in the current.

"There!" I pointed to a cluster of sleek metal craft. In the center was a wooden barge with a heavy, colored canopy over colorful, thickly padded seats. Its prow was carved into the shape of an aggressive bird of prey. A burnock, maybe? It had to be water transport for the Gothori royals, especially since it was flanked on both sides by smaller, sleeker metal patrol boats. Behind a pilot's console, each carried a plasma cannon mounted on a rotating turret.

We sprinted for the lead patrol boat, Archie bounding ahead. I leaped aboard after the Aleal, with Meg close on my heels. Stopping at the pilot's console, I pressed the button to start the engines. A red LED flashed, rejecting the effort, while a projection demanded an access code and provided a floating numeric keypad.

"Hurry!" Meg urged, her gaze locked on the path we'd just come from. The distant figures of the palace guard were spilling out of the corridor between the buildings, their weapons glinting in the harsh light.

"It's passcode protected," I explained, pulling out one of my cracking devices and slapping it against the flat part of the console next to the ignition switch. An eternity seemed to pass as it went to work, the soldiers drawing closer with each thudding heartbeat. "Archie, release the mooring lines."

The Aleal quickly sprouted tendrils to unwind the lines from the side of the boat, setting us adrift. Finally, the device blinked green. The boat's engine rumbled to life beneath our feet.

"Hang on!" I cried, immediately opening up the throttle, the sudden acceleration slamming me back into the seat as we sped away. "Meg, grab the yoke!" I cried, moving aside to let her squeeze in. She took over the stand-up steering and angled us out into the river's main flow.

I scrambled back to the plasma cannon, grabbing the handles and flipping the switch to activate it. The gun hummed as I primed it, the entire base rotating with me until the muzzle faced the rear. I aimed the cannon toward the dock, my finger tightening on the trigger. I still didn't want to hurt anyone, but we needed every second we could buy.

Before our pursuers could jump into them, my plasma bolts sizzled through the air, putting holes in the boats in front of the royal barge. Freezing on the dock, they turned toward the craft behind the barge, the number of available chase boats anchored there was limited to three. I heard the initial loud whine of their engines over the softer purr of our own, and within seconds, the boats pulled out from behind the barge, accelerating rapidly. We had a lead, but it wouldn't last long.

Their first volley of fire seared past us, close enough that I could feel the heat of its passage. Squinting down the targeting reticle, I fired back, plasma bolts stitching the water around the lead boat. I aimed for their hull, trying to breach it below the waterline to either sink it or at least flood the engine compartment and stall it.

The air crackled with our fire, superheated plasma hissing and spitting as it struck water. Meg jinked and wove, trying to present a more challenging target, but in the narrow confines of the river, there was only so much she could do. Every bolt aimed at us drew closer and closer to hitting us.

These fast assault boats were more nimble and faster than our bigger patrol boat. They matched our maneuvers, making them a harder challenge than I anticipated.

Finally, one of my shots found its mark, punching through the starboard bow of the lead boat. It lurched and slewed in the water, smoke pouring from the wound. But still, it came on, the gunner doggedly firing even as their craft began to wallow and sink.

I shifted to the next target, pouring all my concentration

into my shots. The cannon grew hot under my hands, the air around it shimmering with the heat of rapid fire. Meg pushed our engines to their limit, the patrol boat leaving a wake that parted the pursuing boats. It forced me to swing the cannon back and forth between targets. That and Meg swerving slowed my shots and disrupted my aim.

The guards' bolts drew ever nearer to connecting with our stern, the disturbed water drenching me. Finally, as it swerved across the river, trying to avoid my steady stream of bolts, I landed a hit on the second attack boat. A brilliant flare of white sparks marked the hit, a fire breaking out in the stern. The boat spun and launched into the air, throwing the helpless guards into the water just before its plasma cannon and engine detonated.

And then there was only one.

The final boat dogged us, stubborn as a pitbull. Fire rained around us, the shots growing more accurate as the chase wore on. I knew I was tiring, my responses starting to slow. Only Meg's desperate maneuvering had kept us afloat for this long, and I owed it to her to finish off our last tail in reward for the amazing effort.

"Come on," I muttered to myself. "This is just like Star Squadron."

I sighted through the reticle, predicting Meg's next swerve and the maneuver of the boat behind us. Knowing it would only pass through the reticle for an instant, my finger pressed lightly on the trigger, ready for that moment to come.

Our boat shuddered as Meg cut hard to port. Feet already planted, I held on, keeping the plasma cannon level. The last fast-attack boat shifted with us, and my finger tapped down just before they swerved into my crosshairs. I kept the trigger depressed, plasma bolts spewing from the cannon and sinking into the water just ahead of the trailing craft. Return fire stitched the water perilously close to us, one of the bolts grazing the hull with a sharp hiss. Meg changed direction again, throwing off our pursuer's aim, their next bolt going wide. Having lost my aim, I stopped firing, stomach sinking at my failure.

The attack boat sent a few more half-hearted volleys toward us before unexpectedly slowing. I only then noticed how the bow tilted forward in the water, the craft beginning to sink from holes I hadn't realized I'd made in it.

"Whooo!" I cried in excitement as the three soldiers abandoned ship, jumping overboard before the weight of the onrushing water pulled the boat beneath the surface. "Meg, we're clear!"

She immediately stopped her evasive maneuvers and straightened the boat in the water. We zipped along the river, headed for the spaceport.

"They're going to know we're coming," Meg shouted over the wind. "We can't fight our way through the entire spaceport."

"Hopefully, we won't need to," I replied. Retrieving her pad, I almost laughed when it demanded a facial scan for access. As skilled and intelligent as Miss Asher had been, she was also arrogant and overconfident, which had been her undoing before, and would help us again now.

Activating the stealth suit, I scrolled through the projected images of scans I'd captured from Miss Asher, surprised to find she had made one of Lavona and me, and even more surprised to find one of Markan himself. When might she have gathered that scan? Did the syndicate's leader know about it? I tried each face against the security guard on her pad, and I was pleased when one of them unlocked the device. A Nycene woman in formal business attire.

"Noah?" Meg asked, glancing away from the river to notice my new look. "What's your plan?"

"When we reach the spaceport, we'll try to confuse

them," I replied. "Best case, they let us pass without a fight. Worst case, we get the drop on them."

"Worst case, they shoot first and wonder who we are later," she corrected.

"Yeah, I guess that would be the absolute worst case, but not very likely." I looked at Archie, curled up on the deck in Maulvas form. "We need to get you past the guards somehow, bud. Maybe if you duck into the water before we reach the dock, you can sneak around behind them aaand…"

My voice trailed off as Archie's shape-shifted, body elongating, followed by the development of appendages. A second sphere blobbed out from its center, rising and reshaping into a humanoid head. The change paused there, hesitant, as if it wasn't sure how to finish the model. Then it accelerated suddenly, becoming a translucent version of someone all too familiar..

Jaffie.

In full Mandalorian armor.

I cringed at the sight of the simulacrum. Of course, Archie had taken his essence months ago, but this was the first time it had tried to copy him.

I continued watching as the Aleal's Jaffie gained detail, his armor appearing to harden as it became opaque, matching the dull metal hue of the original. In under a minute, a replica of the man who killed my parents stood in the back of the boat.

"What the—?" Meg whispered, looking over her shoulder. "You look so real."

"That's a great job, Arch," I said. "Can you speak, too?"

Archie shook its head, running its hands down the front of its body. I understood the unspoken explanation. The Aleal had chosen a more straightforward human form that didn't require the detail of a face or the complexity of muscle beneath its skin. Apparently, it didn't have complete enough knowledge of a throat, larynx, or lungs to create them, or it just didn't have enough total mass to create a complete life size human copy.

Either way, it was convincing enough to provide a body-guard for my Nycene emissary. And just in time. The dock for the spaceport came into view ahead, an entire unit of spaceport security lining the restricted checkpoint with shock batons at the ready.

"I'm going with the worst case scenario here," Meg muttered as we neared the dock.

I couldn't argue. It would take a strong performance to convince the guards to let us pass without a fight. "I have to try," I replied. "Meg, you're our prisoner. I'll take the wheel. Archie, hold onto her arm, but be gentle."

Meg relinquished the wheel, moving to the back of the boat to allow Archie to wrap a gloved hand around her arm, making it look like he was holding her captive. Reaching the shore, I tossed one of the guards a mooring line coiled in the bow and brought us in. Once the boat was tied up, we clambered out, hands raised in a show of non-aggression. The soldiers, however, weren't taking any chances. They closed in, batons humming with restrained energy.

With a deep breath, I stepped forward, keeping my movements slow and deliberate as I spread my hands placatingly. "What is the meaning of this?" I demanded, playing the role of the affronted dignitary, Asher's impe-rious tone coloring my voice. "I came here at the King's request, and this is how I'm greeted? With threats of violence and baseless suspicion?"

The guard wavered, clearly taken aback, just as I'd hoped. Miss Asher had taught me well.

"I...my apologies," he managed, lowering his baton a fraction. "But there are escaped fugitives we have to—"

"Fugitives?" I cut him off, laying the outrage on thick.

"Do I look like a fugitive to you?" My gaze swept the line of guards, noting how they shifted uneasily under my withering stare.

"That one," I gestured at Meg, "is a fugitive. A criminal wanted by the Nycene authorities for murder. Her transfer from Gothor is the reason I'm here." I pointed at Archie. "That is my bodyguard. I'm certainly not going to touch this murderous filth with my own hands."

The soldier swallowed hard, indecision written plainly across his features. I could practically see the gears turning in his head as he tried to decide which would be worse—letting a potential fugitive slip through, or causing a diplomatic incident by offending a VIP.

"The guard boats are the fastest way to the spaceport from the palace," I said.

"Huh?" the guard replied.

"I assume you're trying to figure out why we came to the spaceport via the river in a patrol boat rather than the royal barge or by some other elaborate means of transportation."

"Uh…right. That's true," he agreed. "It's just that the fugitives also—"

"I repeat, do I look like a fugitive?" I snapped, beginning to enjoy the game we were playing, even if it was wasting our time. "Do we match their descriptions?"

The guard swallowed hard. "Uh…well…not exactly." He pointed to Meg. "She…she does look like one of them. Small…short hair…"

"So you're basing my delay on one match, out of how many escapees?"

"Three."

"Three what?" I barked. "You will address me with respect when you speak to me."

"My…my apologies, Your Grace. We are looking for three fugitives."

"And one of us in this boat matches the description of one of the fugitive's?"

"Y…yes, Your Grace."

I pressed my advantage, stepping forward until I was toe-to-toe with the guard. Up close, I could smell the sweat from fear beading his brow. Every stammer from him only increased my confidence. I never expected to have so much fun with this.

"You have two choices," I said softly, my voice cold as the void. "You can step aside and let us pass, and I'll forget this unfortunate incident ever happened. Or you can continue to obstruct me, and I'll make sure the full weight of my displeasure falls upon you and your men when you bring me back to the King. Choose wisely."

For a long, tense moment, no one moved. Then, slowly, the soldier stepped aside, a bead of sweat trickling down his temple.

"My apologies, Your Grace," he said hoarsely. "It won't happen again. Please, proceed with your business."

I swept past him without a second glance, Archie falling into step behind me and Meg stumbling along beside the Aleal, playing her role as the cowed prisoner to the hilt. Entering the spaceport terminal, I couldn't believe our deception had actually worked.

"Noah, that was amazing!" Meg said as we moved further away from security.

"You played your part perfectly," I replied. "You too, Arch."

Instead of waving a tendril, Archie flashed me a quick thumbs-up.

We'd done it. Against all odds, we'd bluffed our way through. Now there was just the small matter of finding our ship and getting off Gothor.

How hard could that be?

CHAPTER 21

Meg, Archie, and I raced through the spaceport terminal, still following Goloran's map. The promise of freedom, of Burnock waiting somewhere out on the tarmac, spurred us on, lending speed to our desperate flight. We had tricked the guards at the river checkpoint that we weren't the offworlders they were looking for, but I had a feeling once they overcame their shock and gave the entire episode more thought, they would realize they'd been had.

We burst through the doors leading to the tarmac, the harsh heat of the Gothori sun slamming into us like a physical wall. Even the clay beneath our feet struggled to resist the heat despite its cooling properties. Squinting against the brightness, I scanned the small sea of ships stretching out before us, a motley collection of vessels from across the galaxy.

"That has to be it over there!" Meg cried, pointing beyond a pair of larger, slightly rusted and dirty shuttles to a sleek, avian-shaped beauty nestled between two bulky freighters. Its hull gleamed a brilliant crimson and orange, the color of blood and fire. It sure looked like a firebird to me.

Burnock, our ticket to freedom.

We had barely taken two steps towards it when alarms began to wail. All around us, spaceport personnel looked up in confusion and growing alarm, some already reaching for weapons or comms.

"They're onto us," I said. "We need to move. Now!"

We broke into a dead sprint, racing across the tarmac towards Burnock. Behind us, I could hear the pounding of heavy boots and the crackle of shouted orders.

Spaceport security was closing in. Fast.

A plasma bolt sizzled past my ear. I jinked left, zig-zagging away from the line of fire. A few more shots followed, aimed lower to disable rather than kill. The bolts spattered off the tarmac at our heels, leaving chips in the clay.

Burnock loomed ahead, tantalizingly close. I fumbled with Goloran's pad, trying hard not to fat-finger the access code while on the run. Success! A menu of remote operations appeared on the screen, printed in Gothori that blurred in and out of English with each step. I managed to find the button for the boarding ramp and tapped it so hard it was as if my life depended on it.

And it probably did.

For a heart-stopping moment, nothing happened. Then, with a hiss of hydraulics, the ramp began to descend, beckoning us into the ship's cool interior.

A glance back revealed a dozen spaceport guards fifty feet back, racing to stop us before we reached the open mouth of starship. Shifting back to its maulvas form, Archie bounded behind me, nipping at my heels. I didn't understand why it was behaving like it was out for my blood until a plasma bolt that would have caught me in a calf burned into the Aleal instead, melting off thousands of individual organisms in the colony with one shot. Seeing

Archie hit made me want to scream in fury, but it barely registered the loss, quickly filling in the damage.

We hit the ramp at a full run, plasma fire pinging off Burnock's armored hull. I slapped the control pad to raise the ramp as soon as we were all aboard, Archie charging up last. The ship's interior was compact but seemed well-equipped, with space for a small crew, but I didn't have time to take in the exact details. Instead, I moved forward to the flight deck and threw myself into the pilot's seat, my hands working the controls as I initiated the startup sequence.

Meg slid into the co-pilot seat, her face pale.

"Keep an eye on our vitals," I told her, watching the status lights flicker from red to green as Burnock's systems came online. The engines thrummed to life, the deck vibrating beneath our feet with barely restrained power.

"Hang on!" I shouted, activating the anti-gravity systems. Inertia tugged me down hard into the seat as Burnock shot straight up as if fired from a slingshot. Barely clearing the larger ships surrounding us, I pushed the throttle open.

Burnock surged forward with breathtaking speed, pinning us back in our seats. We rocketed away from the spaceport. From the ground, I knew we had to be nothing more than a crimson streak across the sky. Plasma bolts zipped past our viewports, nowhere close to making contact as Gothor's coppery expanse quickly fell away beneath us. We knifed towards the stars, our view outside blurring from blue to black.

"Noah, we've got planetary defense fighters, coming up hot!" Meg warned, eyeing the sensor grid while monitoring system status, including shields.

I saw them. The trio of deadly little ships had taken off from the palace's royal spaceport near the back of the palace.

As one, they sent a salvo of missiles after us, their boosters allowing them to outpace even our increasing velocity. Realizing I couldn't outrun them, I wrenched Burnock into a stomach-churning spiral, doing my best to confuse the missiles' guidance systems. The ship responded beautifully, whipping through maneuvers that would have torn a bigger craft apart. The missiles detonated around us, near misses that flared the shields and shook the airframe but didn't cause any serious damage. Before I could celebrate the success, another group of starfighters appeared on the grid, coming up fast from the main spaceport, spewing energy blasts at our flanks. Enemy fire from two directions criss-crossed around us, forming a deadly web that I swept through without incident as I marveled at Burdock's overall precision and agility.

"Noah!" Meg warned, watching the starfighters closing in.

"We can't fight them," I said. "We have to get past them."

Spotting a gap in the defenders' attack vectors, I pushed the throttle to its limit. Burnock found another burst of speed, but the target lock alarm screamed, warning us of one or more missiles locking onto us. I cut the angle of ascent and shifted into a tight dive. Burnock's frame shuddered but held. We screamed into a dive just long enough to keep the starfighters from once again locking onto us, and then we pulled up, regaining our climb.

The Gothori fighters ripped past, forced to make wide turns to come back around on our tail. Too late and a dollar short, we shot past them at too great a velocity for them to match. Quickly leaving them behind, the stars wheeled crazily beyond the canopy, Gothor's rust-red sphere shrinking to a marble behind us.

"Whoo!" Meg cried. "I think we…" Suddenly, she cursed softly, the sensor grid picking up three more contacts directly ahead of us. A trio of Gothori warships the size of cruisers moved in to block our escape.

"If we try to skirt around them, the fighters will catch up."

My eyes narrowed, jaw tensing. "Who said anything about going around?"

"Head on? Noah, that's crazy!"

"There's no other way. Hang on!"

I didn't reduce thrust or change course, keeping my evasive maneuvers relatively light so we wouldn't bleed off too much speed. Ahead of us, the Gothori ships flared with energy on the grid, a signal they were charging their batteries and preparing to fire.

"Push as much power to the forward shields as you can," I said.

"Already did it," Meg replied.

My heart throbbed like a drum, adrenaline coursing through me as I charged the warships, ready for the sudden onslaught and hoping I could dodge enough of it to survive.

"Noah, we have an incoming hail," Meg said.

"Let's see who it is," I replied.

"Probably Resolute, with orders to surrender," Meg answered before opening the channel.

"Commander Vaas, this is Princess Goloran. I order you to stand down and allow Burnock to pass. Immediately!"

A tense pause, then Vaas' voice filled the comms, tight with strain. "Your Highness, I...I don't understand. Your parents have ordered..."

"Burnock is not a threat," Goloran replied. "Kloth and I are on board. We're on a critical mission related to the Wardenship. Do not intervene."

Another pause, heavy with indecision. Then, grudgingly, "As you command, Your Highness. Burnock, you are clear to proceed."

The warship's energy signatures faded, its cannons went offline, and its comms disconnected. I let out an explosive breath, hardly daring to believe our luck.

"Thank you, Princess," I said fervently. "We owe you again."

"Consider us even," she replied. "And Noah...be careful out there."

"We will," I promised before cutting the comms. "Meg, set a course for Ocypha. Let's go meet up with our crew."

"No," Meg replied. "We can't."

"What?" I said, head whipping toward her in confusion.

"We're two weeks behind Head Case," she explained. "By the time we reach Ocypha, they might have already finished the Warden's task and left the planet to come to us. We need to make sure we can pass a message along to them when they arrive."

"You mean stop at a closer system?" I asked.

"Yes." She pulled up Burnock's star map on her display. Entering commands, she quickly highlighted a planet halfway between Gothor and Ocypha. "Amion. Population one million. It's a mining colony."

"Anywhere but here sounds great to me right now," I replied. "Set a course."

"On it," Meg replied.

I reached for the hyperdrive controls, eager to put some distance between us and Gothor the moment the nav computer finished its routing. But before I could initiate the jump, a new contact appeared on sensors. A massive and menacing ship sat directly ahead of us, filling the sky with its armored bulk.

"What the hell?" My blood ran cold as I recognized the color and texture of the hull, so similar to the stealth suit hugging my frame, it made me sick to my stomach. Had Markan wrapped an entire starship in the material? It didn't surprise me that Asher would travel in something like that. I just didn't think it was even possible.

"We're being hailed again," Meg said.

"Maybe the Princess will rescue us a second time," I replied.

"I doubt it," Meg answered, opening the comms.

"Gothori gunship, this is the Nycene Frigate Vendetta," a cold woman's voice said. "Surrender or be fired upon."

Angular lines bristling with weaponry, the sleek frigate was already spiking with energy, preparing to open fire.

Meg paled. "Noah..."

I stared at the approaching ship, its huge bulk looming in our viewports. Fear and anger warring in my gut, my every instinct screamed at me to run before they could bring their guns to bear. It would be the smart move, the safe move.

But I was tired of running. I was tired of being one step behind, always reacting instead of acting. If we were ever going to gain the initiative, we needed to take the fight to our enemies.

I reached to the comms to mute them, turning to Meg. "We're going to give Markan's goons a taste of what this ship can do."

She looked at me like I'd lost my mind. "Noah, that ship outguns us a hundred to one!"

"In a straight fight, sure," I agreed. "But Markan needs us alive, which means he can't use lethal force. And anyway, who said anything about fighting fair?" Unmuting the comms, I added, "Vendetta, you can kiss my stern."

I wrenched the controls hard over, sending Burnock into a dizzying spiral. Vendetta unloaded, energy pulses flashing all around us.

"Disrupter beams," Meg said. "Spiral tech. Forget this, Noah. Those pulses can punch through our shields in nothing flat."

I swept between two of the bursts, the volume of fire giving me pause. Maybe Meg was right. At the same time, Burnock was Ferrari-quick and as agile as a cheetah. We could win this and send a message to Markan that he couldn't just take everything he wanted. That we weren't pushovers he could shove around like chess pieces.

Rather than make for open space, I opened fire. Our guns blazed, peppering Vendetta's shields with searing bursts of energy. The warship's hull shimmered as the impacts dissipated harmlessly across its defenses.

They returned fire, a storm of energy that lit the void with strobing brilliance. I jinked, weaving an erratic pattern as I pushed Burnock to its limits. The gunship shuddered as one of Vendetta's deadly shots found its mark, our shields flaring brightly with the strain.

"Shields at sixty percent," Meg announced to prove her point. We had lost forty percent with one hit.

"What other weapons does this thing have besides energy cannons?" I asked, spinning us into a tight arc and skimming along Vendetta's flank. Up close, the warship was even more imposing, but its batteries also struggled to both keep up with and target us so close in. We zipped past, buying us a few seconds of safety.

Meg brought up our weapons status. "Looks like she's loaded with rockets," she replied. "I don't know Warexian tech anywhere near well enough to know how powerful they are."

"I guess we're going to find out."

I sent a few more energy blasts into the Vendetta's shields near her thrusters before clearing the ship's stern. Its guns swiveled to follow, spewing pulses I struggled to avoid. A second pulse hit us as I angled to come about.

"Shields at twenty percent. Noah, it's not worth it."

"Just one run," I argued. "They won't hit us again."

"They better not, or the shot after that will blast us to microns."

Coming around on Vendetta, I toggled our rockets. The ship's belly opened, the launchers angling down for the rockets to clear us when fired. Resuming my attack with the energy cannons, I continued peppering the frigate's thrusters, even as disruptor pulses came in so hot and heavy it was like dodging raindrops in a storm. I set the rockets' target and waited for the ship's fire control system to signal a lock.

A disrupter pulse grazed Burnock's starboard wing, setting off alarms as the shields failed on the entire port side of the ship. Old me would have doubted my decision, lost confidence, tried to pull off the attack and wound up blasted and captured. Or dead. But I'd sprinkled useless pieces of the old me throughout Warexia, from Cacitrum to Asterock to Marin, and on Markan's giant robot station and the Wardenship.

The new me refused to give up the attack.

The new me knew he could get the job done.

I rolled hard over to avoid a pair of crossing disruptor pulses, dipping and rising to sweep between at least three more. We were almost out of time before I would need to circle back.

"Come on," I growled, eyes narrow, jaw clenched. "Lock on!"

The reticle changed color. My thumb dropped to the secondary trigger. Rockets spewed from their launchers at the same time I cut the throttle, fired the retro rockets, and pulled Burnock away before we joined the missiles colliding with the frigate's stern.

For a breathless moment, nothing happened. Vendetta's shields held, absorbing our attack as multiple rockets detonated against them. But then, with a flash of brilliant light, they overloaded and failed.

The remaining rockets struck home, tearing into the warship's unprotected hull and engine. Explosions bloomed along its flank, gouging craters in its armored hide. Atmosphere and debris spewed from the wounds, glittering in the starlight.

Vendetta lurched, reeling from the devastating strike. Its guns fell silent, its starboard engine flickering. Electricity crackled along its hull, arcing between the ragged edges of the breaches.

"You did it!" Meg whooped. "Their main power is down! And they're circling like a sailing ship with a jammed rudder!"

"Now we can get the hell out of here," I replied, a huge grin splitting my face. I reached for the jump controls, hesitating a few more seconds to watch Vendetta slowly go dark. "Engaging…now!"

The stars compressed around us as the hyperdrive kicked in. Vendetta vanished behind us, a crippled giant left circling helplessly in our wake.

I slumped back in my seat, sudden exhaustion washing over me as my adrenaline ebbed. We had done it. Against all odds, we had evaded capture and even managed to strike a solid blow against our pursuers. I knew the fight was far from over. But for now, we had earned a moment to catch our breath.

I glanced over at Meg, seeing my own weariness and determination mirrored in her eyes. Archie's maulvas padded back onto the flight deck, extending gentle tendrils out to both Meg and me and squeezing our shoulders in celebration.

"So," I said, "that was fun."

Meg snorted, shaking her head. "If that's your idea of fun, remind me never to go on vacation with you."

I chuckled, the sound edged with exhaustion and relief. "Honestly, I think I'm starting to like this stuff."

"Honestly, you sound like Ben."

"Is that a bad thing?" I asked.

"No…and yes. I am eager to see him again, though. And Matt, Leo, and the others."

"Me, too," I agreed. "What do you say we check out our new ride? It's a bit bigger than the hop racer, at least."

"Not by much, but I'll take what I can get."

I closed my eyes, taking another moment to relax. If my father really had been a Warden, I could only hope he agreed with what I was trying to do. If not…?

Too bad. He had taught me to think for myself. And that's exactly what I was going to keep doing.

CHAPTER 22

Despite its compact size, the two weeks in hyperspace on Burnock were a vacation compared to the hours Meg, Archie, and I had spent inside the hop racer's tight confines. The ship had only a single small deck, with four tiny berths tucked into the stern, a cramped head on the port side that made airplane bathrooms seem spacious, and a small cabinet next to an interlock hatch stuffed with food bars and drinks. What Burnock lacked in creature comforts, it made up for in speed, agility, and firepower, and we at least had enough space to stand up and stretch our legs.

"You know, when I dreamed of adventures in space, this isn't quite what I had in mind," Meg said, unwrapping one of the food bars.

The food and drink on the ship had clearly been designed for Gothori physiology and tastes, which meant they tasted awful. After two weeks of forcing down everything that went into my mouth, the thought of eating even one more awful food bar made me want to vomit.

Instead, I watched Meg try to convince herself she was hungry enough to choke down a bar and a bottle of some brackish pink concoction. Its viscosity and smell had made me question more than once whether or not whoever inventoried the ship had mixed up energy drinks with body wash.

"What do you mean?" I replied. "This is a five-star vacation compared to our trip over on Shelby."

"You're just lucky the Gothori are tall as a species," Meg shot back. "I don't think the berths would have been big enough for you to lay flat, otherwise."

I glanced over at my bottom bunk on the starboard side of the stern. "I still have to bend my knees a little," I corrected. "Any Gothori on board would probably have to tuck up into a fetal position. I'm more grateful the head is large enough to contain me. If the Gothori were your size, I'd be in big trouble."

"I think Archie and I would be worse off than you," she said. "Nobody needs parts of you sticking out through an open door while you take care of business."

Meg grinned, still waffling over her desire to eat the food bar. We had nearly reached Amion, and while there was no guarantee we could score a decent meal there, I was willing to take the risk.

"Are you going to eat that, or are you watching to see if things start growing from it?" I asked.

She took a tentative bite, made a face, and spit it out. "I'm hungry, but I think you're right. I can't stomach one more of these crappy things."

"Which only makes you look smarter for redirecting us to Amion instead of Ocypha. I think you literally saved our lives."

We laughed, the sound easing some of the tension that had settled over us from too much time spent in the cramped quarters. It was good to know that even in the midst of all this chaos, we could still find moments of levity.

In other words, we made do. It wasn't like we had much choice.

"Since I decided I'd rather die than eat this, do you want to look at the data Goloran's techs collected again?" Meg asked.

We'd already spent most of the trip huddled over Goloran's pad, poring over the data her team had collected on the Wardenship. The schematics, the sigil breakdowns, every scrap of information we could glean. It hadn't been much, but it was a start.

Meg had proven invaluable in getting me started on trying to decipher the complex web of sigils. Her engineering background and experience with the complex patterns gave her a learned insight into their function and application, which she had done her best to pass on to me. She'd explained how each sigil was simply a guide for the chaos energy used to power it. The shapes forced the energy into specific patterns that created a specific action, obviously with the sigil as the center of that action.

Who or whatever provided the chaos energy also provided the target. So the sigil for pull would, as if by magic, pull an object toward the sigil, while push would push it away. That part was pretty easy to understand. When Ben used chaos energy, he selected what would be pulled or pushed. A weapon, a hand, or as Meg had informed me while I listened slack-jawed, an entire starship.

Of course, Ben was an outlier. He could innately shape chaos energy without sigils, one of only two beings in the universe who could do it, as far as she knew. She refused to tell me anything about the other one except that he was "as evil as evil comes, and makes both Markan and the Warden look like amateur hour."

Over time, I'd come to understand how multiple sigils could be combined to create more complex effects. For example, how push, contain, and light could be added together to essentially create a laser. And that was just the tip of the iceberg. The machinery within the Wardenship, especially the reactor and the batteries, were loaded with interconnected sigils, creating some of the most complex actions she had ever seen.

Together, we started trying to extract the different sigils based on their overall shapes while also guessing at their functions. Contain, enhance, amplify, extend...the list grew longer with each passing day. It was painstaking work, and there was a good chance we were barking up the completely wrong tree, but it gave us a sense of purpose, a direction to focus our energies.

"I don't know," I answered after considering the question. "How much more are we going to learn in two hours?"

"Two hours more than we know right now," she answered, drawing a smile from me.

"I don't know how you always manage to stay so upbeat."

"Are you kidding? I whiplash between elation and despair at least twice a day, more when I'm on Head Case."

"But you love every minute of it," I said confidently.

"I do," she admitted, tossing her food bar in the small disposal unit under the cabinet.

I retrieved Goloran's pad from my berth, taking three steps to meet Meg in the fuselage's open center near the ramp's hydraulic arms. Without seats outside the flight deck, we'd taken to standing most of the time, with me looking over Meg's shoulder while we examined the data. I handed her the pad, looking back over my shoulder to where Archie lay, curled up in his berth.

The Aleal had continued to grow at an astonishing rate.

Despite the damage it had sustained while escaping Gothor, its maulvas form was now closer to that of a small pony than a dog. It had taken to resting in its own space, no longer content to sleep at my feet.

At first, I felt sad at the growing distance between us. Archie had been my constant companion, a comforting presence on or close to my person through all the chaos and danger. Watching it settle into its new sleeping arrangements, I realized this was a natural part of its development. It was maturing, coming into its own. And like any good friend, I needed to give it the space it needed to grow.

"You know, when we get back to Earth, we could make a killing in the tattoo industry with these designs," I joked as I handed her the pad.

She quickly navigated to the technical images, projecting them into the air ahead of us and creating a second projection with our current notes. "Somehow, I don't think random lines and swirls would be a big seller."

"Are you kidding? Call it tribal ink and we're good to go."

She zoomed in on a small section of the Wardenship's reactor we'd yet to fully examine. I could tell right away she was trying to isolate what she thought was a single sigil, so we could re-draw it separate from the interconnected sigils. "It's too bad David isn't here," she commented. "Ben's brother-in-law. He's a whiz with sigils."

"From everything people have said about him, he sounds like a whiz with everything," I replied.

"Not girls."

"He got married, didn't he?"

"Ben's sister has the patience of a saint."

I laughed at that, settling into staring at the sigil, trying to see it without any other overlaps. It wasn't long before my mind began drifting, and I found myself thinking about the schematics of the Warden's cloning apparatus instead of the reactor's sigils. I conjured a vision of the complex array of tubes and tanks in my mind, thoughts churning with more personal unanswered questions. If my father had been a Warden—a clone grown in a similar device—what had he been like in that role? What had driven him to flee, to turn his back on everything he knew?

I wanted to believe it was because he had realized the fundamental wrongness of the Warden's actions. That some innate sense of morality had compelled him to seek a different path. But I would never know for certain. He was gone, and with him, any chance of getting those answers. The thought left a hollow ache in my chest, a longing for a connection that could never be.

"Noah, are you with me?" Meg's voice kicked me out of my head.

"Yeah. Sorry," I replied. "I'm with you."

"You were thinking about your dad again, weren't you?" Her voice was gentle, understanding.

I sighed, tearing my gaze away from the schematics. "Is it that obvious?"

"You get this look on your face," she said. "Like you're trying to solve a puzzle with half the pieces missing."

"That's pretty much how it feels," I admitted. "I have so many questions, and no way to get answers."

Meg laid a comforting hand on my shoulder. "We'll figure it out, Noah. Together. And who knows? Maybe your dad left clues behind, breadcrumbs for you to follow. Maybe on the Wardenship."

"I hope you're right," I said, mustering a smile. I doubted it, considering his voice in my head when I touched the Wardenship's controls had told me I shouldn't be there. But I didn't want her to worry about me. "Thanks, Meg."

We'd only half-transcribed the focused sigil when we had to put the pad down and return to the flight deck. Finally, when it was time to drop out of hyperspace near Amion, I was nearly punch-drunk with excitement over the prospect of getting off Burnock, if only for an hour or two. The mining colony hung in the void ahead, a dull gray sphere pockmarked with craters and scars overlaid by a series of large hexagonal habitats adjacent to external mines. Not the most inviting sight, but at this point, I would take any port in a storm.

"Noah, we're being hailed," Meg reported.

"Put it through," I replied.

"Unidentified starship, this is Amion Orbital Control," an unenthused voice announced. "Please state the name of your ship, the name of your captain, and your business on Amion."

"Orbital control, this is Kat Zuo, captain of the starship Burnock," I replied. "We've come to Amion to stretch our legs. A pitstop on the way to Ochnya."

"Kat Zuo, did you say? On your way to Ochnya?"

"Yes, that's right."

"My system is showing that our messaging service received a transmission I believe is intended for you. It was encrypted by the sender."

I looked at Meg, who nodded. If the message was from Head Case, she would be able to decipher it. If not? It probably wasn't a message we wanted to hear.

"Please transmit the message, control," I replied.

"There's a five hundred quark transfer fee. We can add it to your three hundred quark landing fee."

I sighed. For a tiny mining colony, landing on Amion wasn't cheap. "Fine. Transmit the invoice."

He did. I used Goloran's pad to pay for it. I figured that's why she had given us unrestricted access to an account with a few thousand quark in it.

"Burnock, you're cleared to land in Dome Seven, LZ Twenty-one. The dome will open for you as you approach."

"Thank you, control," I replied.

The comms disconnected. A moment later, the message reached the ship's computer as a string of alien characters.

"You can decrypt that?" I asked, looking over at Meg.

"Yes. It should be the same encryption algorithm Lantz used on Head Case's network. Even the Warden hasn't been able to crack it yet."

"Nice. In that case, open it up. Let's see what Ben has to say for himself."

She smiled, tapping on her controls to enter the decryption keys while I guided Burnock ever closer to Amion. It would feel so good to have solid ground under my feet again.

"The message is ready," Meg announced a couple of minutes later, tapping on her controls to play it.

"Noah, Meg...it's Ben. If you're hearing this, it means Goloran was right about your destination. She didn't say much in case her message was intercepted, but she told us you were headed our way." There was a warmth in his voice, an undercurrent of relief. "We're still tied up with this damned sea monster, but as soon as we're finished here, we'll meet you on Amion. Sit tight, stay safe. We'll see you soon."

The message ended, and I sat back, grateful that Ben and the others were safe. Princess Goloran had rightly guessed where we were most likely to be, and they were coming for us. After weeks of uncertainty, that knowledge was a balm to my weary soul.

I glanced over at Meg, seeing the same mix of emotions playing across her face. Archie had his paws up on her seat back, head cocked as if listening intently.

"Looks like we've got a welcoming committee inbound," I said.

Meg grinned. "Best news I've heard in a long time."

"Think they'll bring us real food? I'd kill for a burger right about now."

"I'd settle for anything that doesn't taste like sealant paste." Meg stretched in her seat. Her grin faded suddenly, and she looked at me with concerned eyes. "Noah...If Goloran guessed where we were headed..."

"There's a chance Markan has, too," I finished. "But only if they know Head Case is on Ocypha. Which they might. But let them come."

I glanced over my shoulder, toward the main compartment where Archie slept. The bigger the Aleal grew, the more dangerous it became. And it wasn't the only dangerous entity on board. Meg had proven herself more than capable. And I...well, I did my best.

"We escaped Markan's base once. We escaped the Wardenship. We escaped Gothor. We can slip them again."

"And if we can't slip them?" Meg asked.

"We'll make them wish we had."

CHAPTER 23

Burnock glided through the void towards Amion's Dome Seven, as fun to fly as ever. With barely any atmosphere, the ride down from orbit went as smoothly as possible, leaving us on approach to the dome's massive shutters. They began to slide open, a yawning maw ready to swallow us whole.

"Here we go," I murmured, guiding the ship through the opening with a deft touch on the stick. Meg sat beside me, eyes wide and mouth agape, unable to hide her eagerness to be off the ship.

We settled in our assigned landing zone with a gentle thump, the dome sealing behind us. We simply sat there for a moment, letting the reality of our arrival sink in.

"Ready?" I asked, glancing over at Meg.

She nodded, unbuckling her harness. "Definitely."

We returned to the main compartment where Archie waited, still asleep in its berth. I considered leaving it behind, but didn't want to risk it waking, finding us gone, and deciding to venture out on its own. I didn't worry about its ability to navigate the planet. Instead, I worried it might decide it needed more fuel for growth. The last thing we needed was Archie eating anyone else's brains.

"Hey, bud," I said, giving his gelatin body a shake that made it shiver like Jell-O. I always enjoyed doing that to the Aleal.

It lifted its maulvas head, looking back at me.

"We're here," I told it. "Amion."

It rose and jumped off its berth, pacing like a caged animal, as eager for more space as Meg and me.

"I'm going to use the stealth suit to disguise myself," I said. "Make us a little less conspicuous. I hope."

"Good idea," Meg agreed.

I scrolled through the scans I'd pulled from Asher's suit. "How about...this one?" I selected the image of a thin, wiry alien of unknown origin, the holomask shimmering as it conformed to my features. In moments, my reflection in the polished bulkhead was that of a stranger, red-skinned and sharp-eyed.

Beside me, Archie rippled and changed, his amorphous body resolving into the now-familiar form of Jaffie in his Mandalorian armor. The sight still sent a chill down my spine, even knowing it was just a disguise. The Aleal cocked its head at me as if sensing my unease.

Meg watched our transformations with a mix of fascination and trepidation. "I'll never get used to that," she muttered.

"That's kind of the point," I replied, my voice distorted by the holomask. "Shall we?"

We descended the ramp into the cavernous interior of Dome Seven. The air was stale and dry, tinged with the acrid scent of industrial lubricants and metal. From the cracked tiled floor to the stained and patched jumpsuits of the workers going about their business, everything seemed to be cast in shades of drab earth tones and lifeless grays. Even the guards stationed between us and the exit had a weary, disinterested air about them as if the very act of existing on this desolate rock had drained the color from their lives.

I couldn't blame them. Life in a mining colony had to be hard, thankless work. These people probably hadn't seen a blue sky or felt the warmth of a natural sun in years, if ever.

We made our way towards the terminal, skirting the edge of the tarmac. I kept my senses on high alert, scanning the faces around us for any sign of recognition or undue interest. Markan had eyes and ears everywhere, and the last thing we needed was to be made before we'd even had a chance to eat.

Reaching the guards, I did my best to project an air of bored nonchalance.

"Hey, there," I said. "We just landed. Any chance of finding some decent grub around here? Preferably something that won't kill a human."

The guard, a burly being with mottled green skin, barely glanced at me. "Next dome over," he grunted, jerking his head towards a nearby tunnel. "Tram'll take you there. 'Bout as far as visitors want to go, unless you work for the company?"

"No, we don't work for the company," I replied.

"'Next dome over then," he repeated.

"Thank you," I said before we walked through the checkpoint without any trouble. Thin doors slid open as we neared, revealing a grimy tram station on the other side. A few miners waited there, faces sweaty, jumpsuits laden with dust. None of them looked in our direction, completely disinterested in our existence.

I loved it.

The automated tram pulled in less than a minute later, squealing to a stop, its battered doors grinding open. One of them stuck halfway, but we managed to squeeze through. We'd barely dropped into our seats by the time the tram jolted into motion, carrying us down the tunnel connecting the domes.

"I can't decide if that guard was apathetic or just hated his job," Meg said quietly as we rode.

I shrugged. "Probably both. Can't imagine there's much to get excited about around here. Just wonder why what he said sounded so much like a warning."

Meg shrugged. "Just something to keep in mind." I nodded.

The tram shuddered to a halt in the next dome. The difference from the hangar was negligible—the same dull color scheme, the same stale air of wear and neglect—with the addition of what I assumed were prostitutes loitering in the shadows. Tucked between shabby storefronts, I spotted a pub that looked slightly more inviting than its neighbors.

"That's probably our best bet," I said, nodding toward the place.

"Looks as good as anywhere else," Meg replied.

Inside, the pub was uncomfortably quiet. A mismatched assortment of patrons—a smattering of workers still in their jumpsuits, a few haggard-looking spacers, and one or two beings that probably weren't entirely on the up-and-up— huddled around the bar and occupied the patched booths. They were either silent or speaking in hushed voices as if they knew Markan or the Warden was listening. The air smelled of stale booze and body odor.

We slid into the booth farthest from the entrance. A bored-looking server, the same species as the guard, sidled to our table. "What'll it be?" she asked, her voice a raspy monotone.

Meg and I glanced at the flickering holographic menu. My nanites refused to translate the Wardenian text, leaving me to navigate by small pictures.

"What is that?" I asked, questioning what appeared to be soup.

"Bartok stew. Chunks of bartok meat in a broth made from fermented nabi roots," the server replied. "House specialty."

Meg blanched. "And that?"

"Ahh, rockworm. A local favorite. Skewered, grilled, and served still wriggling."

I suppressed a shudder, moving down the menu to something that looked like chili. "How about this?" I asked though I wasn't sure I wanted to know.

The server shrugged. "Xandarian slop. Synthesized protein mash blended with sweet orgato and seasonings. Not my favorite, but at least it won't kill ya."

I glanced at Meg. She looked like she'd lost her appetite. I figured if the waitress didn't like the slop and it had something sweet in it, then it was probably our best bet. "Two orders of the slop, then. And water, please."

"What about you, killer?" The server turned to Archie expectantly.

"Oh, he doesn't talk," I said quickly. "Or eat, actually. He's...on a special diet."

Archie, to his credit, simply inclined his head in agreement. The server eyed him for a moment, then shrugged again. "Suit yourself." She tapped our order into a wrist pad and shuffled off.

"I can't believe we're about to eat something called Xandarian slop," Meg muttered, shaking her head. "I mean, I know we said we wanted real food, but this?"

"Hey, it's not sealant paste," I pointed out. "That's a step up, right?"

Meg snorted. "A small step. Maybe."

"The best thing to do is try to enjoy the moment," I added, leaning back in my seat. Archie mimicked the movement beside me.

Meg relaxed into the seat on the other side, releasing a long sigh. "When we got stuck here, I honestly thought we'd find a way out within a couple of days." She paused before leaning forward. "Hey, your eighteenth birthday must be coming up, right?"

I stared at her. "Without a Gregorian calendar, I honestly don't know. I've lost track of the number of days we've been here."

"So it might have passed already?"

"I hope not. I figure I might have at least another few weeks to go." I let out a sigh of my own. "I never expected to spend it on the other side of the universe, or without my parents."

"On the bright side, if you reach eighteen before we get back to Earth, all of your foster care problems go away."

"At least there's that," I agreed with a grin.

The server returned with our orders, dropping two mugs of water and two bowls of orange paste onto the table. Bits of perfectly round, gray balls floated in it. It actually smelled pretty good.

"I have this for you, too," she said, placing a torn scrap of paper on the table next to my bowl.

"What is this?" I asked, at first nervous she was passing me her phone number or something. I might have preferred that to her answer.

"Don't know. Some random duppa paid me fifty quark to pass it on to you."

I craned my neck to look past her. I didn't see anyone suspicious looking back. In fact, nobody paid any attention to us at all. "Where'd the duppa go?"

"Left after he handed me this." She shrugged. "Hope you like the slop." With that, she moved on to her next customer.

"How is it that trouble finds us wherever we go, even when two-thirds of us are in disguise?" Meg groaned.

"Just lucky, I guess," I replied, picking up the paper.

I unfolded it beneath the table, angling it so only I could

read it, if possible. The words were written in a hasty scrawl as if the sender had been in a hurry. More importantly, either the nanites could translate it, or it had been written in English.

"Dome Five. One hour. That's all it says." I looked up at Meg, my brow furrowing. "No signature."

"A trap?" she asked, her voice tight.

"At this point, isn't everything?" I chewed my lip, thinking. "We should check it out though."

"Are you insane?" Meg hissed.

"No. But I am tired of running away. Besides, I don't think traps are really Markan's style. Brute force and assassins, on the other hand…"

"We should just go back to Burnock. We can wait for Ben and the others in orbit, where we can make a quick getaway." She shook her head. "We should never have come down here to begin with."

I picked up my spoon, spilling a gray protein ball and some of the paste into my mouth. "It's actually pretty good," I said once I'd swallowed. "Worth coming down for, after those Gothori food bars. Try it," I urged.

She did, her frown fading. "You're right. It's better than I expected from something called slop."

"Slop to everyone else is good food to humans, I think," I replied. "But we need to eat quickly. We only have an hour to get to Dome Five."

"Noah—" Meg started to complain.

"We have Archie," I cut her off, thrusting a thumb at it. "We'll be fine. Even if it is a trap, we'll squirm out of it like we have before."

She stared at me again, long enough to make me uncomfortable. "What?" I asked.

"You've changed so much since you boarded Head Case. I barely recognize you."

"I am in disguise," I pointed out.

"You know what I mean."

"Well, it's not like I had a choice. The younger version of myself would be dead by now. Do you like the change?"

She nodded. "I do."

"Then you'll come to Dome Five with me?"

She growled but nodded a second time. "Against my better judgment, yes."

I glanced at Archie, who had been sitting silently through our exchange. "You up for a little adventure, bud?"

The Aleal cocked its head, Jaffie's helmeted visage unreadable. But after a moment, it gave a curt nod.

We rapidly downed the slop. The waitress made her way back to us when she noticed the empty bowls. "Are you sure you don't want to lick it?" she asked, seeing how I had scraped at mine.

"Tempting," I answered. "Hey, uh, weird question. But what exactly is in Dome Five?"

She blinked at me, nonplussed. "Ore processing. Or it was, before the dome breach last month. Damn near vented the whole section before they got it sealed up again. It's supposed to go back into rotation next cycle, but it's still empty now. Why?"

I shrugged, feigning casual curiosity. "Just overheard some folks talking about it. Sounded interesting, is all."

She snorted. "Ain't nothing interesting about vacuum exposure. But suit yourself. You want anything else?"

"No, we're done. Thanks," I replied.

She tapped on her wrist pad. "That'll be sixty-four quark."

I used Goloran's pad to send her eighty. She seemed pleased with the tip. "Enjoy your stay on Amion," she said, offering a smile before she turned on her heel and sauntered off.

"Alright then," I said, getting to my feet. "Let's see what Dome Five has to offer."

CHAPTER 24

A growing sense of unease settled over me as we approached the tram station on the opposite side of the dome. Similar to the first station we'd entered, the platform was lightly traveled, but the passengers were all miners, shabbily dressed and mostly dirty. A few disinterested guards leaned against the walls or stood in small groups chatting, their eyes glazed with boredom.

"There," Meg said, spotting the doorways leading to the platforms that connected the domes. "That station connects to Domes Five, Eight, and Twelve. But the line to Five is closed."

"The waitress said the dome was closed for repairs," I reminded her. The doors had been blocked off with bright yellow barrier tape. We needed to get by it unseen by the guards to meet with the note sender.

I glanced at the guards, weighing our options. They didn't seem particularly alert, their postures slack and their gazes unfocused. "We need to get into that tunnel," I murmured to Meg and Archie. "Follow my lead and act casual. If anyone stops us, let me do the talking."

They nodded, falling into step beside me as we

approached the cordoned-off exit. Every footstep sounded unnaturally loud in the cavernous space, but the guards barely spared us a glance, too lost in their malaise to register our intent.

We slipped past the barrier and through the doors without so much as a *hey you, stop*. The platform beyond was dimly lit, but I could make out the shape of the parked tram nearby and the even darker maw of the tunnel leading to Dome Five.

"Looks like we have to hoof it," I said. "I hope it isn't too far to make it within forty-five minutes. We don't want to be late."

"I wouldn't mind being late," Meg replied nervously.

"Come on," I said, leading her and Archie to the edge of the platform. The tram didn't run on tracks. Instead, a flat band of metal in the center appeared to provide power while the vehicle navigated freely above it. I climbed down into its path, turning back to help Meg down. Archie jumped down, landing slightly awkwardly. He didn't seem fully accustomed yet to his upright, two-legged form.

We stood there momentarily, blinking until our eyes adjusted before continuing into the unlit tunnel, the sudden darkness swallowing us whole. I assumed the slight vibrations I felt under my feet were from the distant operation of mining equipment. The stir sent occasional pebbles from the tunnel walls pinging off the track, the dislodged sand enough to make our eyes sting. The only other sound came from the echoing thud of our heartbeats.

"Well," Meg said, her voice hushed. "No turning back now."

"Guess not," I agreed, trying to inject confidence into my words. "Come on. The sooner we get this over with, the better."

We set off down the tunnel, our footsteps echoing off the

rounded walls. Before long, it felt like the air was pressing in on us, thick and heavy.

Time threatened to lose all meaning in that endless, shadowed passage. We walked at least two miles and burned at least thirty minutes—though they felt like hours —before we finally saw a faint glimmer of light ahead of us. We approached cautiously, hugging the walls, every sense straining for any hint of the ambush Meg expected. We both pulled our blasters while Archie shifted back to maulvas form, ready to fight.

But there was nothing. Just an empty tram platform that led out to an empty tram station. Dome Five connected only to Dome Eighteen, not that Amion's numbering system meant anything to me.

We emerged from the station, blinking in the dim, industrial lighting. The dome stretched out before us, a vast, cavernous space filled with hulking machinery and towering stacks of raw ore. The air smelled of metal and stale grease, the lingering scent of operation even though the conveyor belts and processing equipment stood silent and still. High overhead, a crane still reached to the part of the dome that had lost its seal, a new transparent replace-ment obvious among filthy hexagonal panes.

"Clear so far," I said softly. "You and Arch should find somewhere to wait out of sight. If this is an ambush, we don't want to be grouped together."

"Good idea," Meg agreed.

They melted into the shadows while I focused on the task at hand. I reached up, deactivating my disguise and removing the holomask. My red-skinned alien visage fell away. I felt strange, exposed like I'd shed a layer of armor I hadn't realized I'd been relying on.

My footsteps echoed in the stillness as I moved through the industrial machinery into the open center of the area.

"Helloooo," I called out, my voice ringing in the emptiness. "I'm here. Show yourself."

For a long, tense moment, there was nothing. Just the oppressive silence and the pounding of my heart in my ears.

And then, laughter, the sound of it all too familiar.

It started low, with an amused chuckle that seemed to come from everywhere and nowhere at once. Then it built, rising to a crescendo that sent chills racing down my spine.

He stepped out from behind a hulking ore processor dressed in a dirty miner's jumpsuit, *Warden* printed on the name patch on his breast pocket. I wasn't all that surprised by his appearance. After all, who else could it have been?

I'd driven myself crazy, questioning whether or not I should try to contact the Warden about everything I'd learned. Now, he'd wasted all that hand-wringing by deciding for me.

"Noah," he said, spreading his arms wide in mock welcome. "So good of you to accept my invitation. I must say, you've led me on quite the merry chase. Well done."

I fought down the surge of anger and fear that threatened to choke me, forcing my voice to remain steady. "How did you find me? How did you even know to look here?"

The Warden tsked, wagging a finger at me. "Oh Noah, you ought to know better. Did you really think disabling your nanites would be enough to hide from me?" His smile sharpened, becoming a predatory grin. "I'll admit, you surprised me with that little trick. It took me a while to figure out what had happened. But I'm nothing if not resourceful."

He began to pace, circling me slowly, though his eyes remained fixed on me, his foppish grin glued to his face. "You see, while I may not be able to track you directly anymore, I can still follow those around you. Your dear Princess Goloran, for instance. And of course, your little friends back on Head Case. It's simple enough to extrapolate your movements from theirs to put the pieces together."

I felt a flicker of worry in my gut. If he could trace Goloran, he likely knew about our harrowing escape from Gothor. And if he could track Head Case... "Are my friends okay?" I demanded, my hands clenched into fists at my sides.

The Warden waved a dismissive hand. "Oh, don't worry about them. They're still on Ocypha, dealing with that delightful sea monster I sent them after." His eyes narrowed, his smile becoming more sinister. "Though I'm not very pleased with Captain Murdock right now. He lied to me about Markan. He told me the upstart was dead."

"It's only fair, isn't it?" I asked, refusing to be cowed by his fury. "You sent us after a Gilded you knew had access to Sigiltech. You knew he had a sigilship and didn't bother to warn us. We're lucky we made it out of there alive."

"That remains to be seen." His amused smile returned. "I'm willing to forgive Ben's transgression for the entertainment value. And I even appreciate you disconnecting your nanites, since it provided insight into how Markan escaped my purview."

"Glad we could help," I said sarcastically. "Are you here in person, or is this a really good hologram?"

He stopped circling to step toward me, sticking out his arm. "Go ahead. Touch me."

I pinched his skin. It sure felt real. "I didn't see your ship on our way in, but you were already here to pass a note to the waitress."

He laughed again as he backed away, the sound grating against my nerves. "You've seen the inside of my lost Wardenship. You know it has its own hangar, and its own complement of smaller craft. Why would I frighten everyone by bringing my ship to this wretched excuse for a colony? That would have made our meeting much harder to arrange." He pointed at the repaired part of the dome. "I already had to take drastic measures to ensure our privacy."

"How many died during the breach?" I asked.

"Only three," he replied. "A pittance."

I forced myself to breathe, to focus, fighting my disgust and anger. "It's not a pittance to the three miners you killed and their families."

The Warden sighed. "Come on, my boy. I thought your experience might help you come into your own, and see the bigger picture. Instead, you sound just like your father."

I froze at his mention, the chill sweeping throughout my entire body. "So it's true?" I asked, my voice barely above a whisper. "My father was a Warden."

"Yes," he said simply. "He was."

Even though I had already suspected as much, the confirmation still left me feeling like the floor had dropped out from under me, the foundations of my world ripped away. My father, a Warden, an inhuman clone tasked with overseeing a corner of the universe, was too much to wrap my mind around.

The Warden must have seen the shock on my face because he chuckled softly. "It's quite the revelation, isn't it? To know that your father was so much more than human." He resumed his pacing. "Do you know how long I searched for him, Noah? How many centuries passed without a trace, without a whisper of his whereabouts? Two hundred years. Two hundred years of silence, of not knowing what had become of him."

Two hundred years. The number hit me like a physical blow. "But...he didn't look old. He...he aged like a normal human."

"He wanted you to see him age like a normal human," the Warden corrected. "He used his nanites to do it. Did you know that's how I found you? By the nanites he passed to you by having a child with your mother."

"You…you found me? When?"

"Let's back up a little. It's easier to tell you the whole story than answer your questions piecemeal." He reversed course in his pacing circles, moving backward while he spoke. "Your father was a Warden clone, like me, but not like me. An earlier model, for one. Not quite as handsome and charming as I am today. He was also defective. I don't know how it happened, but like you, he had an overdeveloped sense of fairness and justice. He knew what we were supposed to do, but after some time, he began refusing to do it. Threatened with elimination and replacement, he disappeared."

I smiled in response to the first part of the story, relieved to know that even if Dad had been an asshole of a Warden at one point, he hadn't stayed that way. The man I had known, loved, and respected was real.

"And then," the Warden continued, his voice hardening, "Through Levain, I caught wind of a rumor. A whisper that while searching for Sigiltech, the mercenary Jaffie had discovered a Warden hidden away on some backwater planet on the other side of the universe. A planet called Earth. Plans were put in place to retrieve him."

His lip curled in a sneer. "But I was too late. By the time I arrived, your father was already dead. Killed by that miserable little worm"

He paused, fixing me with a piercing stare. "But then, I learned something else. Something incredible. The wayward Warden had a son." His smile returned, sharp and predatory. "You, Noah. The son of a Warden, with all the potential to replace what I had lost."

"What do you mean, replace what you had lost? You're all clones."

"No. We create clones. But there's always a master copy.

A source. One per ship. When your father left his ship, we lost his source. The ship went derelict and disappeared from my sight, leaving a large part of Warexia to evolve without guidance."

I shook my head, trying to process the onslaught of revelations. "The black ship that attacked Head Case. That was you!"

"It was," he admitted. "As I said, I came to Earth to retrieve your father. I discovered him dead, but you, alive. Before I could pick you up, your friend Ben swooped in and grabbed you. I saw him come out of the rift. I knew right away he was from the same place as Markan, and had the same power. At first, I considered confronting him and destroying him outright. But then, a different idea sprouted."

"You attacked Head Case after he picked me up, knowing he would open a rift to escape. Knowing you could force him to Warexia."

"A beautiful plan, wasn't it?"

"You told us you didn't know how we got here. You lied to us."

"Lying comes with the territory, Noah. You'll need to get used to it."

Anger surged through me, hot and bright. "You bastard," I snarled. "You manipulated us. Used us. You trapped my friends here. You put their lives in danger. And for what? What's the damned point?"

The Warden threw back his head and laughed, the sound echoing off the dome's walls. "Oh, Noah. Don't you see? Everything I've done, every move I've made, has been leading to this moment. To you, standing before me, the inheritor of your father's legacy."

I felt sick, my stomach churning with a mix of rage and revulsion. All this time, all these machinations, and for what? To claim me as some sort of prize, a pawn in his endless schemes?

"Why tell me now?" I asked, my voice rough with emotion. "Why not just keep manipulating me from afar, if that's what you wanted?"

The Warden's smile faded, something almost like regret flickering across his face. "Believe it or not, Noah, I had no intention of revealing the truth to you. Not yet, at least. I had hoped to guide you, to shape you, from behind the scenes. To mold you into the tool I needed you to be. The tool your father once was."

He sighed, a sound of frustration and grudging respect. "But then, you just had to go and activate your father's ship. Oh, I felt it, the moment you sat in that command chair. Like a bolt of lightning across the cosmos."

My mind raced, pieces clicking into place. The way the ship had responded to me, the strange visions and sensations. It hadn't just been a fluke or a quirk of fate. It had been a connection, a recognition of the Warden blood flowing through my veins.

"I came immediately, of course," the Warden continued. "To recover the ship and bring it back under my control. But Markan got there first, and snatched it out from under me."

He fixed me with a hard, calculating stare. "Which brings us to the matter at hand, Noah. I have a task for you, a chance to prove your worth and claim your birthright."

I laughed, the sound harsh and bitter in my throat. "You're kidding, right? After everything you've done, you expect me to just fall in line? To be your good little soldier?"

The Warden's face hardened, all pretense of charm and civility falling away. "I expect you to be smart, Noah. To understand the opportunity I'm offering you. You're the son of a Warden! With the right experience, you can become one of us. You know where to find Markan. You'll find the

Wardenship there as well. Recover the ship for me, and you'll have the greatest boon anyone could ask for."

I shook my head fiercely. "No. I won't be a pawn in your games anymore. I don't care about any boons from you, and the last thing I want to do is be a Warden. My father had the right idea getting away from you. I won't help you."

The Warden's expression turned dangerous, his eyes glinting with a cold, cruel light. "Oh, but you will, Noah. You see, I tried to at least give you the illusion of choice when in reality, you have none."

He leaned in close. "Let me make this perfectly clear. You will retrieve the Wardenship for me. You will deliver it into my hands. And if you refuse, if you even think about defying me...let's just say I'll make sure everyone you've ever cared about suffers the consequences. Your little engineer friend, Meg. That overgrown puddle of goo you call a friend. And of course, dear Captain Ben and the rest of your motley crew."

He tilted his head, a mocking parody of sympathy. "It would be such a shame if something were to happen to them, wouldn't it? A tragic accident, perhaps. Or maybe a run-in with some of Markan's more unsavory associates. Or, oh, I have an idea! How horrible would it be if they accidentally got lost in the void? The universe is a dangerous place, after all." He rubbed his hands together in glee as he spoke, almost preferring my refusal so he could find creative ways to convince me to help.

I couldn't breathe, the weight of his threats crushing the air from my lungs. He had me, and he knew it. As much as I hated to admit it, as much as every fiber of my being rebelled against the idea, I couldn't risk the lives of my friends.

"Noah," the Warden said softly, almost gently. "The ship

belongs to us. It's a rightful part of our domain, our legacy. Surely you can understand that."

I met his gaze, my hands clenched so tightly at my sides that my nails bit into my palms. "No, I won't," I ground out. "There is no us. You're a monster, not a savior. My father would have never left otherwise."

The Warden sighed, a sound of deep, profound disappointment. "So be it. If you will not embrace your destiny willingly, then I suppose I'll have to give you a little incentive. You have two months to retrieve the ship. I'll know immediately when you have it. If you fail, well, I think you know what will happen."

His amused grin returned as he backed toward the shadows to leave. He stopped after a few steps, putting up a finger. "You know, there is one thing I have yet to figure out."

"Good," I replied.

"Maybe Meg knows. Meg!" He shouted. "Come on out!"

Meg moved out from her hiding place on one side of the clearing. Archie came into view on the other, teeth bared menacingly.

"What do you want?" Meg asked.

"I had a question for you. Why did you pick up Noah?"

"Wh…what do you mean?"

"On Earth. Why did you pick up Noah?"

Meg glanced at me before shaking her head. "I'm sorry, I don't—"

"Eight billion humans on Earth, and you picked up the only one I wanted," the Warden explained. "Are you going to lie to Noah and tell him it was a coincidence?"

"It wasn't a coincidence," Meg replied. "Our algorithm selected him as—"

"Liar!" the Warden cried before calming with a laugh. "She's lying to you," he told me.

"I am not!" Meg insisted. "I swear."

"Then maybe your captain is lying to both of you," the Warden suggested. "You should ask Ben, the next time you see him."

"Are you done?" I replied, eager for him to leave. "Or should I have Archie kill this copy of you? I wonder what would happen if he absorbed your essence. If you even have one."

"I'm a clone. I probably don't. In any case, I'm leaving. Toodles!" He wiggled his fingers at us, disappearing back behind the machinery.

I turned to Meg and Archie, my mind still reeling from everything I had just learned. "Let's get out of here."

CHAPTER 25

We made our way back to Burnock in silence, each of us lost in our own thoughts. I barely registered the journey, my mind churning with the revelations the Warden had dumped on me.

As we boarded the ship, Meg shot me a concerned glance. I could see the questions in her eyes, the worry etched in her features. But I couldn't bring myself to talk, not yet. I needed time to process, to try and make sense of everything the Warden had confirmed for me and everything he had said that I hadn't already guessed.

I went directly to my berth, climbing up and lying down, exhaling huge breaths and trying to calm my frayed nerves.

"Noah," Meg said from her side of the ship, less than ten feet away. "If you want to talk, I'm here."

"Thanks, Meg," I replied. "I just want to think right now."

I probably shouldn't have been surprised when Archie climbed onto my mattress and settled on my feet, its head resting across my legs. I reached down to pet it, hands brushing through individual gelatin hairs.

I sighed again, closing my eyes. My father's face came into focus behind them, his warm smile, his kind eyes. I tried to reconcile that image with the revelation of his true nature and fit the pieces together in a way that made sense. There was still so much I didn't know, so many things I would never know. What had my father's life been like before he came to Earth? What had he seen, what had he done, in the nearly two centuries before he met my mother?

It was a staggering thought. Two hundred years...a span of time that was almost impossible for me to fathom. What had he experienced in all those long years? What had he learned, what had he endured?

I thought back to the Warden's words, how he had spoken of my father as something defective. A broken tool, a malfunctioning cog in the machine of his grand design.

But at the same time, I couldn't help but feel a flicker of pride. My father had broken free. He had chosen his own path, love, family, and humanity over the cold, ruthless calculus of the Warden's schemes. That took courage, a strength of will I could only hope to emulate.

As I lay there, I couldn't help but pore over old memories of my dad, searching for any clues I'd missed, any signs of his true nature. But he'd hidden it well. There was nothing overt, nothing that screamed "inhuman clone from beyond the stars." What would that even look like, anyway?

But there were tiny details that took on new meaning in light of what I now knew. He'd sometimes get a knowing look in his eye as if he understood something far beyond the mundane world around us. The uncanny knack he had for always knowing just the right thing to say, the perfect piece of advice to offer, even if I often refused to follow it.

And of course, there were the stories. My dad had always been a master storyteller, weaving tales of far-off worlds and incredible adventures. As a kid, I'd always assumed he was just making them up, letting his imagination run wild for my entertainment.

But now, I couldn't help but wonder. How many of those stories had been based on truth? How many were memories carefully edited and repackaged into something a young boy could understand and enjoy?

The thought made my heart ache. All that time, all those years, and he'd never said a word. He'd carried the weight of his past, the burden of his secrets, and never once let it show. And he'd done it all for us, for Mom and me. To keep us safe, to give us a normal life.

Except it hadn't worked out that way, had it? It had taken two centuries for the past to catch up, but it still did. And my father, along with my mother, had paid the ultimate price.

I sucked in a shaky breath, trying to center myself. It was hard. Everything I thought I knew about myself, about my family, had been upended. I was adrift, untethered, struggling to find my way in a universe that suddenly seemed larger and more complicated than I'd ever imagined.

What did it mean to be the son of a Warden? The Warden seemed to think it meant I was special and had some grand destiny to fulfill. But I didn't feel special. I just felt lost. And afraid of what the Warden would do to my friends if I failed. Afraid of what I might have to do, what I might have to become, to protect them. But beneath the fear, the doubt and the confusion, there was something else. A flicker of...what? Hope? Determination?

I remembered that moment on the Wardenship when I'd sat in the command chair. The rush of power, the sense of connection, of rightness. It had been terrifying, overwhelming, but also exhilarating.

Was that my birthright? The legacy my father had left me, knowingly or not?

That was the strangest thing about the Warden coming to me with his ultimatum and tasking me with recovering the Wardenship.

I would have done it anyway. He didn't need to threaten me or my friends over it. All he had to do was sit back and watch. Maybe that would have been too boring for him.

The hours ticked by. At some point, I tried to rest, warm and comforted by Archie's presence on my feet. Maybe it wasn't mankind's idea of a best friend, but it was mine.

As it turned out, my mind was too full, too busy trying to sort through my tangled knot of thoughts and emotions for sleep to find me. The Warden's words kept playing repeatedly, a taunting loop of information.

I found myself thinking about my dad again. With the Warden's revelations, I opened memories like precious boxes, more carefully examining each one for new significance.

That was when I remembered a camping trip we took when I was eight years old. Just the two of us, out in the woods for a long weekend. I'd been so excited, practically vibrating out of my skin at the prospect of an adventure with my hero.

And it had been an adventure. We'd hiked, swam in the lake, and toasted marshmallows over the campfire. Dad had taught me how to fish, pitch a tent, and find the North Star in the night sky.

In retrospect, one moment stood out, sharp and clear. We'd been hiking a trail, and I'd been chattering away, peppering Dad with an endless stream of questions the way kids do.

I'd asked him why the sky was blue, how fish could breathe underwater, and what made the wind blow. And he'd answered each one patiently, thoughtfully, taking the time to explain in a way my young mind could grasp it.

And then, I'd asked a question that made him pause. I couldn't remember now what it was exactly. Something about the universe and the stars. Something big and profound and probably far too weighty for an eight-year-old to even think of asking, much less comprehend.

I remembered the look on his face. The way his eyes had gone distant, his expression turning inward. For a long moment, he hadn't said anything at all.

And when he did speak, his voice was soft, almost reverent. "There's so much out there, Noah," he'd said. "So much wonder, so much mystery. More than we can ever imagine."

At the time, I didn't understand the weight of those words. The depth of feeling, of knowing, behind them. I'd just been happy that my dad was sharing a moment with me, imparting some grown-up wisdom.

But now, looking back, I could see it for what it was. A glimpse behind the curtain, a fleeting peek at the man beneath the façade. At that moment, he wasn't just my dad. He was a Warden, ancient and wise and burdened with secrets I was only now beginning to comprehend.

Oh, Dad…what now? If only he could give me an answer.

The Warden had said I had my father's potential. That I could become like him, given time and training.

Did that mean I had other abilities lying dormant within me? Abilities that I'd never known about and never had reason to tap into until now?

The thought was both thrilling and terrifying. On one hand, any advantage, any edge I could get in the fight ahead was welcome. We were up against forces so far beyond us, powers we could barely comprehend, let alone match. If I did have some latent Warden abilities, they could be the key to turning the tide, to protecting the ones I cared about.

But on the other hand, the idea of being more than human, of being something other, something unknown was scary as hell. The thought that I might be something else, something more was a lot to wrap my head around. If I did have abilities and could tap into the same well of power that my father and the Warden drew from, then what did that make me?

Whatever abilities I might or might not have, whatever secrets lurked in my genes didn't define me. My choices did. My actions, my beliefs, my unwavering determination to do what was right.

I was still Noah, and I was my father's son—not just in blood but in spirit. He had chosen to be more than what he was made to be, to choose love, family and honor.

If I had his abilities, I would use them the same way he did: to protect, defend, and fight for what was good and right and true. I would make him proud and continue to honor his memory by being the best version of myself that I can be, special powers or not.

I was done letting shadows of the past and threats of the future control me. With my friends at my side, my memories of my parents in my heart, and the strength of my convictions as my guide, I would find an honorable way through this mess.

Maybe even a way to Wexaria free from Markan and the Warden.

With that settled, blissful sleep finally came.

I was ready for whatever the universe had in store for me.

CHAPTER 26

Even though I woke rested from my nap, my stomach coiled back up in knots as Meg, Archie, and I made our way around the other starships parked in the dome. Excitement and apprehension built with every step. Coming around the squared corner of a supply vessel, I couldn't hold back my grin at the sight of Head Case resting on the tarmac. It had been weeks since I'd seen any of my friends, and I missed them. At the same time, I knew our path forward wouldn't get any easier from here on out.

The ship's ramp lowered as we approached, revealing a group of familiar, smiling faces.

"Noah!" Ally cried, breaking out from the pack and bounding down the ramp to engulf me in a fierce hug. "You made it!"

I laughed, returning her embrace. "Did you ever doubt me?"

Tyler was next, his grin wide as Ally moved aside so he could grab me in a tight bear hug. "Nah, man. We knew you'd pull through. But damn, it's good to see you in one piece." His eyes flashed to Archie. "Geez, you've grown."

Archie huffed what could only be a laugh before nuzzling Tee's outstretched hand.

"Good to see you too, ya big booger."

I looked past them to see Ben, Matt, and the rest of the crew descending the ramp and greeting Meg. Relief and joy mingled on their faces, especially Leo, who wrapped his arms around his twin and held her close, happy tears spilling down both faces.

"So glad you're back and in one piece," I heard him say. "I worried about you every day."

"I missed you, too," Meg replied.

"Katzuo." I turned away from the group to find Lavona at my side, eyes warm with emotion.

"Lava!" I said, my wide smile stretching a little more as we embraced. "How are you feeling?" I pulled back just far enough to gaze down into her eyes.

"Much better," she replied. "I had a lot of motivation to heal up before we reached Ocypha. I really wanted to help with that monster."

"You're all accounted for instead of in sick bay, so I assume that went okay?"

"It did. Tee punched a hole in its thick hide with his rocket fist, and Ally used the exposed soft spot to kill-shot it while the rest of us kept it distracted."

"Did you get video of it by any chance?"

"Sure did," Tyler said. "I'm totally posting it when we get home."

"No one will believe it's real," Ally said.

"No, but who cares?"

"Noah, welcome back," Ben said, his eyes crinkling with a smile as he approached. The tightness in my gut twisted a little, and I was happy to see him but nervous about what I had to tell him. I'm sure we have a lot to talk about."

"We do," I agreed, the smile disappearing. "Things have gotten...complicated."

"Then let's not waste any time." Ben raised his voice, gesturing back up the ramp. "We can finish the reunion later. I want all hands in the lounge, immediately. Time isn't on our side."

Ben led the rest of us back to the elevator and up to Deck Three. In the meantime, I hugged and shook hands with as many of the others as I could, happy to see them all again.

"Hmmsss," Ixy said upon seeing Archie. "I mightsss not havesss enough ratssss for yousss anymoresss." Her hissing chortle sounded like she was choking on one of those rats.

Archie's attempt to repeat her laugh sounded almost demonic, drawing Matt's attention. He had gotten used to the Aleal over time, but I could tell from his reserved expression that Archie's increasing size and maturity worried him. I couldn't deny my little bud wasn't so little anymore, and it had only become more dangerous as it had grown. But it was still loyal to me and, by extension, to the rest of the crew, including Matt. He had nothing to worry about, though I doubted I could ever convince him.

We made our way to the lounge, everyone finding somewhere to sit or stand in our de facto meeting space. Our group had grown large enough that we'd become a crowd in the small area. I took a moment to look around, drinking in the sight of them all: Ben, Matt, Tyler, Ally, Meg, Leo, Lantz, Lavona, Cade, Karpov, Shaq, Ixy, and, of course, Archie.

My crew, my friends. My family.

As I settled onto the sofa between Lavona and Tee, Ben leaned forward, his gaze intent. "Alright, Noah. We're all ears. Tell us everything from the moment you and Meg left Head Case on Shelby Cobra."

I took a deep breath, organizing my thoughts. There was so much to tell, so much to explain.

Matt interrupted before I could. "I assume my hop racer

is parked somewhere nearby? I didn't spot her on the way down."

While Ben had hailed us the moment Head Case came out of hyperspace, it had been a quick exchange necessitated by our shared concern for Markan's spies.

"Yeah, about that…" I replied hesitantly.

"You lost her, didn't you?" Matt said, face falling.

"No," Meg said. "We know exactly where Shelby is. It just isn't here. Your racer's still on Asterock."

"Assuming Markan hasn't confiscated it and it hasn't been stolen or anything," I added.

Matt groaned, dropping his head into his hands. "This always happens to me."

"I'm sorry about the racer," I said. "We didn't have a choice. We had to leave her, but on the brighter side, Princess Goloran did give us a gunship named Burnock. It's pretty amazing."

"And probably not race legal," Matt lamented, still looking forlorn as he raised his head. "Oh, well."

"Look, maybe we can get Shelby back somehow," Ben pointed out. "But right now let's try to stay focused on the more important issues. We can think about Shelby later."

"Where's Twama, by the way?" I asked. "I didn't see her in the hangar."

"We moved her back to the Captain's Quarters. It was too much effort to keep her locked up anywhere else."

"You aren't worried about her sneaking messages to Markan?"

"I took care of it," Lantz said.

It was all the explanation I needed. "Goloran's very eager to have her back."

"I'm sure she is," Matt said.

"Noah, go ahead," Ben prodded. "The sooner we get moving again, the better."

"Right," I said, out of excuses to stall.

Slowly, haltingly, I began to recount the tale. I told them about my father's true identity, about his escape from Warexia and his life on Earth. I told them about the Warden's ultimatum, his demand that I recover the missing Wardenship from Markan or else.

As I spoke, I watched their faces cycle through a range of emotions. Shock, disbelief, anger, and finally, a steely resolve.

"So let me get this straight," Tyler said when I'd finished. "Your dad was a Warden, and now the current Warden wants you to get his ship back or he'll take us out like garbage?"

"That's the threat," I replied. "I mean, I would have suggested going after the Wardenship anyway, but—."

"But we can use the disabler to get him off our backs, right?"

"Directly off our backs, sure," I agreed, "but he found me here pretty easily without a direct connection to the nanites. He still has plenty of resources at his disposal. We have to play it smart, or we'll all pay the price."

"I can't believe the black ship belonged to the Warden," Ally mused, her brow furrowed. "But if he got to Earth…"

"Then there's no question that he knows how to do it," Matt finished, his expression thoughtful. "And if Markan was involved with Levain, odds are Sigiltech is the key. There has to be a way to use that to our advantage to get around the Warden's blockade."

"I have an idea!" Tyler announced, his eyes alight with sudden inspiration. "What if, instead of trying to get the Wardenship back from Markan, we help Markan with the Wardenship instead? We could make a deal, and he can help us deal with the Warden."

"Absolutely not," Lavona cut in, her voice sharp. "Markan is a bigger monster than the Warden."

"Is he, though?" Tyler questioned. "Are you sure about that?"

"He's responsible for the war on my home world. The deaths of millions of Vicons. And that's only *my* planet."

"The Warden's wiped out planets too," Ally said. "Remember the Oron?"

"I agree," I added. "Markan's too dangerous, too unpredictable."

"And the Warden isn't?" Tyler argued.

"Better the devil you know than the one you don't," Matt said. "Not to mention, we know how to fight a Gilded, even a powerful one like Markan. We have no idea how to defeat the Warden. We already know killing one doesn't work."

"From what I understand, we need Sigiltech to counter Markan's Sigiltech," Lantz said. "Or more accurately, we need chaos energy."

"Which we don't have nearly enough of," Ben agreed.

"But Markan does," Meg said, excitement kindling in her gaze. "And so does the Warden." She dug Goloran's pad out of her pocket. "We have three dimensional scans and imagery of the Wardenship's chaos energy reactor and battery setup. Noah and I spent hours breaking down the sigils, trying to figure out how it all works. If we can reverse-engineer it, build even a simple, terribly inefficient version…"

"Then I can combine it with the sigibellum to even the odds," Ben finished. "Well, not exactly even. A sigilship is more suited for battle than Head Case."

"Maybe, but even a Gilded isn't equal to you," Matt said. "That should help balance the equation."

"It might. But a battle royale between two experienced Sigiltech users isn't a given win for either side. And believe me, nobody wins. At least not without a cost."

Ben's tone sent a chill down my spine. I hated everything about this situation, but what choice did we have? We couldn't run away. There was nowhere to hide. Not from Markan. Not from the Warden.

"It's our best option right now," Karpov said. "And I've seen your glowy hands at work. I think you can win."

"I appreciate the vote of confidence," Ben replied. "Meg, how soon can you start working on reverse-engineering the system?"

"Right away," she replied, already rising from her seat. "But I'll need your feedback, too. You're the expert when it comes to sigils."

"I'll do what I can," Ben agreed. "Take it as far as you can right now, and let me know when you're stuck."

"Sounds like a plan. Lantz, Leo, Karpov—feel like unraveling magic?"

The three other engineers offered affirmation, also getting to their feet. "Lead the way, boss lady," Lantz said with a mock salute.

As they filed out, Ben turned to the rest of us. "In the meantime, we need to get moving. Markan will be hunting for us, and I don't want to be here when he comes knocking."

"About that," I interjected. "The gunship I mentioned. Burnock. I don't want to leave it behind. It's fast, well-armed, and frankly, I've grown kind of attached to it."

Ben's eyes crinkled with amusement. "I had a feeling you'd say that. We should take Burnock with us. We can tether it to Head Case once we reach orbit. It should be a nice addition to our arsenal." He glanced at Matt. "An no offense, it's a huge offensive upgrade compared to Shelby."

"I can't really argue that, can I?" Matt asked.

"I can fly Burnock to orbit for retrieval once we're done here," I said. "I need to talk to you about something in private, Ben."

Ben's eyes turned my way. I thought I saw a flash of

guilt ripple across his face when our eyes met. I knew the sharpness of my look had to have spoken volumes. "Sure, Noah." He turned to the others. "The rest of you are dismissed."

They didn't need to be told twice. I watched them go, my gaze lingering on Tee, Ally, and Lavona as they filed out of the lounge toward their respective quarters to offer us privacy. Archie remained behind, resting on its haunches beside me.

"I meant you, too, Archie," Ben said, his attention shifting to the Aleal.

"It's okay if Archie stays," I told him.

He glanced back at me. "You aren't going to sic him on me, are you?"

"That depends." I tried to make light of the tension and roiling anxiety in my gut, but I knew I didn't quite accomplish it.

"Then I'll have to be careful what I say. What's on your mind?"

CHAPTER 27

I paced the lounge, trying to find the right words. There was no easy way to say it, no gentle phrasing that would soften the accusation. So, I just came out with it.

"When I spoke to the Warden, he said something very enlightening. He implied it wasn't a coincidence that you picked me up when you did."

Ben stilled, his expression carefully neutral. "What are you trying to say?"

I stopped pacing, turning to face him head-on. "I'm saying, I need the truth, Ben. Did you really choose me because of an algorithm? Or was there something more to it? Did you know about Jaffie, about what happened to my parents? About who and what I am? Is that why you came for me, why you brought me on board?"

For a long moment, Ben didn't answer. He just stared at me, a wealth of emotions playing across his face. Grief, guilt, regret...and beneath it all, a bone-deep weariness.

Finally, he sighed, his shoulders slumping. "Yes," he said quietly. "I knew."

The admission hit me like a punch to the gut, stealing

the breath from my lungs. "Just like Markan and the Warden…you wanted to use me." I'd suspected it, but to actually hear him say it—

"No…I'm not like them. Everything I did was to help you, not hurt you"

"How?" I managed, my voice tight with barely leashed anger. "How did you know about my father? About me?" Beside me, Archie rose to its feet, muscles tensing in anticipation.

Ben ran a hand through his hair, eyes meeting mine and locking on. "Please believe me when I say that I never intended for any of this to happen."

"I want to believe that," I replied. "Convince me."

Ben nodded, exhaling sharply before speaking. "Even Head Case's old comm system was highly advanced compared to Earth tech," he said. "Maybe you can imagine my surprise when we exited the rift from the Spiral near Earth and Levi immediately picked up an unexpected transmission passing in the clear over frequencies humans on Earth don't use."

"Jaffie?" I asked.

Ben nodded. "It had to be. I didn't know who he was or where he was from. Levi captured his transmissions, which I assumed were intended for a ship hiding beyond Earth's ability to see it. When we encountered the Warden's black ship, I thought it was Jaffie's ride. I realize now his ship was probably on the other side of the planet, making it impossible for us to see it too. I learned about the Warden's existence the same time you did."

My hands clenched into fists at my sides, my nails biting into my palms. "And you didn't think to tell me this? To warn me, warn my parents?"

"I didn't know who Jaffie was or what he was after. This was before the Warden pilled us so we couldn't speak or understand his language. I had no idea what he was about, but If there's one thing I know, it's when an alien comes to Earth, they're generally up to no good. So, we triangulated his position and tracked him. We now know his first target was the *reflect*-etched Sigiltech ring he gave Zariv. He might have used it as a cover to satisfy Zariv while he went after your father for Levain and Markan. I don't know, and it's way too late to ask him, unless Archie can speak now."

We both looked at Archie. It shook its head.

"He can shift into Jaffie's armored form," I said. "We haven't gotten further than that. So you knew someone was being hunted, but you didn't know who? If you were monitoring Jaffie's position, why didn't you tail him on the ground?"

"I did," Ben replied. He lowered his head, apparently ashamed. "I..." He breathed in, head snapping up to look me in the eye once more. "I was there, Noah. At the intersection when Jaffie rammed his SUV into your car. I...I saw him run the light. I tried to stop him. I tried to *pull* the car, to slow it down with Sigiltech. And maybe I did, just not enough." Moisture pooled at the corners of his eyes, and a tear slipped free, his sincerity overwhelming me with emotion, wetting my cheeks. "I'm sorry."

"Or maybe just enough to save my life," I replied.

"I wanted to save all your lives, and find out what he wanted with you. I tried to chase him, but he vanished into thin air. Knowing what I know now, he might have had a stealth suit. After that...I didn't understand your father's significance, or why Jaffie was after him. But I knew you had survived, and I was worried you might still be a target, that you were still in danger."

"So why didn't you come and get me right away?" I asked, wiping my eyes with my sleeve. Recalling the events of that day was reopening wounds not properly healed.

"Like I told you when we met at the farm, I can't exactly

go throwing chaos energy around like it's no big deal. I have other people to think about, too."

"So you what, decided to manipulate Tyler into bringing me to VR Awesome so you could enlist me on a star tour? Without telling me the truth and putting Tyler and Ally's lives at risk?"

Shame flickered across Ben's face. "Mistakes were definitely made, and I'm sorry for every single one of them. I underestimated the situation, underestimated the forces at play. I thought I could keep you safe, that I could get answers without putting you and your friends in harm's way. I let Tyler and Ally come along because I honestly believed you'd all be safer with me than left behind. But I was wrong. And I'm very sorry for that."

I stared at him, my anger warring with the pain in my chest. On some level, I understood. I truly believed Ben was a good guy at heart. He had been trying to protect me, to do what he thought was right. But the lies, the secrets felt like a betrayal, a knife twisting in my gut.

"You should have told me," I said at last, my voice rough with emotion. "I deserved to know the truth from the beginning."

"You're right. I should have, but how could I explain that a being from another part of the universe had hunted down your father, and that I had no idea why? Or even where he had come from? I needed answers, and I never had a chance to get any of them. Please believe me when I say I was only trying to do what I thought was best. And please don't blame Matt or the others. They follow my lead, and wouldn't say anything to you without my approval."

I closed my eyes, taking a shuddering breath. The hurt was still there, raw and aching. But beneath Ben's desire to help me, it wasn't that he'd lied to me in the beginning that bothered me, it was the fact that he'd continued to lie to my face while I'd come to respect him more than any man I'd ever known, except my father.

And that's when it hit me.

My father had lied to me and probably my mother, too, undoubtedly for the same reasons Ben and his entire crew had chosen to continue lying to me. To protect me, Tee and Ally.

Suddenly, I could feel the first stirrings of understanding. Of forgiveness. Ben wasn't perfect. He'd made mistakes, but his heart had been in the right place.

And right now, with everything we were facing, we needed each other.

"I understand why you did it," I said softly, finally dropping my hands and looking up at him. "And I forgive you. How could I not, when your effort probably saved my life. But no more secrets, Ben. No more lies. From here on out, we face everything together, as a team. Okay?"

Relief washed over his face, followed by a fierce nod. "Deal," he agreed. "No more secrets. I promise."

"Me, too," I agreed. "I should go back to Burnock. I'll meet you in orbit." I turned to leave, but Ben's voice stopped me before I could take a single step.

"Noah...for what it's worth, I'm proud of you. I'm sure your parents would be, too. You're facing all of this with so much strength, so much courage. Never doubt that."

Tears pricked at the corners of my eyes, a fresh swell of emotion choking my throat. I nodded. Not trusting myself to speak, I headed for the elevator, Archie at my side.

My mind raced, trying to process everything that had happened and had been said.

It was a lot to deal with, but I couldn't afford to dwell on it, couldn't let myself get lost in the swirling maelstrom of grief, anger and confusion. We had a job to do. A mission, a purpose. To stop Markan, to free ourselves from the Warden's grasp.

And to find a way back home.

As I neared the elevator, a new thought crept into my mind. A way for us to potentially hedge our bets and give the others better odds of escaping this craziness and getting home.

What was the point of being the son of a Warden if I couldn't use it to help my friends?

CHAPTER 28

I settled into Burnock's pilot seat, my heart heavy with the weight of my decision. Archie remained nearby in maulvas form, a silent but steady presence. I could feel its eyes on me, assessing and questioning, ready to accept whatever I intended to do.

I took a deep breath, my hands hovering over the controls. This was it. The moment of truth. I'd decided, but that didn't make it any easier.

I activated the comms. "Amion Control, this is Burnock, requesting departure."

"Burnock, this is Amion Control. Departure granted. The shutters will open in two minutes. You're the third ship in line."

"Copy that, control," I replied, cutting the connection. Archie stretched a tendril forward, resting it on my shoulder. It could sense my unease, my anxiety, and my determination. "Thanks for being here, bud."

I sighed more than once while waiting, casting my eyes upward when I heard the loud clang of the shutter at the top of the dome release. Immediately, one of the supply vessels nearby lifted from the tarmac, antigravity emitters carrying it almost straight up toward the opening. It had nearly reached the shutters when Head Case jumped from the surface, rising steadily behind the bulkier craft.

"Here we go," I said, eliciting a tighter squeeze on my shoulder from Archie's tendril. With a heavy heart, I guided Burnock out of Dome Seven, following in Head Case's wake. We rose through Amion's thin atmosphere, the rusty landscape falling away beneath us as we ascended into the star-strewn darkness.

A flashing light on the console signaled an incoming hail from Head Case. I stared at the blinking LED, deciding if I should answer. Finally, I opened the channel. I couldn't bring myself to leave in silence.

"Noah, is everything okay?" Matt asked over the comms.

"Yeah," I replied, though I couldn't convince myself. "I just had a little trouble finding the right controls to answer. Meg handled the comms on the way here."

"Uh-huh," Matt replied suspiciously. "Well, we're ready for you to dock. Bring her in nice and easy."

I hesitated, my fingers tightening on the controls. But I didn't steer Burnock toward Head Case or make any moves to synchronize with them.

"Noah?" Matt prompted. "Are you sure everything is okay over there?" Even if he had chosen to believe my first excuse, he wouldn't fall for another.

I closed my eyes, steeling myself for what I had to say next. "Matt...I'm not coming with you."

Silence. Then, "What do you mean, you're not coming with us?"

I could hear the confusion, the dawning realization in his voice. It cut me to the core, but I had to stay strong.

"I'm going back to the Wardenship," I said, my voice barely above a whisper. "I'm going to make a deal with Markan."

"What?" The shock in Matt's tone was palpable, even over the comms. "Noah, you can't be serious. After everything he's done, everything he's capable of, you—"

"I know," I cut him off, my throat tight. "Believe me, I know. But this...this is our best chance. Our only chance, maybe, to get everyone home safe."

"Noah." Ben's voice broke in, steady but stern. "Think about what you're doing. We can find another way. Together."

I shook my head, even though he couldn't see me. "No, Ben. We can't. We're stuck between a rock and a hard place. What if you can't reverse-engineer the chaos energy siphon? That's the only way we can beat Markan. But if you use the disabler to cut off the Warden, he can't hurt you, at least not right away. And if I can convince Markan to tell me how to get you back to Earth in exchange for my help with the ship, then at least you'll be safe."

"But you'll still be stuck here," Ben grated, anger and regret heavy in his voice.

"I know. But maybe I'm supposed to be stuck here. I don't have anything back on Earth without my parents. Maybe this is home for me now."

"I don't think that's what you want."

"It doesn't matter what I want for myself. It matters what I want for Tee and Ally, and you and Matt. I'm the son of a Warden." I swallowed hard. "This is my responsibility. My burden to bear."

"Noah, please," Ally's voice now, tearful, pleading. "You don't need to do this. We have some of the smartest engineers in the galaxy on board. They'll figure out the siphon. We'll deal with Markan together."

My heart clenched, a physical pain in my chest. But I couldn't waver. Not now.

"And then what, Red? The Warden won't ever let us leave. I think you know that by now. And he definitely won't ever let me leave. He told me only original Wardens can use the Wardenships or make clones. They don't do copies of copies. Dad would have been irreplaceable, except for me. I'm doing this for you. For all of you. So you can have a chance at a normal life again. A chance to go home."

"But what about you?" Tyler, his usual bravado stripped away, leaving only raw concern. "What happens to you?"

"I'll be fine. I have Archie. And I have my father's legacy. Markan has no reason to keep me in Warexia. In fact, it's better for him if I leave—"

"Or if you're dead," Ally interrupted.

"I don't think he'll renege on a deal."

"A criminal mastermind with scruples. A novel thought," Tee groused.

"It's a chance I have to take," I insisted. "I won't change my mind, and there's nothing you can do to stop me. I only answered the comms so I could say goodbye. So you would know what I was going to do and could adjust your strategy accordingly."

A long pause. Then, finally, Ben spoke again. "Noah... are you sure about this?"

"I am," I said, and I meant it. "Ben, I do need you to do something for me, though."

"What is it?"

"Tell Lavona..." My voice caught, emotion threatening to overwhelm me. "Tell her I'm sorry. I know this will hurt her, but please try to make her understand why I'm doing this."

"I will," Ben promised. "But Noah, I'm not sure I fully understand it myself."

I laughed weakly. "That makes two of us. I have to trust my instincts on this one. It's my fault you got trapped here. And it's my responsibility to get you home. Ally, Tee, if this is goodbye…" Tears blurred my vision, and I blinked them away, taking a shuddering breath. "Thank you for being there for me, when I needed someone more than I ever had before. Thank you for being my friends, and for joining me on this crazy ride. I'm sorry for everything that's happened."

"Don't be," Tyler replied. "I, for one, am having a blast. And I got a rocket fist out of the deal, which is freaking awesome."

"We're going to miss you, Noah," Ally said. "Be safe, and come back to us."

"I'll do my best," I answered, choking back emotion. "Goodbye."

I disconnected the comms before I could lose my nerve, peeling Burnock away and entering the coordinates for the Wardenship into the nav computer. Head Case didn't change course to follow, and Ben didn't hail me again, either. He respected my decision, and I respected him for that.

Sensing my emotions, Archie whined softly, pressing its head against my leg in a gesture of comfort. I reached down, burying my fingers in its thick fur, drawing strength from its solid presence.

The nav computer returned the course and ETA. Five weeks. That's how long it would take us to reach the Wardenship. Five weeks in the black, with only Archie and my own thoughts for company.

It was a daunting prospect. But it was nothing compared to what waited on the other side. I had to do it. For my friends, for the family I'd found among the stars. They were counting on me.

Activating the hyperdrive, I leaned back in my seat, closing my eyes. In the ensuing stillness, a sudden realization hit me. My birthday. Somewhere in the vast emptiness of space, in the long weeks ahead, I was pretty sure I would reach eighteen.

It was a milestone I'd always imagined celebrating with

my parents and friends. Candles on a cake, off-key singing, laughter and love.

Instead, I would mark the occasion hurtling through the cosmos on a desperate mission. No cake, no candles. Just the soft hum of Burnock's engines, the weight of my own choices, and Archie repeatedly beating me at every game we played.

But that was okay. It was a small price to pay in the grand scheme of things. I would gladly give up a thousand birthdays, a million small joys if it meant giving my friends a chance to resume their lives back where they belonged. On Earth. Because that's what you did when you loved someone. You put their needs above your own. You made the hard choices and walked the difficult paths.

Just like my father had all those years ago.

I understood him now in a way I never had before. Understood the courage it must have taken to leave behind everything he knew for the sake of what was right. To go against his nature to be a better man.

I could only hope to live up to his example. To be the man he had believed I could be, even if he weren't here to see it. "I'll make you proud, Dad," I whispered into the stillness. "You and Mom both. I promise."

Archie looked up at me with its dark maulvas eyes, sighing and pressing harder against my leg in a show of support. Together, we sailed through the star-strewn abyss, chasing an uncertain and possibly deadly future.

But I wasn't afraid.

Not anymore.

CHAPTER 29

The weeks crawled by like a tedious slog broken by eating, sleeping, the occasional game of Aktak with Archie, which I always lost, and working out as best I could in the cramped space of the small gunship. But even those distractions could only hold my attention for so long. Most of the time, I found myself staring into the emptiness of hyperspace, my thoughts chasing themselves in circles.

I was pretty sure my birthday had come and gone somewhere along the way, enough so that I'd marked the occasion by digging out the best-tasting of the Gothori ration bars, which still managed to be barely palatable. As I choked it down, I tried to summon some sense of accomplishment, some flicker of joy at reaching the milestone, but all I felt was a hollow ache in my chest, a longing to be back on Head Case, or even back in VR Awesome with Tyler and Ally. When I'd started this adventure, I could never have imagined I would want to undo the whole thing. That I would wish it never happened. But I did.

There was one silver lining. Now that I was eighteen, I wouldn't have to deal with Child Protective Services whenever I made it back to Earth.

If I ever made it back to Earth.

The thought sobered me, as it always did. There were no guarantees in this mad quest of mine. No certainties beyond the fact that there were so many ways for things to go wrong. But what choice did I have?

Despite my trepidation, I felt immediately relieved when Burnock finally dropped out of hyperspace near Levain's station. Anything was better than the endless waiting, the ceaseless anticipation. At least we'd finally arrived.

My relief didn't last. Alert tones began sounding before Burnock's sensors could finish rendering space around me, warning me of incoming fire.

"Archie, hold onto something!" I shouted, my eyes narrowing to limit the glare from incoming energy blasts fired by warships I could barely see on the sensors.

I cursed, throwing the ship into evasive maneuvers just as Archie launched tendrils to grab onto the co-pilot's seat. Most of the energy blasts flashed past, but a couple scored hits on the ship's previously battered shields, setting off more dire alerts from the ship's computer.

I tried to continue evading the heavy barrage while trying to switch up the comms channel to a frequency I knew the syndicate used. But I couldn't prevent another blast from hitting the shields. The emitters on the port side sizzled out as I finally got the comms tuned. "Hold your fire!" I shouted. "This is Katzuo. I know Markan is looking for me. I've come to bargain!"

For a heart-stopping moment, the only response was the continuous sizzle of energy bolts flashing past my viewports. But then, miraculously, the barrage slackened and then stopped.

A familiar voice crackled over the comms. "Katzuo!" Janelle's tone was a mix of surprise and amusement. "You're the last person in Warexia I would have expected to show up here."

"I could say the same about you," I replied. "This is a big step up from casino security."

"Yes, well, at least in part, I have you to thank for it. You've created a few open positions in the syndicate, and I was fortunate enough to be in the right place, at the right time, with the right willingness to do what needed to be done to claim my place."

I could only imagine what that meant to someone like her. She hadn't hesitated to kill Hzzt for getting too close to the syndicate.

"I need to speak to Markan," I said.

Janelle scoffed. "Not in the mood for small talk, then? Markan isn't here."

"I'm sure you have a way to contact him. I know he'll want to talk to me."

A long pause followed while Janelle tried to decide how best to proceed. In the meantime, my gaze shifted to the sensor grid, which had finished populating during our initial exchange. A half-dozen warships disguised as cargo haulers were arranged around the station. I immediately recognized Deepling, approaching from the far side of the outpost.

"Fine," she bit out at last. "Deepling's on an intercept course. Land in the hangar bay when you reach the ship. I'll meet you there to coordinate a meeting. But I warn you, Katzuo. If you're planning anything stupid, you won't live to regret it."

I swallowed hard, my mouth suddenly dry. This was it. No turning back now. "Understood," I replied, proud of how steady my voice sounded. "Katzuo out."

Breaking off, I watched Deepling drawing ever closer. When it neared, a rectangle of light appeared in the side of its hull—the hangar bay doors opening to allow me entry. I flipped the gunship over to quickly reduce velocity, drifting back behind the warship before regaining forward momentum and angling cleanly into the hangar. Only two other small shuttles waited inside, giving me plenty of room to land.

"This is it, Arch," I said when our skids hit the deck. I shut down the engines and unstrapped myself from my seat. "Don't attack without provocation, okay?"

Archie nodded its maulvas head in agreement before changing shape, stretching and growing into Jaffie's form. The Aleal had continued growing over the last five weeks and now possessed enough organisms to create an uncanny copy of Levain's bodyguard. It looked and felt so real it had given me nightmares the first time it had taken on the nearly finished form, though it still couldn't or had chosen not to speak.

Janelle was waiting when I descended Burnock's ramp to the deck. Her rigid posture and unreadable expression failed to hide a moment of surprised confusion when she laid eyes on the Aleal walking beside me.

"I thought you were coming alone," she said.

"When did I say that?" I replied.

"Do you have a name?" she asked, focusing on Archie.

It stared at her in silence.

"His name is Jaffie," I said. The name tasted like acid on my tongue, but I wanted to know if Janelle recognized it. "He doesn't talk."

"A mute? Is that why you wear the helmet?" Archie remained still. Janelle quickly lost interest, turning her attention to me. "I could have my people subdue you and take you prisoner. No deal required. What do you think of that, Katzuo?"

"I think it would be a huge mistake on your part," I replied.

"I heard you trained with Miss Asher, and also killed her, so that's probably true. Lucky for me, the syndicate is a criminal enterprise. That means it's a business, and businesses who don't treat customers well tend to fail."

I wasn't about to correct her misinformation that I had been the one to kill Asher. It worked in my favor for her to think I was much tougher than I felt. Or looked.

"In any case," she continued. "I've arranged for the meeting you requested, though I can't guarantee the boss will attend himself."

"I need to speak to Markan himself," I pressed. "Not some middle-management ass-kisser."

By the sharpness of Janelle's laughter, I figured I'd called it pretty true. "Any deal you make will be honored, no matter who you make it with."

I nodded and motioned to the hangar bay's exit. "Lead on."

She brought us to a conference room near the bridge, the door whispering shut behind us. With a few taps on the control panel, she opened a comms channel and leaned back in her seat.

Then we waited.

And waited.

And waited.

"I thought you said you arranged the meeting," I said after twenty minutes had passed, and we still sat there in silence.

"I put a message out to my superior," Janelle replied. "That's the limit of my ability to control the situation. They will answer. It's just a matter of time."

"Maybe you should have someone bring pillows so we can take a nap."

Janelle smiled. "You've gained an edge since I nabbed you at the casino. I suppose you've realized you're a terrible thief."

"But a pretty good assassin," I added, meeting her gaze. "And the son of a Warden."

Janelle's face blanched so quickly I realized she had no idea why Markan wanted me. "The...what?" She swallowed hard, suddenly nervous. "So that's why you're here."

"To make a deal. I can give Markan access to the Wardenship."

She smiled as it dawned on her how happy Markan would be with her over my arrival, even though she had nothing to do with it. She leaned forward, tapping on the comms again.

"Upper command, this is Janelle," she said crisply. "I need a direct line to Markan, now. Code Blue."

Finally, someone picked up on the other end. "Code Blue?" By the voice, I think it was the same big alien in the pinstripes that Janelle had contacted from the casino. But he didn't activate his camera. "This had better be good, Janelle."

"It is, Rolo. I promise."

The other speaker grunted and the comms went dead.

"Does this mean we continue to wait?" I asked.

Before she could answer, the viewscreen at the head of the conference room flashed on.

And there he was—Markan himself—standing in what appeared to be the interior of the giant robot's head, which he had destroyed three months earlier. While there wasn't as much clutter behind him now as when we'd been there in person, he'd obviously reconstructed the space and resumed his research.

His eyes widened fractionally as he caught sight of me. "And there he is. I hope we're meeting under better circumstances this time, Kat Zuo."

I squared my shoulders, meeting his gaze head-on. "My name is actually Noah. You already know I can access the Wardenship. I'm here to bargain."

Markan stilled, his expression sharpening. "I see. You've led my people on a wild chase the last few months. Killed one of my finest assets, and disabled one of my frigates in a Gothori gunship. It irks me that I didn't realize who and what you were when you visited me here. I would have done more to prevent your departure."

"You should be thankful you failed, or you would have pulverized me and lost your only means of entering the Wardenship without damaging it."

"I suppose that's true. Well, I take it you and the Warden aren't seeing eye to eye? Not surprising, all things considered."

"The Warden gave me a task. To recover the Wardenship...and to kill you."

Markan threw his head back and laughed. "Of course he did. When you've followed his antics as long as I have, you realize how predictable he truly is. And yet, here you are, offering me the prize instead. I have no love for that arrogant wannabe god, but surely you know how risky crossing him is."

"I do," I replied. "I put your nanite disabler to good use. He can't hurt me."

"Not directly. But he has other ways. Other targets."

I met his gaze unflinchingly. "I know. That's why I want your help getting my friends safely back to Earth. From what I've learned, I'm convinced you know how to get there, despite what you said about the rifts. Show them the way home, and I'll give you full access to the Wardenship."

Markan ran a hand through his hair, considering. "And what about you, Noah? Don't you want to go back to Earth, too?"

"Of course. I want you to help me get there after you're done with the Wardenship. But I need them to go as soon as possible, to keep them safe."

Markan laughed again, but the tone of it had changed. More resignation than amusement. "Oh, Noah. Haven't you learned by now? There is nowhere safe from the Warden."

"You can't really believe that. You're trying to overthrow him."

"Render him irrelevant," Markan corrected. "But I still do it from the shadows. Through the wormholes and beyond his easy reach."

"Why? What do you know about the Warden? What makes him that dangerous?"

"I destroyed a Wardenship once," Markan said. "Did you know that?"

"How would I?" I replied.

"It required quite a bit of effort, a number of ships, and a massive supply of chaos energy. To destroy. One. Single. Ship." He paused to let the statement sink in. "That was when I realized that I could never defeat the Warden head-on. That I could never overpower him, so I would need to undermine him. But, it's easier to play the long game when you're immortal."

I shuddered, chilled by the admission. "Do you know where the Warden came from?"

Markan shook his head. "No. By all accounts, he's always been here."

"But you don't believe he's a god?"

"I suppose that depends on your definition. It doesn't meet mine."

I nodded. "Mine either."

"Good. To suggest the Warden is all-powerful is to admit defeat before you even fight. Very well, Noah, you—"

"Wait," I said, struck by inspiration. "I have additional terms."

Markan's eyes narrowed, his glare turning cold. "Go on."

"One, I want you to ensure the security of Gothor. I know you made a deal with the King, but I want your personal assurance. Two, I want you to do what you can to end the war on Viconia."

Markan continued glaring for long enough that my nerves began to fray, but I refused to give in. "Is that all?" he growled.

"It's enough," I replied.

"Very well. You have my word that the syndicate will do no harm to Gothor. And I will look into how to end the strife on Viconia."

"I don't want you to look into it," I pushed back. "I want you to end it. Period."

"Of course," Markan said. A flicker of respect passed over his face, eyes glittering with anticipation. "Very well, Noah. You have a deal. I'll meet you at the station in one hour. Once you open the Wardenship for me, I'll instruct the syndicate to locate your friends and communicate the terms of our deal. To be clear, my method for escaping Warexia is not entirely pleasant, and will require leaving their ship behind."

The screen went dark before I could ask any follow-up questions, leaving me in a ringing silence. Janelle eyed me warily, clearly uncertain what to make of things.

"I'll prepare the contract," she said at last, rising to her feet. "It will all be contingent on your opening the Wardenship once Markan arrives." She paused, as if it had suddenly hit her that the leader of the syndicate would be at her doorstep in an hour. I doubted she'd ever met him in person before. In fact, our conversation may have been the first time she'd ever seen him at all. "You wait here. I'll post guards outside the door, so don't try to leave." She paused, smiling at me. "If this all works out, I could be in for another promotion. I need to shower and change my uniform. Do you know, does Markan have a wife?" My confused stare elicited a nervous laugh. "Right. I need to go."

She hurried out of the conference room, leaving Archie and me staring at one another.

CHAPTER 30

I stared in stunned disbelief as Janelle returned to the conference room, transformed into a polished executive clearly eager to impress her boss. Her uniform was crisp and perfectly pressed, not a wrinkle in sight. Her hair, previously loose, was now pulled back into a sleek bun, a small officer's cap perched atop her head. The scent of body wash and perfume wafted from her as she approached, and I noticed the subtle touch of makeup on her face.

She carried a data slab in her hands, which she promptly handed to me. "The contract," she explained, her tone all business despite her primped appearance. "Please review it carefully."

I took the slab, my eyes growing heavy as I scrolled through the lengthy document. For such relatively straight-forward terms, the contract seemed unnecessarily verbose and complex. Just like back on Earth. Janelle leaned over my shoulder, pointing out various clauses and stipulations as I read.

We were midway through the review when a chime sounded from the comms panel. Janelle straightened, a flicker of excitement passing over her features. "Markan is arriving," she announced, tapping a command into the console.

The main viewscreen came to life, displaying a feed from Deepling's external cameras. What I saw left me stunned. Markan's robot was emerging from the shimmering maw of a rift, intimidating as anything as it glided through the void. I had expected him to come in a ship, not bring his entire base of operations.

Like the Wardenship, the colossal machine drifted through space, lacking an obvious form of propulsion. It moved into position near the station, dwarfing the outpost with its sheer scale. Awe and fear warred within me at the sight. Markan was clearly intent on making a statement, on demonstrating the extent of his power.

Janelle's voice snapped me from my reverie. "It's time," she said, unable to contain her eagerness. "We'll meet Markan on the station. Come."

She guided Archie and me out of the conference room, through the corridors of Deepling, and back to the hangar.

"We'll take a shuttle across," Janelle said, pointing to one of the two basic craft.

"I'll take Burnock," I replied, pointing to the gunship.

I thought she might argue, but she only shrugged. "A ride is a ride," she said.

We boarded Burnock. Janelle dropped into the co-pilot seat while Archie loomed behind us, still in its Jaffie form. Within minutes, we crossed from Deepling to the station, landing in the hangar bay and departing onto the deck.

"Oh my," Janelle said as we moved away from Burnock, her eyes turned toward the open bay doors. I turned to follow her gaze, shocked for the second time.

A figure emerged from the void, gliding through the protective energy field as if it weren't even there. My breath caught as I recognized Markan, propelling himself through space unaided, the protective aura of a Sigiltech shield shimmering around him.

He had opted to show up in the most intimidating fashion possible, a show of strength and power that I couldn't help but let rattle my nerves. Taking a deep breath to calm them, I steeled myself for the confrontation.

Janelle practically vibrated with excitement as Markan touched down lightly on the deck, his expression cool as he took in our small party.

"Mr. Markan, sir," Janelle gushed, dipping into a deep bow bordering on groveling. "It's an honor to welcome you aboard. We have—"

Markan silenced her with a raised hand, his smile indulgent but dismissive. "Thank you, Janelle. Please stand up, I'm your boss, not a deity to be worshiped. You've done well." His gaze slid to me as she straightened, sharpening with interest. "Noah. I'm so glad we were able to come to an agreement."

I fought down a shiver at his tone, keeping my expression neutral. "Me too. I'm sure it will benefit both of us."

Markan chuckled, the sound devoid of genuine mirth. "Of course." His eyes slipped to Archie. "I knew you had a creed to always work for the highest bidder. What I can't imagine is how these visitors could afford you."

Archie replied with a noncommittal shrug, at which point Markan lost interest in the Aleal. If he knew Archie wasn't Jaffie, he didn't let on. And I was happy to at least have confirmation that Markan had known the mercenary.

"Did you go over the contract with him?" Markan asked, turning to Janelle.

"Yes, sir," she replied.

He looked back at me. "Any questions? Concerns?"

"I have a million questions, but not about the contract," I replied.

"I'm sure you do. We'll have time for all of that." He held his hand out toward Janelle.

She hastily presented him with the data slab, and he skimmed through the content with practiced efficiency, nodding before affixing his signature with the sweep of a finger. He passed it to me, and I did the same, my heartbeat quickening as I formalized the agreement and returned the slab to Janelle. No turning back now.

"Excellent," Markan said. "How is Rena, by the way?"

I wanted to spit back something like, *Great, now that she's away from the father who wanted us to kill her in front of him.* Instead, I settled for, "She's fine."

"Shall we?" Markan asked next, motioning us toward the exit. "I believe you know the way."

I nodded. "Is this your first time here?"

"It is."

"I can hardly believe that."

"I have plenty of other matters begging for my attention, and no need to stare at the outside of a Wardenship. My arrival here so soon after our conversation should give you an idea of how important this is to me."

"I'm honored," I quipped.

"You should be," Janelle said.

"What about my friends?" I asked. "You said you would pass the message about our deal on to them."

"Of course. Janelle, make the arrangements."

"Yes, sir," she replied. She cast me a hard side-eye as she turned to leave, jealous and angry that I'd caused her reassignment.

"So," I said as we crossed through the maze-like corridors leading to the Wardenship. "How does your system to get back to Earth work, anyway?"

"I prefer not to divulge my secrets," Markan replied.

"Of course not. But maybe you can give me a general explanation. Does it use chaos energy?"

"Yes."

"Is it related to the wormhole generators?"

He paused to glare at me. "Are you telling me, or just guessing?"

"Guessing," I replied, struggling not to feel intimidated.

"Intelligent guesses close to reality," Markan agreed. "My original intent in building the technology was to return to the Spiral. I'd abandoned the whole idea for centuries, until Levain came to me about a ship he had found. A Wardenship with no Warden. I never would have imagined."

"Yeah, it's pretty wild." I held my tongue again before I could blurt out, I *especially liked the part where you helped Jaffie get to Earth to kill my parents.*

"It must have been amazing, the first time the ship responded to you," he continued.

"To be honest, it scared the hell out of me. It seems half the universe knew my father was a missing Warden, but I had no idea."

"It's quite a way to discover your birthright."

"I guess so."

We silently finished the walk, passing through the sanitizer to the platform leading to the ship. An entire unit of armed and armored soldiers stood guard there, and they snapped to especially stiff attention when their boss came into view.

I swallowed the lump in my throat and exhaled sharply. Something felt off about this situation, a gathering dread that I couldn't shake.

"It's okay, Noah," Markan said with surprising softness. "In a few moments, we'll both get exactly what we deserve."

I glanced at him, dread growing into alarm bells ringing sharply in my mind. Markan's idea of what we each deserved was radically different than mine. His statement was something a boss-level enemy would say in a poorly written roleplaying game, but I had come this far. I couldn't falter now, not when I was so close. I could only hope Archie sensed my fear and would be ready to act if things went sideways.

"Getting cold feet?" Markan asked, moving closer to me. The Sigiltech ring on his pinkie glowed slightly, ready for use to prod me forward. "We have a contract, Noah. We both made commitments. Open the ship."

Taking a steadying breath, I steeled myself for whatever lay ahead and approached the Wardenship's hatch. Like before, the portal opened up the moment I grew near. I didn't need to look back at Markan to feel the sudden shift in the atmosphere surrounding us, his anticipation turning to pure elation. A softly uttered incantation seemed to freeze Archie in an invisible grip, while his guards surged forward, hard hands clamping down on my arms with bruising force, preventing me from crossing the threshold.

"What the hell?" I snarled, straining against their grip. I'd known this was a huge risk from the beginning and had seen the betrayal coming. I didn't expect Markan to be smart enough to disable Archie first. "We had a deal! A signed contract!"

The Gilded's lips curled in a cruel smile, his eyes glinting with fresh malicious amusement. "Indeed we do, Noah. And nowhere in that contract does it stipulate that you will remain free for the duration of our partnership."

My blood ran cold at his words, fear and anger warring in my gut. "But my friends! Their safe passage home is in the contract."

"And they'll have it," Markan replied. "I don't need them, and frankly, returning them to Earth will upset the Warden, so I'm heavily in favor of it."

"I said I would help you willingly," I ground out,

relieved at least that he intended to hold up his end of the deal. "You don't need to restrain me."

"That's where you're mistaken." Markan stepped closer, his voice dropping to a silken purr. "I don't anticipate you'll be quite so willing to part with your brain."

CHAPTER 31

I stared at Markan, uncomprehending. "My brain? What are you talking about?"

"The nanites, Noah. Warden nanites. The precious little machines your father passed down to you. They're the reason you can control the Wardenship. The only thing that makes you special. They're woven through your neural pathways, integrated into your very being. Your DNA." His smile sharpened, predatory and hungry. "And I want that power for myself."

Horror dawned on me like sickness, bile rising up my throat. He didn't want my cooperation. He wanted to dissect me, to rip the Warden's legacy from my skull and claim it as his own.

"You can't. We…we have a contract." It was a pathetic response, but it was all I had.

"I'm sorry, Noah. I'm not usually so diabolical, but then again, it's rare that anyone possesses anything I want so badly. I hope you understand."

Before I could swallow back my terror and muster a witty response, Janelle ran out onto the platform. "Mr. Markan, sir!" Her shout echoed throughout the hangar bay as she ran toward us, breathing hard from dashing all the way from the hangar bay. "We're under attack!"

"The Warden?" Markan asked, unperturbed.

"No, sir. It looks like a robot head, and it just crumpled Juggernaut like the ship was made of paper!"

Head Case!

Markan's face twisted in anger while my heart leaped into my throat. I could hardly believe they were here, much less their impeccable timing. But why were they here? They knew how dangerous Markan was. The Gilded would tear Head Case apart and leave all of my friends floating in the airless infinity of space. Except...Janelle had said they crumpled a ship like paper. There was only one person and one way they could do that.

Somehow, they had succeeded in reverse-engineering the Wardenship's siphon.

If Ben had access to unlimited chaos energy, the entire equation had changed.

Too bad I was stuck like a fish on a hook.

"Sir, what should we do?" Janelle asked, panicked.

"First, you'll calm down. One robot head starship is no match for our fleet. I'm sure our forces will take care of it before—"

The station suddenly shuddered, an echoing rumble rippling through the superstructure. The vibration was enough to throw the guards holding me off balance, their grip loosened, and I took advantage of it, wrenching one arm free. Immediately, I drove my elbow into the guard's face with a sickening crunch. He reeled backward, the other guard's grip weakening just enough for me to tear myself completely free.

Archie stood frozen mere inches from me, and it took everything in me to turn away, to leave it behind. I felt sick at the thought of abandoning the Aleal, my constant companion through all of this. But I had no choice. If I stopped now, if I hesitated for even a moment, we'd both end up dead.

I hurtled through the open hatch, my boots pounding on the decking as I raced deeper into the ship. Behind me, I heard a furious roar, Markan's bellow of rage echoing over the cacophony of ongoing destruction outside the station. Worry for Archie tugged at the corner of my thoughts, reminding me of how I had left Lavona to Markan, too. I had run then, and I was running now, and I hated it. But I didn't look back.

I couldn't. Not now. With my friends buying me precious time, with the hope of salvation so tantalizingly close, I could only hope I'd find a way to turn the tables and get back at Markan for his betrayal.

I sprinted through the corridors of the Wardenship, my heart thudding in time with my footsteps. Behind me, I could hear Markan's guards giving chase. But I didn't dare look back, didn't dare slow down. I had to get to the command seat. It was the only chance I had to help Ben, and with any luck, save Archie.

My mind raced as I ran, desperately trying to map out the twists and turns of the ship's interior. I'd only been here once before, a fleeting visit that now felt like a lifetime ago. But the knowledge of the structure was there, buried in my subconscious.

Or rather, stored in the nanites melded into my mind.

I veered left, then right, hurtling down hallways that all looked the same, yet somehow I knew they were leading me closer to my goal. The shouts behind me grew fainter, the footsteps more distant. I was losing them, if only for the moment.

Up ahead, I spotted a familiar hatch. With a final burst of speed, I flung myself through the opening. With little more than a desire to stop the guards from reaching me, the door sealed shut at my back.

For a moment, I simply stood there, chest heaving as I fought to catch my breath. The command seat sat empty in front of me. The ship nearly drove me mad the last time I sat in it.

But I had no choice. We would lose if I refused to interface with the ship, tap into its power, and make it my own.

I gritted my teeth and approached the chair, my palms slick with sweat. Every instinct screamed at me to turn back, to run as far and as fast as I could. But I couldn't. Not now. Not with so much at stake.

I sat down gingerly, bracing myself for the onslaught. For a sickening moment, nothing happened. Then, like a tidal wave crashing over me, the ship's systems surged to life.

It was just as overwhelming as the first time, a cascade of data and sensory input threatening to drown me. But I knew the truth now. I knew what to expect. I didn't fight the current or try to stem the tide. Instead, I let it flow through me, surrendering to the strange synchronicity between the nanites in my mind and the ship's vast neural network.

Slowly, painfully, the chaos resolved into order. The random noise coalesced into coherent data streams, flickering behind my eyelids in dizzying patterns of light and color. I could feel the Wardenship around me, its every bulkhead and conduit mapped out in exquisite detail. I could sense its systems as if they were part of me. The chaos energy reactor, my heart. The batteries, my lungs.

And more than that, I could feel its weapons. The immense destructive potential thrumming beneath its hull, waiting to be unleashed.

I was only vaguely aware of pounding on the hatch behind me, the reinforced metal holding up to the onslaught for now. Somehow, Markan's guards had found me. It was only a matter of time before they broke through.

But I wasn't defenseless anymore.

With a thought, I activated the cloning tanks where pralls were born, awed by the unbelievable machine three-dimensionally printing the aliens as if they were little more than resin.

I felt a flicker of hope for the first time since this nightmare began. The Wardenship was mine now, responding to my every whim and desire. With its power at my fingertips, maybe, just maybe, I stood a chance.

But even as that hope kindled in my chest, a cold dread crept up my spine. Because I knew, with sinking certainty, that this was only the beginning. Markan wouldn't rest until he had what he wanted.

And what he wanted was lodged firmly in my skull.

I closed my eyes again, reaching out through the ship's sensors, desperate to locate Head Case. There! Amidst the frenzy, fighting tooth and nail to rescue me. But the battle was fierce, and Markan was right. Even with chaos energy, they were badly outgunned. Matt was one hell of a pilot, but even he couldn't fly in seven directions simultaneously.

I had to help them.

The pounding on the hatch behind me grew more persistent, and I glanced over my shoulder when I heard a sharp hiss. A thin laser beam pierced the metal near the base and began to rise, the guards trying to cut their way in.

Except my pralls were ready. Through the nanites to the Wardenship, I could sense each of them individually, but one stood out among the rest: my new commander. Silently, I ordered it to arm the newly created guards and bring them to me. A smile split my face at its immediate compliance.

While I waited for the pralls to arrive, my attention returned to the ship's controls. I had to back it out of the station, to get into space to help Ben fight. But I only knew how to fly with a stick and throttle, not with my mind. I tried to picture the Wardenship moving, but at the same time, I could sense its stillness, as if it waited for me to change gears out of park or something.

The laser had climbed nearly halfway up the hatch when I heard screams from outside, followed by the whining thump of return fire. By focusing on the prall commander, I could see through his eyes and watched him and his fellow prall exchange fire with Markan's soldiers. They gave better than they got and cleared the corridor in seconds, a job well done.

Footsteps heard through the prall commander's ears turned him around. Walking down the stark white passageway, a dark wraith, glowing with chaos energy, face twisted in fury.

Markan.

He only needed to lift a finger to send the commander's prall soldiers crashing into the bulkheads with enough force to topple them like bowling pins. The commander opened fire, bullets reaching the Sigiltech glow, vanishing before they could connect. Another hand motion, a wet crack, and my ability to see through the commander's eyes was gone.

And Markan was right outside the door. How long could it hold him at bay?

More prall had finished printing, and I urged them out and on the offensive. I was vaguely aware of the Warden's cloning pods, empty and unused. I could make copies of the ship's Warden, I realized.

Copies of my father.

The thought sent a cold chill through me, and I forcibly refrained, shying away from the apparatus in my mind.

The first prall reached the corridor, returning my view of Markan as he stalked towards the sealed hatch. He hadn't noticed the prall yet, so I held it back to observe.

"Noah!" Markan called out, Sigiltech enhancing his

voice and allowing it to penetrate the metal barrier between us loud and clear. "I will tear this ship apart piece by piece if I have to. I will rip every last secret from your mind, even if it means scooping your brain out with a rusted spoon. The Wardenship is mine, Noah. Give it up now, and I'll spare you as much pain as I can."

I wanted to scream back at him, to rage and curse and defy. But what would be the point? What chance did I stand against a powerful Gilded with unfettered access to chaos energy?

And then, through the despair, a flicker of warmth and hope. Because out there, beyond the confines of this ship, my friends were fighting for me. They were risking everything, putting their lives on the line, all for the chance to save me.

And that meant something. It had to.

I thought of my dad, of the courage it must have taken for him to betray the nature of being a Warden and leave Warexia behind—to choose kindness and justice over the cold calculus of power and control. He had been one man, too, standing alone against the weight of expectation as a ruler of a galaxy.

But he'd done it. He'd found the strength, somewhere deep inside himself, to forge his own path. To be more than what he was made to be.

And now, it was my turn.

I straightened in my seat, squaring my shoulders. "You're wrong," I said, my voice steady despite the hammering of my heart. "This ship isn't yours. It never was."

Markan's eyes narrowed, his jaw clenching with barely contained rage. "You insolent little—"

With that, I reached out to the Wardenship, the vast well of power humming beneath my fingertips. I let it flow through me, let it fill me up until I was brimming with it until I could feel every atom of my being vibrating with barely contained force.

And then, I pushed it out.

A wave of iridescent energy burst from the ship's hull, a shimmering tsunami of light that passed through the surrounding station and swept through Markan's forces with the wrath of an angry god. I couldn't see the results, but I knew what was happening because it was exactly what I had asked for. Because the Wardenship wasn't the weapon at all.

I was.

Beyond the confines of the suddenly powerless station, the warships touched by the light flickered and went dark, leaving them adrift. Markan's ships...but not Head Case. The light bent around the ship, swirling and changing impossibly to avoid hitting my friends. It could do that because the light came from nothing but from nanites. Trillions and trillions of nanites, so many they might as well be infinite, so many they overwhelmed the enemy ships' shields, so small they passed right through their hulls and into their engine rooms, where they burned through conduits and connectors.

And they weren't limited to movement outside the Wardenship.

Markan roared, a sound of mingled rage and fear cut off by frantic incantations, a shield of energy enveloping him just before the prall guards' plasma or the nanites could break through. Casting one last angry glare toward the hatch separating us, he turned and charged my prall defenders, pushing them aside and vanishing around a corner.

The nanites I had sent out returned home, passing through the hull or clinging to it. The chaos energy batteries discharged some of their power into them, recharging the microscopic machines.

I located the Wardenship's comms in my mind, sending a transmission at a frequency I felt certain Head Case would hear.

"Ben, Matt, it's Noah," I said aloud. "Do you copy?"

"Noah!" Ben replied. "Where are you? Did you do that?"

"Yeah," I answered with a grin. "Markan's ships should all be disabled."

"They are, mostly. How?"

"I'll explain later. What do you mean, mostly?"

"Do you have visual? You need to see it to believe it."

CHAPTER 32

My mind's connection to the Wardenship allowed me to sense its surrounding environment. I had an innate understanding of objects' positioning in space and time. Yet, as I focused on Markan's giant robot, a strange absence tugged at my awareness. Where the station and warships stood out in stark detail, the massive automaton remained an empty void in my perception.

"No," I said, replying to Ben's question. "I don't see it. The Wardenship doesn't have cameras. However it works, somehow the robot is invisible to me."

"If I transmit the feed, can you receive it?" Ben asked in reply.

"There's only one way to find out."

"Transmitting," Ben said. A moment later, an image from Head Case's external cameras flickered to life in my mind's eye, overlaying my own senses.

What I saw left me stunned. The robot base glowed from within, shafts of light spilling from its many open wounds and forming a shield around it, like the one Markan had used to escape the nanites.

"The robot has sigils etched on the inside?" I asked. "Like Head Case."

"It appears that way," Ben said grimly.

"But Markan is here on the Wardenship."

"He is? Where? Are you in danger?"

"No. He ran off after I disabled the ships. I think he's retreating."

"No," Ben countered. "Men like Markan don't retreat. They regroup. This isn't over." He paused, tension hanging thick between us. "If Markan is on the Wardenship, then he must have someone else at the base who can use Sigiltech. Noah, we need to get you out of here."

"I can't fly the Wardenship," I replied. "I haven't figured out how to make it go yet."

"We can't pick you up in the station. The power's out, which means life support and gravity are offline, too."

"I know. That's why you shouldn't have come for me. I risked my life to save you, not to have you end up dead because of me."

"Markan was never planning to keep his word," Ben answered. "Rena confirmed as much after you left."

"Then why did you let me go?" I asked.

"We both know that nothing I said would have stopped you. Your heart was in the right place, but you don't know people like Markan the way I do. I've dealt with his kind before."

I didn't want to believe it, but after what Markan had tried to do to me, that he would renege on the contract didn't seem like much of a stretch. Especially since, according to the document, the terms were null and void when I ceased to exist.

"I'm sorry I got you into this."

"Don't apologize yet. You can still help us get out."

I opened my mouth to reply, but the words died on my

tongue as movement caught my eye on Head Case's visual feed. A lone figure, wreathed in the telltale glow of chaos energy, launched from the station towards the waiting robot.

"Markan," I hissed. "He's heading for the base!"

Ben cursed under his breath. "He'll never be more vulnerable than he is right now. We can't let him get there. Matt!"

"On it," Matt said. Head Case surged forward, ion cannons swiveling to target the Gilded. He seemed like easy pickings alone as he drifted across the black at low velocity.

But he didn't remain that way for long.

Before a single shot could be fired, a swarm of smaller craft began to burst from the openings in the robot like angry hornets from a swatted nest. Sleek starfighters joined barely-armed shuttles and other ships, suddenly bearing down on Head Case with deadly intent.

"Damn it!" Ben yelled over the comms, struggling to evade the onslaught. Plasma bolts and energy beams streaked across the void in a deadly barrage that threatened to make quick work of Head Case. "Noah, you need to figure out how to get the Wardenship out here. The siphon and battery the engineers built is unstable. We need your help."

Gritting my teeth, I tore my focus away from the harrowing scene, turning my attention inward to the Wardenship's systems. I had to get this ship out of the station. I had to get out there to fight.

But how? The Wardenship didn't have thrusters or engines. There was no machinery or other technology I could sense dedicated to propelling the starship. It moved through some arcane means I couldn't comprehend or control.

Only that was impossible. I sat in the command seat,

linked to the rest of the Wardenship through the nanites. I had to be able to make it go.

Sensing Head Case outside, I could tell how frantically Matt maneuvered through the horde, desperately trying to reach Markan despite the overwhelming odds. I could imagine how much of a beating my friends were taking, the shields quickly losing power, threatening to fail at any moment.

"I need to get out there!" I cried, slamming a hand down on the console in front of me out of frustration.

I felt like an idiot the moment the realization hit me. The nanites! If I could use them to disable Markan's ships, why couldn't I use them to propel this one?

I took a calming breath and reached out with my thoughts, ordering trillions of the machines clinging to the bow to activate whatever small amount of thrust they possessed. They were so tiny, but like with Archie, the scaling effect made them more powerful than they seemed.

Archie. I wondered what had happened to the Aleal, even as I felt a shudder that reverberated through my bones as the Wardenship broke free of its moorings. Slowly at first, then with gathering speed, it backed toward the massive bay doors behind it.

With the bow nanites pushing us out, I sent the forward nanites streaking toward the bay doors in a swirl of light and energy which quickly ate away the metal, creating a hole for the Wardenship to pass through. Returning to the hull, they pulled energy from the batteries to recharge, ready for their next command.

"I got it!" I shouted over the comms. "I'm on my way!"

Elation surged through me in a wild, giddy rush of newfound power. But it was short-lived. Because at that moment, a bang sounded from the sealed hatch at my back, the metal denting inward from a tremendous impact.

My heart skipped a beat. Had Markan's guards

remained on the ship? Were they trying to break through, to drag me back to their master? I shifted my senses to the prall in the outer corridor to see what was happening on the other side of the hatch.

And froze. Because there, visible through the prall's eyes, was a sight I had never dared to hope for.

Archie. My faithful companion, my friend, slamming against the hatch with all the considerable might of a maulvas.

Instinct took over, and with a thought, I commanded the hatch to open. Archie bounded through, sleek and deadly, skidding to a halt at my side.

I wanted to leap from my seat and throw my arms around the Aleal. But there was no time. Not now, with the battle raging beyond and my friends in desperate need of aid.

"Welcome back, buddy," I managed, my throat tight. "I'm so happy to see you. Now hold on tight. Things are going to get rough."

Archie sprouted tendrils, wrapping them around any purchase it could find. My friend's presence gave me just the confidence boost I needed, and with a thought, I sent the Wardenship hurtling forward, angling to join the fray.

Head Case wove and spun through the chaos, ion cannons blazing as it fought to hold off the enemy swarm. But it was badly outnumbered, the smaller craft darting in to strafe its shields before darting away again. Matt and Cade were doing an incredible job of flying and shooting, but it couldn't last.

Not against these odds.

I connected with the nanites on the Wardenship's bow, directing them towards the enemy craft. They launched into the fray like a swarm of angry locusts, boring through hulls and ripping into vital systems. Damaged fighters spun out of control while larger shuttles went dark, powerless against the onslaught.

"Damn it!" I cursed in frustration as Markan reached the robot base, vanishing through a gash in the thigh to safety within. We'd stopped his forces from overwhelming Head Case, but we hadn't stopped him from making it home. And now he would be that much harder to defeat.

A chaotic maelstrom of nanites and enemy ships swirled around the Wardenship with Head Case herding the enemy ships closer, making it easier for me to take them out. Trails of the micro-machines smashed through the vessels, leaving them powerless and adrift while Head Case passed through the storm untouched, the nanites swirling around it in a bubble of safety.

"We've got them on the run!" Matt announced as the smaller ships turned tail, retreating back toward their robot base.

Only my senses told me something different.

Until now, the robot base had been invisible to me. But now, I could clearly pick up its beating heart, the thing suddenly alive and filled with energy. "Damn!" I replied. "They're making way for Markan's attack."

"Oh, hell," Matt cursed, Head Case's visual revealing what I had already sensed through the Wardenship. Huge panels on the robot's surface faded to reveal Markan's sigilship, glowing brightly.

Cold sweat breaking out across my brow, it took some effort to swallow past the sudden lump in my throat. "Ben, the nanites can't pass through Sigiltech shields."

A beat of silence. Then, "Understood." Ben's voice was grim but determined. "Can you go to hyperspace?"

Making the ship move with nanites was one thing. Going to hyperspace, something else entirely. "I...I don't know how."

"It's okay, Noah," Ben answered calmly. "We'll just have to get creative."

"Creative," I echoed, nodding even though he couldn't see. "Right. I can do creative." I hoped.

Narrowing my focus to a laser point, I sent the Wardenship racing towards the sigilship, nanites swarming ahead of me like a living shield. The best I could do was distract Markan so Ben could try to find a way through the chaos energy barrier surrounding the enemy vessel.

The sigilship's weapons spoke out loudly, lances of searing light hammering into my nanite shield, instantly destroying millions of the machines.

I pushed forward, refusing to back down. I had Markan's attention, which was all I wanted. It gave Head Case the opening it needed to wheel around in a tight arc, flanking the sigilship. Its ion cannons opened fire, hurling heavy matter against the enemy's shields. In retaliation, Markan launched a massive gout of flame at Head Case.

Matt juked and wove, putting all his considerable piloting skill into evading the sigilship's tracking fire. Markan was relentless, displaying his immense control over Sigiltech and chaos energy.

I knew Ben had traded energy shields for chaos when the flames from Markan's ship reversed toward it, forcing Markan to end the attack on Head Case. He continued pounding the Wardenship, defeating the line of nanites and hitting the shields. The ship absorbed the attack like a champ, with plenty of power available to defend against the assault.

I redoubled my efforts, driving the Wardenship hard to buy Ben the time he needed to send his gout of flame at the sigilship. He quickly replaced it with what looked like lightning. The bolt made it through the sigilship's defenses, ablating some of its armor but failing to pierce its tough hide.

We continued our attack, maneuvering around the sigilship, and for a few glorious minutes, it seemed as if we had the upper hand. We peppered the ship with everything we had, two targets making it difficult for Markan to put up a unified defense.

And then, disaster.

"Noah!" Ben's shout came across the comms edged with raw panic. "This is taking too long. Our chaos energy stores are almost drained. We need to end this now or Markan will end us."

Was it possible Markan had somehow intercepted our communications? Had he chosen that moment to break off his attack on the Wardenship so he could turn his attention to Head Case?

In tandem, energy lances and stretches of flame belched out from the sigilship toward Head Case, forcing Matt to pick his poison, and Ben to raise chaos energy shields to absorb the firepower. They slipped the noose, streaking past the sigilship, but Markan was already bringing it about, adjusting vectors to keep up the pressure.

Desperate to regain Markan's attention, I sacrificed nanites by the millions, throwing them into the sigilship's shields. It didn't work. He remained trained on Head Case, another burst of flame practically roasting the smaller ship before Matt could steer clear.

"That's it," Ben announced, his voice weak. "We're out of chaos energy. We won't survive the next hit."

I felt his words like a physical blow, despair crashing over me in a frigid wave. We were going to lose. Markan would take my brain, my friends would die, and there was nothing I could...

No.

The idea burst into my head like a nuclear light bulb. Markan was powerful, sure, but that wasn't why he was winning. It was simple math. He had more fuel. Greater resources.

But I had one last desperate gambit, one final roll of the dice.

"Ben!" I yelled into the comms. "I have an idea! I'm going to release all of the Wardenship's stored chaos energy! Get ready to draw it in!"

"What?" He sounded shocked, disbelieving. "Noah, I don't—"

"You can control it! I know you can!" I was already reaching into the batteries with my mind. I could feel the energy there, a roiling tempest straining at the edges of its confinement, begging to be set free. "You know what to do!"

I didn't wait for his response. Couldn't afford to hesitate a moment longer. With a mental twist, I released the floodgates.

Chaos energy erupted from the Wardenship, released into the universe in one massive expulsion that Markan could seize as well as Ben. If he were quick enough.

He wasn't. As a space wizard, Ben had him completely outclassed.

And I had just fanned his flames.

Without warning, Head Case came to a sudden, impossible stop in space, rotating to face the sigilship as Markan's final attack went way wide, its Sigiltech shield falling away to provide extra power for the failed killing blow. At the same moment, Head Case lurched backward from the force of all the ship's ion cannons firing into a single point in front of the ship. Instead of crossing through one another, they coalesced into a single beam of utter destruction molded by Ben's control. Combined and focused by chaos energy, the beam lanced out, a spear of pure, unbridled power, striking the sigilship dead center.

Desperately launched shields flared to impossible

brightness as they fought to repel the attack. For half a ragged breath, they held before shattering like glass.

The beam punched through in a spray of molten metal and sizzling energy. It cored into the heart of the sigilship through decks and bulkheads, leaving utter devastation in its wake. Secondary explosions rippled across the hull, gouts of flame jetting into the darkness before running out of oxygen and dissipating.

For a long, frozen moment, the sigilship simply hung there, a gutted, dying hulk. Then, with a soundless implosion that I felt in my bones, it crumpled in on itself, consumed by a storm of energy and debris.

Just like that, Markan was gone.

CHAPTER 33

"Yesss!" I shouted, doubling my fist and punching the air over my head. Archie jumped on its hind legs, grunting joyfully, tendrils springing out to shiver in excitement. I could hear Ben, Matt, and the others on Head Case cheering along with me, whooping and whistling as pieces of the sigilship drifted away, sparkling like fairy dust before dying out.

Through Head Case's feed, I watched as many of Markan's remaining forces turned tail, fleeing back to the giant robot base, while others peeled off to the disabled ships, no doubt to rescue their stranded comrades. For the moment, at least, we had been forgotten.

The Wardenship's power suddenly winked out. Darkness enveloped the command deck, broken only by the dim glow of emergency backup lights.

Concerning but not enough to kill my vibe.

I reached out with my senses, trying to tap into the ship's systems, picking up on what amounted to a damage report. The rapid discharge had damaged the siphon and batteries, leaving the ship truly dead in space.

"Hey, Ben?" I said into the comms, my concern growing over the outcome. "We have a problem."

"What is it?" Ben asked, his tone still edged with the excitement of victory while echoing his exhaustion from the fight.

"The Wardenship is done for. No power, no systems. Just emergency backups." I grimaced, realizing the extent of our predicament. "And no life support." I'd gotten so excited I only now realized I was in zero gravity, too. We'd worked so hard to gain the Wardenship only to lose it. But it was still better than losing our lives.

"Do you have enough power left to open the hangar bay?" Ben replied. "We need to get you out of there."

"I'll try," I replied. I sent the command to seal off the hangar bay, knowing it was the only way to preserve the ship's existing atmosphere when I opened the outer doors for Head Case. The ship resisted the command at first, signaling it would drain too much power too quickly. I reiterated the desire, overriding the warning. The entrance to the hangar bay closed, and I opened the outer bay door. I'd be lucky if it had enough juice left to close it again so I could get to Head Case. We could worry about opening the outer door again once I got that far. I knew, if need be, Cade could blow up the hangar door to facilitate Head Case's escape.

"Hangar door's open," I reported.

"We're coming in now. Just hold on."

I watched on the viewscreen as Head Case maneuvered towards the open bay, its running lights a beacon in the darkness. The moment it was inside, I commanded the doors to close and opened the interior hatches.

I slumped back in the command seat, exhausted. The adrenaline of the battle was fading, leaving me drained and shaky.

"Archie, help me out of this thing, will you?" I asked, looking over at the Aleal.

It shifted into Jaffie's form for the task, reaching out and releasing my restraints before gently easing me out of the seat. My mind disconnected from the Wardenship when I lost contact with the station. Immediately, a wave of dizziness washed over me. Without the ship's artificial gravity, my magboots kept me stuck upright to the deck.

Archie held fast to me, guiding me away from the command seat and out into the passageway, where the bodies of both Markan's guards and the pralls floated, along with globs of their blood. I choked back a wave of nausea, eager to get through the horrific obstacle course.

"Come on, bud," I mumbled. "Let's get to the hangar bay."

Together, we made our way through the darkened corridors of the Wardenship, Archie's tendrils doing as much to keep me anchored as my boots.

By the time we reached the inner hatch to the hangar bay, I was not only dizzy and weak, my vision blurred at the edges. Head Case sitting there in the hangar a sight for sore eyes.

"Noah!" Tyler and Matt were there in starsuits, rushing forward to help me.

"Damn, man," Tee said on reaching us. "You look like crap." I didn't have the wherewithal to respond. It was all I could do to keep from passing out.

"Let's get him to sick bay," Matt said.

"We've got him, Arch," Tyler said. Archie reluctantly let go of me as they each slipped one of my arms over their shoulders and carried me to the ship, Archie following close behind.

"No...not sick bay," I choked out, my throat bone dry.

"Yeah, man," Tyler said, his face tight with worry. "We gotta get you to the autodoc."

"No," I repeated, shaking my head and immediately regretting it as the world spun. "Just...need rest. And drink."

They guided me up Head Case's ramp into its hangar bay, Matt moving to switch me to a fireman's carry once the anti-grav kicked in.

"I can walk," I said, wriggling out of his grasp. I would have stumbled and fallen flat on my face without Tee's arm still wrapped around my torso.

"Noah," Matt chided.

"I can walk, damn it," I pressed more forcefully.

"Suit yourself," he answered, throwing his hands up. By the time I had both feet solidly under me and Tee had cautiously let me go, Lavona had appeared in front of me, eyes wide with worry and relief. She hit me so hard I had to take a step back to keep my balance as she wrapped me in a fierce hug, her strength just enough to steady me.

"I was so worried," she whispered, her voice rough with emotion. "When you left like that..."

"You're not mad at me?" I asked.

"I *was* mad. At first." She drew back far enough to look up at me with tear-filled eyes. "I still don't understand why you'd think Markan would ever give you a fair deal, much less let you live."

"It seems everyone knew that but me," I mumbled.

Then she smiled. "How can I be mad at someone who's so loyal to his friends he's willing to sacrifice his life for them?"

"You wanted to help us so badly, you were blinded by it," Ally said, approaching from my left. "Idiot," she added, gripping my arm tightly.

Everyone else, except for Cade, who likely had the con, gathered around, relief and exhaustion etched into every face. Ben moved between Matt and Tee, clapping a hand on my other shoulder, his grip warm and steady. "You did it,

Noah," he said, pride shining in his eyes. "You saved us all."

"No," I replied. "We did it, Ben. I couldn't have beaten the sigilship without all of you."

"Fine. *We* did it," Ben corrected. "The point is, we stopped Markan."

"Yeah, but we still don't have a way home," I said. "It feels like a hollow victory."

"Keeping you alive is hardly hollow," Lantz said. "We've missed you around here, kid."

"More than you know," Lavona added.

"So what happens now?" Ally asked, looking around at the assembled crew. "With Markan gone, I mean."

Rena stepped forward, her expression a mix of sadness and determination. She knew her father was a monster, but he was still her father, and now he was gone. "The syndicate will spend the next few months, if not longer, eating itself alive. With all of them vying for power, trying to fill the vacuum left by my father's death it will relieve pressure on other parts of the galaxy." She looked at Lavona, hope kindling in her eyes. "Viconia, for example. The usurper government will lose its source of weapons and intel. It will give the freedom fighters a better chance at victory."

"That's a wonderful thought," Lavona agreed.

"It is," Ally added. "But what I really meant was what's next for us? We unintentionally did the Warden's dirty work, just like he asked, and now we're no closer to getting back to Earth."

"I wouldn't say no closer," I replied. "Markan did suggest the road home leads through a wormhole too small for a ship, even as small as Head Case, to pass through."

"And I still have my father's data," Rena added. "Maybe we can find more detail in there."

"If not, maybe Leo can cook something up," Matt said. "He got one of the boons."

"He's like Space MacGyver now," Tee said, giving Leo a playful nudge with his elbow. "He built a rudimentary siphon and battery with duct tape and paperclips."

"A bit of an exaggeration," Leo said. "And the design was a team effort."

"You're just being modest," Meg said, beaming at her twin's success.

Before anyone else could speak, Cade's voice erupted through Ben's comm badge, urgent and strained. "Captain, Matt—I need you on the flight deck, right away!"

"Cade, what's wrong?" Ben asked, already frowning.

"You…you need to come see this, Captain."

"On my way."

He glanced back at us, unspoken command in the nod of his head toward the stairs before he rushed up them to the elevator. Tee helped me up the stairs as we all hurried after him, Lavona supporting my other side, Archie trailing directly behind me.

We crowded into the elevator, taking it up to Deck Three, where we burst through the doors, practically stampeding onto the flight deck. Once we got a look through the forward transparency, none of us needed to ask what was happening.

Tee groaned, his shoulders slumping. "It freakin' figures. Couldn't we get like…I don't know…five minutes, just this once?"

Three Wardenships, vast and imposing, hung in the black before us, all of them pointed at Head Case as if daring us to even twitch.

For a moment, no one spoke. No one breathed. We stared, shock and dawning horror creeping through our veins like ice. My heart hammered, a sickening, stuttering beat. We'd just barely survived one battle. And now this…

This was something else.

A force beyond reckoning.

Battered as we were and without my father's Warden-ship, it was a threat we couldn't hope to stand against. But we would. Together. Because that was the only way we would ever have a chance to survive.

A chance to go home.

"Captain," Cade said from the pilot's seat. "We're being hailed."

CHAPTER 34

With my heart in my throat, I stood on the flight deck, staring at the three massive Wardenships looming in front of Head Case. Beside me, my friends were a mix of tense silence and nervous energy, equally worried about what the next few minutes would bring.

"Captain?" Cade repeated, still looking back at us over his shoulder, waiting for Ben to decide what he wanted to do.

Ben glanced at me, his expression stiff, as if he knew what would come. And maybe he did. "Answer the hail," he told Cade.

A familiar holographic projection flickered to life in front of the viewscreen. The Warden's eyes glinted with an unexpected measure of amusement. "Captain Murdock!" he exclaimed, his voice jovial. "And the rest of your intrepid crew! So good to see you all again."

I stared at the screen, uncomprehending. This wasn't the reaction I'd expected. Where was the anger, the fury at our defiance? The Warden seemed...pleased.

"What do you want?" Ben asked, his tone carefully neutral.

The Warden's grin widened. "Want? Why, to congratulate you, of course! And especially to congratulate Noah. I have to admit, when I tasked you with recovering the Wardenship, I thought it would be a lot harder than you've made it seem. And you also made up for your Captain's terribly transparent lies about taking care of Markan. Although, I suppose I shouldn't be that surprised. You are a Warden, after all."

I blinked, confusion warring with a sudden, irrational surge of pride. He was congratulating me?

"A…a Warden?" I said. "Me? My father was a Warden. I'm only half, at best."

The Warden laughed. "There's no such thing as half a Warden, Noah. You activated a Wardenship. That makes you a Warden. Period. End of story."

I wasn't sure what to think of that. On one hand, I felt a swell of pride to follow in my father's footsteps. On the other hand, being a Warden wasn't exactly a good thing. This one was, at best, an asshole and, at worst, a complete tyrant.

"I don't understand," I said slowly. "I thought you'd be angry. Especially since the ship is disabled."

The Warden waved a dismissive hand. "I could repair the damage, but considering the changes I've made since then, it's better to retire this particular vessel. The important thing is, you did exactly what I hoped you would do. You embraced your legacy, your birthright. You showed Markan who the true power in Warexia belongs to. Us."

"If you're so happy with the outcome," Matt cut in, his voice tight with barely restrained anger, "then why the show of force? Why surround us?"

The Warden's eyes flicked to Matt, his smile turning sharp. "Insurance, Matthew. I had to be ready to jump in when you failed, which honestly, was more likely than not. I couldn't risk Markan slipping away again. But you exceeded my expectations. Truly. Bravo." He offered Matt a condescending golf clap.

"How did you even know we were fighting Markan?" I asked, a cold suspicion taking root in my gut.

The Warden's gaze snapped back to me. "I think you already know the answer to that."

I did, and it sent a shiver down my spine. The nanites in my brain. Warden nanites. I didn't think the Warden could track me anywhere I went with them, but once they connected to the Wardenship, my mind joined the Warden Network, allowing all of them to sense me. And if I'd had more experience, I probably could have sensed them, too.

"My connection to the Wardenship," I said, for the sake of my gathered friends so they would know the answer to my question.

"Precisely," the Warden replied. "I believe you're beginning to understand."

"Enough games," Ben said, his voice hard. "We did what you wanted. We dealt with Markan and recovered your precious Wardenship for you. I think we've earned our way home."

The Warden tutted, shaking his head. "Ah, Captain. For once, you aren't wrong. Since I can no longer reward you with boons, then perhaps offering you a ride back to your galaxy is a fair exchange."

"Really?" Ally said, surprised he would agree to the request.

"Yeah, are you serious?" Tee seconded. "And, do I get to keep the rocket fist?"

"I'm completely serious, Tyler. and I will let you keep your fist, if that's what you want. And all of you can go home...except Noah, of course."

My blood ran cold, even though it was nothing I hadn't expected. Beside me, I felt the others tense, the atmosphere on the flight deck edged with anxiety.

"What do you mean, except Noah?" Ally asked, her voice low and dangerous.

"I'm sure if I were really here, you'd shoot me again, Alyssa." The Warden's smile gained another level of sick amusement. "Noah will be coming with me, of course. The rest of you can return to your inconsequential lives. Noah, on the other hand, is a Warden. His father abandoned his post. It's his duty to take it up again."

"No," Ben said immediately, his tone brooking no argument. "Absolutely not. Noah is one of us. He belongs back on Earth with his friends and family."

Family. The word sent a pang through my chest, even as a swell of love and gratitude rose to meet it. These people, this crazy, wonderful crew—especially after coming here to face off against Markan and rescue me—had truly become my family.

Which was why I had left them to make the deal with Markan. And why I had to leave them to make the deal with the Warden now, even if it was the last thing I wanted.

"Ben," I said softly, hating how my voice shook. "He's right."

Ben whirled to face me, his expression stricken. "Noah, no. You can't—"

"I can," I interrupted, forcing myself to meet his gaze. "I have to. If it means getting the rest of you home safely...I'll do it." I looked at the Warden. "I'll go with you."

"Like hell, you will!" Tyler exploded. Ally and the others were quick to voice their agreement, their faces set in stubborn lines. But I knew, with a terrible, sinking certainty, that this was the only way, the only choice.

The Warden had us dead to rights. We were outgunned. Outmatched. If I refused, if we fought, I knew he would kill my friends.

And their blood would be on my hands.

"Please," I said, my voice cracking at the word. "This is

my decision to make. And he's right. I belong here." Of course, as much as I tried to convince myself, I didn't believe it. However, I had to convince them of it to make it easier for them to accept.

"Noah," Lavona whispered, her eyes bright with unshed tears as she eased her hold on me, touching the back of my hand with her fingertips.

I turned my hand around and entwined my fingers with hers, squeezing. "It's okay," I lied. "I'll be okay," I assured her. Then I looked up at everyone. Almost as much as I could feel Lavona's anguish, I could feel everyone's desire to change my mind. But there was nothing they could do. Not this time. "This is my choice," I told them. "I'm asking you to accept it."

Silence fell, heavy and oppressive.

"Very touching," the Warden drawled, shattering the moment. "It always brings a tear to my eye when people care so much for one another." He said it, but of course, there was no hint of tears in his eyes. "Prepare to be boarded, Captain."

Ben's jaw clenched, his hands balling into fists at his sides. For a moment, I thought he might attack the hologram.

"Wait," he said. "Not everyone on board wants to go to Earth. Some of my crew will certainly want to stay in Warexia. We need to drop them somewhere before you can send us home."

The Warden's face flashed impatience, but he continued grinning. "In that case, I propose a neutral site. The station, perhaps? I'll send a shuttle there, and Noah can come to me of his own free will. Any of your crew who want to remain in this galaxy can all disembark as well. Acceptable?"

Ben nodded. "Acceptable. We'll be there shortly."

"I'll be waiting," the Warden purred. The hologram winked out, plunging us into silence once more.

It was really happening. I was going to give myself over to the Warden. To leave behind everything and everyone I cared about, hoping it would save them.

Archie whined softly, pressing closer as it sensed my distress. I laid a hand on its head, trying to draw strength from the contact.

"Noah..." Ben started, but I shook my head.

"Don't," I said softly. "Just...let's just get this over with."

He sighed heavily, his unhappiness clouding his eyes, but he didn't say anything more before turning away from me. "Cade, take us in. But no sudden maneuvers. I don't want the Warden to get the wrong idea."

"Aye aye, Captain," Cade replied. Head Case eased forward, angling towards the gaping wound in the chest of Markan's robot station, where a few other ships that had attacked us minutes before were also headed. They had picked up the crews of some of the vessels the nanites from my father's Wardenship had disabled, bringing them home.

When we slipped into the robot's cavernous hangar bay, Markan's people stood in scattered groups, watching our approach with fear and awe. They had seen Head Case destroy Markan's sigilship. They knew better than to challenge us now.

"I'll meet you in the hangar," Ben said quietly as we filed off the flight deck. "There's something I need to do first."

Last in line, I nodded, not trusting myself to speak as I followed Lavona, her shoulders stiff with tension. My throat felt tight, my eyes burning with the tears I refused to let fall—not yet, not until I was alone.

"Ixy," Matt said over his comm badge as he stepped into the elevator ahead of us. "Please report to the hangar."

"Yesss, Bosss," she replied.

Everyone clustered around me in the elevator was a bittersweet comfort. Lavona held my hand, her grip almost painful. Tyler and Ally stuck close to my other side, shoulder-to-shoulder, like an honor guard.

All too soon, we reached Head Case's hangar bay. My steps faltered as I started down the steps, a sudden, visceral fear spiking through me. This was it. The point of no return.

"Noah..." Lavona's voice cracked, again squeezing my hand when she noticed my terror. "You don't have to do this. There has to be another way."

I shook my head. "There's no other way."

"Maybe..." She paused, hesitant. "Maybe I can come with you. Miss Asher paired us together. We're a team."

I smiled at her. "I wish you could come with me, but you can't. I wish I could go with you. To Viconia, or Earth. Anywhere but here. But like the Warden said, this is my birthright. My destiny."

"Yeah, like the plot of a lame video game," Tyler grunted from where he and Ally stood on a nearby step. "I'm getting tired of saying goodbye to you, man." He halfheartedly punched me in my shoulder.

"Yeah, me too," Ally agreed, wiping away a tear running down her cheek as she turned and scampered down the steps.

Ever stoic, Matt looked up at me as Ally passed him. "We won't forget this. Or you." He didn't wait for me to reciprocate. He just turned and went down the stairs. Tee, Lavona and I followed quietly behind.

We reached the bottom of the steps and continued to the middle of Head Case's hangar bay, where everyone else but Ixy waited. I nodded to each one, memorizing their faces. Meg, Leo, Karpov, Lantz... Even Rena managed a watery smile.

Archie. My faithful companion, my friend. It butted its Maulvas head against my hand, a low whine building in its throat.

"Take care of them for me," I murmured, almost breaking down completely. "Keep them safe."

"Noahsss!" Ixy called from the top of the steps. Rather than use the stairs, she scrambled down the arm of the Hunter mech to reach us. "Don't leavesss withoutsss sssaying goodbyesss." She wrapped me in her pedipalps, pulling me close. "Will misss you."

"I'll miss you too, Ixy. Make sure Archie has enough to eat, okay?"

"I triesss."

"Noah," a voice said from the bottom of Head Case's ramp. We turned as one to look down at the Warden, or at least a copy of him, waiting impatiently in front of a translucent sphere that reminded me of a hamster ball.

"Coming," I said, quickly offering silent goodbyes to the others. They were all so hard to part with, and it hurt so bad to know I would never see any of them again. I battled back tears as I started down the ramp leading out into the robot base's hangar bay.

Toward the Warden.

Toward my destiny.

He grinned as I neared, waving his arm toward the hamster ball. "You made the right choice," he said.

"I made the only choice you gave me," I replied.

"True." He laughed as I stepped up to the ship, looking back to see my friends, my family, standing at the top of the ramp, looking down on me with sour, sad, tearful faces. "For them, you'll soon fade into nothing more than a distant memory. For you, they'll be dead for generation after generation, and eventually you won't remember them at all."

"No," I countered. "I'll always remember them."

"Ever the optimist, eh, Noah? We shall see. Hop in!" He paused. "Ah, wait. You favored the Gothori ship, didn't you?" He raised his eyebrows, and I watched in amazement as his shuttle reconfigured in front of my eyes, morphing from the oversized hamster ball into a replica of Burnock. "I'll even let you fly us over."

The power that the Warden possessed amazed me. I would have a chance to share in that power. Only, I didn't want it.

I wanted to go home.

"You're home now," the Warden said. I knew he had read my thoughts by the look on my face, not the nanites fused to my brain.

"And you'll keep your promise? You'll send Head Case back to Earth?"

"I'll allow the ship to bypass my blockade on the Void," the Warden agreed. "I'll keep my end of the bargain. I have what I wanted."

I exhaled a breath I didn't realize I was holding and stepped into the shuttle, the hatch closing behind me.

One story ends. Another begins.

"Then, yeah. I guess I am home."

———

Thank you for continuing Starship For Rent! For more information on the next book in the series, please visit mrforbes.com/starshipforrent5

OTHER BOOKS BY M.R FORBES

Want more M.R. Forbes? Of course you do!
View my complete catalog here
mrforbes.com/books
Or on Amazon:
mrforbes.com/amazon

Starship For Sale (Starship For Sale)
mrforbes.com/starshipforsale

When Ben Murdock receives a text message offering a fully operational starship for sale, he's certain it has to be a joke.

Already trapped in the worst day of his life and desperate for a way out, he decides to play along. Except there is no joke. The starship is real. And Ben's life is going to change in ways he never dreamed possible.

All he has to do is sign the contract.

Joined by his streetwise best friend and a bizarre tenant with an unseverable lease, he'll soon discover that the universe is more volatile, treacherous, and awesome than he ever imagined.

And the only thing harder than owning a starship is staying alive.

Forgotten (The Forgotten)
mrforbes.com/theforgotten
Complete series box set:
mrforbes.com/theforgottentrilogy

Some things are better off FORGOTTEN.

Sheriff Hayden Duke was born on the Pilgrim, and he expects to die on the Pilgrim, like his father, and his father before him.

That's the way things are on a generation starship centuries from home. He's never questioned it. Never thought about it. And why bother? Access points to the ship's controls are sealed, the systems that guide her automated and out of reach. It isn't perfect, but he has all he needs to be content.

Until a malfunction forces his wife to the edge of the habitable zone to inspect the damage.

Until she contacts him, breathless and terrified, to tell him she found a body, and it doesn't belong to anyone on board.

Until he arrives at the scene and discovers both his wife and the body are gone.

The only clue? A bloody handprint beneath a hatch that hasn't opened in hundreds of years.

Until now.

Deliverance (Forgotten Colony)
mrforbes.com/deliverance
Complete series box set:

The war is over. Earth is lost. Running is the only option.

It may already be too late.

Caleb is a former Marine Raider and commander of the Vultures, a search and rescue team that's spent the last two years pulling high-value targets out of alien-ravaged cities and shipping them off-world.

When his new orders call for him to join forty-thousand survivors aboard the last starship out, he thinks his days of fighting are over. The Deliverance represents a fresh start and a chance to leave the war behind for good.

Except the war won't be as easy to escape as he thought.

And the colony will need a man like Caleb more than he ever imagined...

Man of War (Rebellion)
mrforbes.com/manofwar
Complete series box set:
mrforbes.com/rebellion-web

In the year 2280, an alien fleet attacked the Earth.

Their weapons were unstoppable, their defenses unbreakable.

Our technology was inferior, our militaries overwhelmed.

Only one starship escaped before civilization fell.

Earth was lost.

It was never forgotten.

Fifty-two years have passed.

A message from home has been received.

The time to fight for what is ours has come.

Welcome to the rebellion.

Hell's Rejects (Chaos of the Covenant)

mrforbes.com / hellsrejects

The most powerful starships ever constructed are gone. Thousands are dead. A fleet is in ruins. The attackers are unknown. The orders are clear: *Recover the ships. Bury the bastards who stole them.*

Lieutenant Abigail Cage never expected to find herself in Hell. As a Highly Specialized Operational Combatant, she was one of the most respected Marines in the military. Now she's doing hard labor on the most miserable planet in the universe.

Not for long.

The Earth Republic is looking for the most dangerous individuals it can control. The best of the worst, and Abbey happens to be one of them. The deal is simple: *Bring back the starships, earn your freedom. Try to run, you die.* It's a suicide mission, but she has nothing to lose.

The only problem? There's a new threat in the galaxy. One with a power unlike anything anyone has ever seen. One that's been waiting for this moment for a very, very, long time. And they want Abbey, too.

Be careful what you wish for.

They say Hell hath no fury like a woman scorned. They have no idea.

ABOUT THE AUTHOR

M.R. Forbes is the mind behind a growing number of Amazon best-selling science fiction series. Having spent his childhood trying to read every sci-fi novel he could find (and write his own too), play every sci-fi video game he could get his hands on, and see every sci-fi movie that made it into the theater, he has a true love of the genre across every medium. He works hard to bring that same energy to his own stories, with a continuing goal to entertain, delight, fascinate, and surprise.

He maintains a true appreciation for his readers and is always happy to hear from them.

To learn more about me or just say hello:

Visit my website:
mrforbes.com

Send me an e-mail:
michael@mrforbes.com

Check out my Facebook page:
facebook.com / mrforbes.author

Join my Facebook fan group:
facebook.com / groups / mrforbes

Follow me on Instagram:

instagram.com/mrforbes_author

Find me on Goodreads:
goodreads.com/mrforbes

Follow me on Bookbub:
bookbub.com/authors/m-r-forbes

Made in the USA
Middletown, DE
11 May 2025